I0628294

Part of Your World

by Gabrielle Chavela

Published by Dymaxicon
An imprint of Agile Learning Labs
San Francisco, CA

ISBN 978-1-937965-07-5
www.dymaxicon.com

edited by Nancy Rommelmann
design & typography by Hillary Louise Johnson

Part of Your World

Pou 'Javier,' ak lespri kap mache ave nou.

Avant-propos

You say that you can't imagine all that, that East Timor is much too far? This evasion is worthless; Dili is only two or three hours by air from your favorite vacation destination, Bali or the Maldives. Under the stamp of globalization, there are no more faraway islands, and every point on the globe has been practically rushed to your doorstep... And if we go instead to Kosovo? Pristina is only two hours by air from Berlin or Paris, if you want to, you can even get yourself there by car... To my rhetorical question: are you not curious about the state of the world in which you live?—you reply by indicating that your receptivity to foreign suffering is limited, and you let me know that you have troubles enough and that you prefer practical love for your neighbor to abstract love for those far away... However, there is an objection which leaves you thoughtful: might it not be that what is possible elsewhere could appear tomorrow, or the next day, in front of your own house? The town of Prizren, whose assistant police chief Milan Petrovic, according the findings of UN investigators, tortured Kosovar civilians to death, is only an hour and half from Munich by plane...

Hans-Christophe Buch
Archipel de Douleur

One

Javier didn't believe in numbers, but it was the third
time he and Eva had met. The first had been in
Morisco Park, last Saturday, with Kristina. Daddies'
day with the toddlers in the park, Daddies pushing
the black rubber socket swings, boosting tots to the
saddles of the garish-colored plastic giant caterpillars that rocked on huge steel springs. Daddies waited for the toddlers to come slipping down the orange
slides that extruded them from the red blue and yellow tubes of habitrail. Daddies scooped up the ba-
bies from the spongy safety mats, wiped their noses,
brushed off the thin grimy sand. Now and then, his
own nose wrinkling, a Daddy might change a dia-
per. On Saturdays the Daddies all wore the same stiff
long-billed caps and looked awkward in the casual
garb they seldom wore. Javier hoped he seemed more
at his ease in a pair of fatigue pants faded almost to
white and a loose pale gray guayabera, though in fact
he was on edge, just a little anxious, the day he met

the au pairs at the park.

He'd set the rendezvous on the web, posting a picture of himself—with Kristina so the girls could believe it wasn't a pick-up or some other scam—but Kristina's face was turned into his shoulder, so eyeballs got nothing but the tip of her nose and a wave of her long snarly strawberry hair. Eight girls had arranged to meet Kristina and Javier Connell in the neutral zone of Morisco Park. The place was always busy on Saturday. The sand around the safety mats was natural. Two hundred yards east, across a low hump of dunes, low surf beat feebly on the South Florida strand.

The first was Annika—German au pairs had a good reputation, and this one was blonde and sharply pretty, like a dozen others he'd seen in the park. Her eyes were as brilliant as tiny blue icebergs. Kristina flinched when Annika touched her hair and said to Javier, "Is not praktical. You must cut it schort." Kristina turned her face to his shoulder, the same pose as in the photo on the web. Javier was looking for a girl to comb the child's hair, not cut it off, but he didn't see the point in saying so. The girls were coming at twenty minute intervals, as Kristina was good for about two hours in the park. He didn't mind if they overlapped. If they found it stressful, then he could see how they managed the stress. Annika stiffened and stalked away when the second arrived, another German, her arm buried to the shoulder in a huge stripy stocking puppet which she made talk in the voice of Barney, the purple dinosaur, though with a slightly German accent. Kristina seemed fascinated and repulsed by this approach; she stared and sometimes smiled but never let go of Javier's pants leg.

The third was a Jamaican woman, whom Javier took to in a way—she was older than the others, a broad-shouldered Amazon (taller than he) with a crown of stubby dreadlocks around her wide, cheerful face. Her calm seemed to relax Kristina, who left the shelter of Javier's knee. She didn't engage with the Jamaican though, but wandered off toward the edge of the playground, where she could dance with her shadow, broken on the weave of the waist-high cyclone fence. Kristina swung the hem of her blue and white calico dress, stuffing a lock of her hair in her mouth, which was a nervous habit of hers. The Jamaican watched from a nearby bench and gave the dancing child an easy, bright white grin.

This one might work, Javier was thinking, then noticed that Kristina's attention had shifted. Another woman was coming in at the playground gate. It was the movement that made you look, a symmetrical wave that rolled from her heels to the top of her purely African head with every step she took. She wore a T-necked dress that fell to her ankles, and in spite of the heat a chiffon scarf, long enough to swing at her heels and printed with dolphins and sea turtles in black oriental brush strokes.

If she was there for Javier and Kristina she was a good quarter-hour early, and maybe she wasn't, since she scarcely glanced in their direction. She sat on a bench in the shade of a frangipani, took out a book and lowered her eyes. But no one ever came to this park unless on baby business.

The Jamaican must have felt the same. She tried a little harder, but try-harder was not her game. Eva wasn't wearing a watch, but at exactly the appointed hour she put her book away and walked toward Javier, a slow smile dawning on her face. She would not meet Javier's eyes, offering her hand in a clasp completely pressureless on her side. She curtsied then— no other word would really do—to give her hand to Kristina, and her smile. With a ripple she straightened up and by the turning movement of her hip and shoulder the dolphins and turtles appeared to swim through the pale translucent blue of the scarf.

Kristina followed, as if on a string. Javier was holding his mouth shut and noticing that it took conscious effort to do it. The word *glissando* appeared in his mind. He couldn't think where she'd put her book. She had no purse and surely an object in a dress pocket would have put a visible hitch in her flow. Where had he seen a walk like that? So easily, effortlessly centered.

"Who do you want to see again?" he had asked Kristina that night, over a meal of fish sticks, mashed potatoes and spinach, which she would eat if he used an equal proportion of butter and spinach. "Eva," Kristina told him. "Eva Ah—Agee..."

"Aguilar," Javier said. "Don't do that." He reached across the patio table to pull the tress of buttery hair from the corner of her mouth. The hair was a problem, it was true, but he wouldn't cut it against her will. "All right," he said to her. "We'll see Eva."

They saw three of the women at the house, the Jamaican, and Eva, and one of the others who had come after Eva to Morisco Park. Javier didn't even remember her name. It was a done deal for Eva from the moment she appeared; he'd followed up with the others just in case she declined. Eva moved in on a Sunday night. Her luggage was minimal, a canvas Gladstone bag with leather straps and a small string bag which contained a red bandanna, a long thick scented candle that filled a cylindrical glass jar, a blue and white porcelain statue of Our Lady of Sorrows, and the book that Eva had been holding in the park. A gilt cross was stamped on the white leather cover, so it must be a Bible or a prayer book.

Javier had made pasta and a spinach salad by the time Eva arrived. The three of them ate together on the patio—at the iron table framed by hibiscus, bougainvillea, a couple of small orange trees. Eva folded her hands and seemed to say a silent grace before she lifted her fork. They spoke little, though Eva urged Kristina to eat her salad, and Kristina did eat some of it, to please her, which startled Javier since no butter was involved.

Afterward he washed the dishes and let Eva give Kristina her bath, wondering if his daughter would call for him, but there was no sound of complaint. In fact he could hear Kristina giggling. When the dishes were done he hung up the rag and went through the steaming bathroom that connected his room to Kristina's. Eva had seated the girl in a chair before her mirror, and the child watched their reflection, rapt, as Eva patiently worked out the tangles. To reduce the pulling, she started at the end of each snarly lock, slowly working the comb's teeth toward the scalp, just as Javier would have told her to do, if he had needed to tell her.

Javier caught his head stupidly nodding, like a dashboard car ornament with its head on a spring. Eva's own hair must have taken some effort, a hundred glossy tight-woven braids, each with an iridescence of henna, wound in a bun at the nape of her neck. He was thinking about that when Eva's brown eyes caught his in the mirror, just an instant before they dropped the task at her hands.

Javier bowed out and went to the music room, where he sat on the piano bench, fingering melodies without depressing any key far enough to sound a note. He was listening but all he could hear was the infrequent hiss of a car passing on the street outside the house wall, the voices of insects and tree frogs rising as the crepuscule deepened into hot velvet night. When he went back, Kristina was sleeping, white sheet folded neatly under her chin. Eva was standing at the foot of her bed, in a pose reminiscent of Our Lady of Sorrows. She might have stood there as long as a tree.

"Well," said Javier. His voice felt awkward, somehow too loud. "I'll show you your room."

Eva poured out of her stillness and followed him. In the courtyard she stopped for a moment, one hand on her sternum, between her breasts, facing the small fountain in the corner of the courtyard, where water purled over the lip of an overset clay jar at the foot of a clematis trained against the wall. Javier watched the slim hand rise and fall with her breath: one, two, three. Then she stooped to lift her bags from the square red tile of the patio and followed him along the diagonal to the room on the opposite corner.

Simple enough—a bed and a night stand, a table and chair. Maybe it was too spare, Javier thought. The previous maid had left a couple of kitsch paintings on the walls; he told Eva she could get rid of them, hang anything she wanted. He opened the door to the small white bathroom and turned on the light inside. When he looked back, Eva had arranged the candle and the statuette on the night stand.

"The sheets are clean on the bed," he told her. Again his voice seemed too loud, and his throat felt oddly constricted.

"I am too far away to hear her in the night."

"I'm there," Javier said quickly, then considered. "The doors between us stay open all night. If she even turns over, I hear."

"Yes," said Eva. "But when you are away."

She was right, Javier realized, he should rig up an intercom. Or maybe, when he had to travel, Eva should be installed in his bedroom. He hadn't really thought of that. There were a lot of things he hadn't thought. He hadn't realized how tired and how tense he really was. There was a hot flush rising from the hollow of his collarbone and he felt himself whirling down a spiral of desperate lonely need. Eva dropped the red bandanna over the statue, veiling the Virgin from her head to her toes. Javier was looking at the floor for some reason and for the first time he noticed that she was wearing shoes at odds with her decorum, spike heels with red leather straps wrapping toward the swell of muscle on her calf. Her first step was tentative, both delicate and poised; he remembered gazelles he had seen on TV. The second step was stronger, it pushed the sinuous wave through her hips with a rolling thrust and lifted the nipples of her small breasts up toward him, hardening against the white cloth of the dress she'd worn to the playground. He could find no way to defend himself. At the touch of her fingernail on the inside of his wrist he was instantly hard as a stone. The small square table rattled its legs on the floor as he sagged back against the wall. She had shucked him quick and clean as an ear of white corn. His cock sprang up to meet her warm heavy lips. She took him all the way up to his root, one, two, three wet deep suctions, then pulled away, teasing the underside of his glans with the rasping point of her tongue. He had not been with a woman since... he bit the inside of his lip to hold silence. His fingers curled and twitched in his palms. He did not feel that he could touch her anywhere. Wrapped around his cock, her mouth smiled up at him, lascivious, but her eyes were empty as dead stars. She closed them then, and pushed her head against his palm; he went straight to the back of her open throat. The shaft of his cock was being massaged by three contracting rings of small muscles at once. With one hand she gripped the back of his leg and with the other lifted his balls and circled a finger around the delicate crinkle of his rectum. When he came it seemed to go on forever. He thought he might faint, and maybe he had—when he came to himself she was seated primly on the straight-backed chair by the table, her ankles crossed, the mouth still smiling faintly, distantly, the dead eyes looking nowhere at all.

He pulled up his trousers and fastened the fly. The idea of touching her still seemed impossible—not a handshake, not a caress. No more could he think of anything to say. She was, he saw, indifferent to his presence. In the end he bowed to her slightly, from the waist, and walked out of her room, softly closing the door behind him.

A Chopin Nocturne was open on the stand of the piano, but instead he fingered the first few bars of Round Midnight, sounding the notes with his lightest touch, then stopped because his hands were shaking. Kristina still slept quietly, unmoving, in her bed. He closed the bathroom door and locked it. He washed himself thoroughly, over the sink, then scrubbed out the sink with scouring powder. It took him an effort to open the door on Kristina's side and leave it that way. Once he had done it, he stared at his hands until they were still.

When he lay down it all came rushing back at him. What had he done? He had done nothing, only stood there letting his reflexes operate while all his conscious intention was null. He didn't know when he had ever felt so weak or so humiliated. His dick was telling him even now that his reflexes would be happy to let it happen again.

He switched if off. Normally, he could choose to switch it off. Two minutes later he was drowned in the dense black oily sleep of exhaustion, from which he woke in a rush of adrenaline, one leg coiled under him and the other cocked, both hands up to protect his head. But there was nothing, of course there was nothing. He strained his ears toward the chant of the frogs, then rose and padded through the bathroom. Kristina had turned over and slept on her belly, her parted lips dampening the pillowcase. He lifted a lock of hair away from her cheek and stepped back to stand in the doorway, listening to her breathing. Moonlight outside the iron bars of her window cast shadows of leaves on the vine that climbed there over her still face.

The same barred shadow lay across his bed, the same dancing shadow of the vine. In the room with Kristina, his heart had stilled; his shrinking glands left him weak but calm. His background check on Eva Aguilar had been, well, perfunctory. It was not usual for Javier to be so slack. He had felt too strongly that she was the one. He'd known it, looking through Kristina's eyes. Her 'résumé' amounted to a single sheet of tasteful café-au-lait-colored paper—someone must have advised her that the off-white shade would stand out in a pack. It stated her age as twenty-two, and the number checked with her driver's license, which Javier had asked to see on the pretext that she might be required to do some driving, though she didn't own a car and Javier had no immediate plan to lend her his. He might have taken her for younger, but at his age the twenty-somethings all looked like children anyway. Jesus Christ! He had her social because he meant in fact to pay the taxes. It would cost him more but it was worth it for the information.

All that and he hadn't bothered to really crunch her vitals. Eva Aguilar. Her accent dropped half a syllable from her name, which became Èv'. She'd tried a phrase or two on him in Spanish, till he'd explained he actually didn't speak it. Ms. Aguilar had only recently moved down from New York city, so couldn't provide any local references. Javier had jumped to the conclusion that he was okay with that. Eva was born in the Dominican Republic, moved to New York with her family at the age of six. She'd adapted well, said the off-white paper, and graduated from a magnet high school in Brooklyn. But after two years at SUNY Buffalo, she'd dropped out. Too cold up there, she said, with a mock shiver—they doan' have snow in Santo Domingo. The softness of her accent dropped off final t's. She'd wanted to get away from her family but after all it was too far. For the next two years or so she'd worked in child care, a daycare center (she wasn't sure if it was still in business), then in people's homes. But you might say she'd been in child care all her life. She was the second child but the oldest girl and yes, Javier did know what that meant in a Latin Catholic family of eight. When her house began to feel too small and crowded again, she'd headed south, for warmer weather. One day she meant to finish her degree, but she was in no hurry about it. She'd been picking up a class or two at a Miami-Dade community college but it would be easy enough to switch to a branch nearer Javier's home.

He returned to the intangibles. Kristina's eyes. They followed Eva and her scarf from the moment they made contact, the turtles and dolphins teased into life by the light humid breeze off the ocean. And Javier felt that Eva's mind was with Kristina's, the whole time Eva was talking to him. When Kristina wanted to mount one of those spring-loaded caterpillars, Eva knew as soon as Javier, and Kristina let Eva hoist her into the shiny yellow saddle, though often she would flinch at a stranger's touch.

Kristina was still rocking on the caterpillar when the fourth girl appeared and Eva withdrew. But Eva did not leave the park. She sat in the same place on the bench as before, the missal open on her knee, throughout the next two interviews. A smooth move Javier had thought at the time; she'd won the game by submerging her quiet magnetism. Kristina was awkward, getting down from the caterpillar, and when she slipped and fell to one knee, Eva caught her with a glance, though since the child was unhurt, getting up on her own, she didn't interfere.

Kristina circled Eva's bench, surrounding her with coy looks, pretending to be caught up in other things, walking her doll through a patch of sand, teetering atop a row of short round posts. The last girl in the series tried taking her hands to help her balance, but Kristina pulled away, jumped down and ran toward Eva's bench, then caught herself up and turned away, affecting to ignore her.

The last two girls were almost jealous, Javier felt, frustrated by the rapport which Eva and Kristina had invisibly achieved. As he lay beneath the flirting shadows of the leaves beyond the bars, that rapport seemed too real, but what had happened in Eva's room did not. The moon was setting. Soon he would sleep, for fifty minutes. Then get up and be gone. Where Eva had come by her consummate abilities, who knew—but he did know there had been nothing personal in the transaction. Nothing at all. There was a light in Eva's eyes when she looked at Kristina, but when she looked at Javier, the light went out.

Two

I keep my girl safe, that's why I'm here, and she is there to keep my flame alive. In the cave on the mountain top, above the spring, beyond the red-trimmed shoots of aloe, three candles burn in three clay jars. It's Eve that keeps them burning, though she doesn't know she does. I saw her born there, and one day I'll see her die, although today she doesn't know she ever knew the name of *Brise*.

My girl can't be in her own head all the time. I know why that would be too much for her to bear. I let her be Solange instead. I let her be Trix or be Solange. Eduardo made Solange, with honey on the skin of his chicken neck and steel wire heated white on the electric eye of the stove. He sold Solange five thousand times, but Solange is there to help take care of Eve, though Eduardo never knew it. And Eve had a hand in the making of Trix herself, though she couldn't have finished the job without *Brise*.

You could think of my hands, if I had any hands,

as moving three shells on top of a rolling pea, and sometimes when I pick up a shell, Trix comes out. Sometimes Solange. Eve can hardly ever come out. It's not safe for her. She's safe in my cave.

Trix had a hand in the making of Eva. Eva was mostly Trix's idea. Eve might have been looking, because of the name, she might have been peering out of the cave. But Eva Aguilar was already there. She had been emptied all the way out and was waiting for someone else to come fill her.

That wasn't my doing. I don't have that power. That was because of the will of God.

But there's more than one pea. There's more than a thousand. Every time the shell comes up there's a different pea, its blue-green pattern blurring into turquoise, like the planet Earth seen from a distant star. Crack one open on the points of your teeth and there's a whole panorama inside; carved in intricate crazed detail like the work of those mad monks in the Middle Ages. Just one more piece of Eve's or Solange's or Trix's life that she's mislaid.

There's this one pea that likes to roll out from under its shell and pop itself open, though usually it shows just one of the stations of its cross. There's Eve all dirty from her work, and dirtier still from hiding in the latrine in back of the fine house in Bel Air, just a little concrete box crammed into a corner of the wall, where the gardeners and the house servants go. Mops and buckets and hoes and spades are kept there too, along with a lot of old PVC pipe and plumbing fixtures not yet put into service, so it made an excellent place to hide. Eve went there quietly, when the shooting started and stayed what felt like a long time to her after it stopped. Red Mickey stuck his head in once and didn't see her. She waited until the dogs switched from barking and growling to gurgling their guts out on the ground. The women only screamed a time or two and then fell silent, though Eve knew, from indirect experience, that often women would scream for hours before they stopped. With men it's quicker. Generally speaking, men shout once or twice and then they are quiet.

Eve waits till the shooting stops, and the shouting and the screaming stop, until she hears the four-by-fours backing out through the gate where they came in when it all began, and she waits for quite a long while after that, until it's *really* quiet. A thousand years later she'll still remember this mistake—she should have waited past that silence, till the ordinary sounds of the day had resumed, chickens and guinea hens clucking and scratching, black crows chattering in the tops of the tall palms, the sound of cars and wagons lumbering by and voices calling to one another, beyond the eighteen-foot-high wall with its wreath of razor-ribbon on top. She should never have stepped into this dead silence, like the silent empty void behind the moon.

But if she had not, but then, but then... where

would she be? Where is she?

She's mostly worried about her work, because obviously there will be more cleaning than usual today, and yet if she does not finish at the usual time she will fall irremediably behind in her other chores and there will be punishment, and after the official punishments Marie Angélique will humiliate and torment her, off the record, and probably pull the braids out of her hair. Eva was carrying her mop when the whole thing started, she carried it to the latrine with her, and now she goes back to the pump where she left her bucket when the two four-by-fours rolled in and the dogs jumped up snarling, hackles high, while Eve walked quietly, invisibly, to her hiding place.

The bucket has already been filled and in all the commotion, no one has spilled it. She swings it to balance on the crown her head and walks smoothly toward the steps of the big house, with an easy effortless gliding step, her back string-straight and the mop trailing lazily from one hand, bare feet silent in the bloody dust. She doesn't pay much attention to the carcasses of the Rottweilers (they eat or they ate more meat every day than her family out beyond Vaudreuil would see in three or four ordinary weeks) nor does she really notice Monsieur Duclos's huge white Explorer skewed short of the gate, the doors hanging open and all the glass shattered. But the dead guinea hens on the ground disturb her, because Man Brigitte should have come to gather them up and pluck them and clean them and get them ready for the pot. The hens have been battered and shredded by bullets and if Man Brigitte does not take care of them soon they are sure to spoil, for the heat is already rising.

It's the steps that really set her back, the white stone steps, all thirty-eight of them, that spill down from the wooden floor of the gallery. Every morning Eve must scrub them till they shine. Today it will be impossible, almost impossible, because of the waterfall of blood that runs down all the steps from the gallery—from the still caramel hand hanging open over the top step, as if it had carelessly spilled all that blood from its pale palm. Eve knows from direct experience that the stone steps are porous and easily stain. Once, to remove a few drops of chicken blood, she actually had to file down the stone, and this is, this is—

Her mind won't contain it. The slow viscous tap of blood dropping from one step to another really is the only sound. It's not a noise behind her that makes her turn. It's a smell: burnt gunpowder dusted over the acrid sweat of furious action.

Eduardo is there when she turns, his olive skin glossy from his exertions, his pulse still thrumming fast in his throat, assault rifle dangling from his right hand, the barrel pointed at the ground. She starts and the water slops to the lip of the bucket, but it stays on her head; nothing is spilled.

Eduardo smiles, a considering smile. Eve's fear, which makes her knees tremble though her back and her head and the bucket stay straight, changes to a paler shade.

Then Red Mickey is there, and Eve's fear brightens. Even without what he says next, Eve has always disliked him and has always been a little afraid of him. Red Mickey is white but his face has tanned the color of brown leather and shrunk from too much time in the sun; it is all shriveled up like a monkey's face. His head is small like a monkey's head, and under the rolled bandanna he always wears tied around his brows (like RAMBO in a poster Eve once saw outside the cinema on the Boulevard de Mer) his eyes are yellow and narrow and mean.

"What are you waiting for?" Red Mickey says. Eve can't understand a word of his harsh Conch English. She has picked up quite a lot of French, in the years that she has stayed in the Duclos house, and already a little Spanish on the street, but the only English she knows is the phrase the ragamuffins always shout at the UN soldiers down by the bay, Eh! Yo! Geef me wan doala!

Red Mickey's eyes are jumpy, like grains of popcorn on hot iron. His eyes always see Eve—in spite of her insignificance—they see her as a threat.

"What are you waiting for?" Red Mickey says. "Who knows what she saw?"

Eduardo doesn't really look at Red Mickey. The

barrel of his gun floats up to cover the bone between the two small buds that will become Eve's breasts. Eve doesn't feel much threatened by that gesture, and she's right. The gun barrel is like a schoolmaster's forefinger pointing at a blackboard.

"Miko," Eduardo says. It's a pet name. Eduardo always treats Red Mickey like a little nervous dog. "She doan see nozzing, Miko. And you know? She doan say nozzing. No matter what she see."

It's true. Eve knows in her bones how true it is. Eduardo and Red Mickey and the other men in the commando who are still prowling, making sure that every vertebrate organism in the Duclos compound is honestly and completely dead—they don't really care if anyone knows what they did. Or rather, they do. They want everyone to know, and to understand.

Eduardo's gun barrel drifts softly back down toward the bloody dirt. "And you know, Miko? Nobody see her. Nobody, nobody ever see her. Only Eduardo."

Now Eduardo is seeing Eve, or rather the horse on which she rides: her body. Her limps are supple and also straight—no sign of rickets, no sign of yaws. She doesn't really know there's human blood between her toes. The body is just ten years old so the legs are still stork-like, but Eduardo notes a sweet little swell beginning in the hips and the buttocks. He sees the quick straight line from her coccyx to the top of her head. Her velvety black skin is clear, and so are the whites of her eyes. Eva hasn't found a lot to eat in the Duclos compound, but she isn't absolutely starving. Her stomach is scarcely swollen at all and her hair has not turned red from malnutrition. In fact her hair is thick and strong. The two dozen stumpy braids are tied with blue and white striped ribbon—or no, there are strips of plastic bag she's scavenged and trimmed to adorn herself. The effect is curiously charming.

"Smile," Eduardo says. "Hmmm? A little smile for Eduardo."

Eve smiles, lips tight and strained against her gums. Her teeth are good. They're white and strong. She is practically unaware of the enormous weight of the bucket, which is slowly, gradually, crushing all the discs in her spine, squeezing the gel out from between each pair of her vertebrae. In just a moment more, Eduardo will tell her to put down that bucket and come with him. She'll carry many other burdens, but not that one.

Red Mickey's shoulders sag—a relief to Eve, because at the same time the machine gun he's been clutching to his chest relaxes.

"Oh Eddy," says Red Mickey, "You are a sick fuck, man."

"Yes," says Eduardo says, in that same slow reflective way. "I am a seek fock, maybe, hmmm? But she doan mind. No, she doan mind..." His eyes scan Eve from head to toe. "Digame, querida—what's your name?"

Êve, O Êve O Êve... that's my girl. About to disappear. She doesn't taste the apple because she wants it. No.

Maybe it's Solange who takes the apple, accepts it because, in the end, she has no choice. Solange has not as yet been born, but here is the moment when Solange is conceived, in this first flash of mutual understanding between Eduardo and Eve. Eve doesn't know at all that she won't be hurt but she does know that she won't be killed. Not killed today. Choose life! That's what she chooses.

So then, when the shells have shuffled and the peas have rolled, it's Solange, not Eva Aguilar, who stands in the maid's room, alone with Javier Connell. Solange reacts according to experience—her experience is deep but not very broad. She knows his naked desperate need and does what she must to disarm it. She accepts the hard red knob of his sex, temporarily, but completely. She knows it is the lesser pain, and that it won't be fatal. The truth is, for a long time now, Solange has not been able to feel pain.

Three

In the maid's room, on the table by the bathroom door, a five-by-eight card is propped against the wall. Birds and bees and blossoms surround a sentence in flowery script: Today is the First Day of the Rest of Your Life. When Eva's eyes open to it, she edits out the middle phrase.

Today is the first day of your life.

Outside the light is coming up fast; she hears the chatter of birds in the trees. The windows let only onto the courtyard- there are none onto the street outside.

She brushes her teeth, gargles with care, turns her face from left to right, scanning the fine lines of jaw and cheekbone: all clear. She pulls a loose blue top over drawstring white pants, steps out the door and closes it with a barely audible thump and click.

The red tiles are warm under her bare soles, still holding a blush of yesterday's sunshine. During the night it has cooled just slightly. She pauses, turns toward the sound of trickling water, stands facing the overturned olla that spills its contents perpetually into a pool of water lilies.

Intermittent scatterings of be-bop licks stitch in and out of the conversation of the birds. It takes her a moment to realize that the piano is live. Then Kristina comes bursting out of the French windows which separate the music room from the patio.

"Eva! Eva—"

Eva's smile is brilliant when she meets the child. Kristina blunders into her, warm and urgent.

Teletubbies tumble in silence on a flat screen TV, the sound turned off. Mister Connell is sitting at the bench of the baby grand. His quick glance doesn't quite meet Eva's eyes. The swift sharp riffs he's laying out are furnishing a different soundtrack to the Teletubbies. Kristina squeals her pleasure, pointing at the television to be certain Eva understands. Getting it, Eva laughs out loud.

Mister Connell raises his hands and pulls the lid down over the keys. Standing, he takes a look at his watch, an ordinary Timex on a web band- no bling. He's wearing tan pants, Madras jacket over a white shirt, open collar and no tie. The jacket, oversized, hangs loose on his lean shoulders.

"Well." His gray eyes skate all around her face and never quite find it. "You know what to do—right?"

Eva smiles and nods. "I am ready."

He bends to scoop Kristina up, kisses her cheek

and the top of her head. Her hair, Eva notices, has relapsed into anarchy during the night.

"Be sweet to Eva," Mister Connell says. "Don't wear her out. We want to keep her, no?"

Kristina nods fervently—she wants to keep Eva—bumping her head against his collarbone. He sets her down, and slings a slim case for a laptop to his shoulder. A quick smile in Eva's direction and Mister Connell is on his way. She stand in the frame of the French windows to watch him go. In the arched portal he stops and turns back, holding up his special key.

"You have yours, right?"

Eva nods. "I have the key."

"Remember when you go out, set the alarm."

She bobs her head. "Yes, I will set it."

Mister Connell unlocks the iron gate on the inside of the archway, passes through and relocks it before opening the solid door to the street. He's noticing Eva noticing just how it is done. Then he is gone.

"Eva, come look, Eva..." Kristina again, tugging the pants leg—drawing her toward the red clay olla and the lily pond.

Javier can reach his garage from inside the house enclosure if he wants to, for instance if it should be raining hard, but he can just as easily go down from the street. The car is nondescript, a Toyota sedan, though with glove-leather seats and an excellent sound system, which Javier does not turn on. He keeps it clean but still the interior smells something like Kristina, less an odor than an aura. Her car seat is permanently strapped into the back. The guys at work stopped kidding him about that long ago. The passenger seat has a dock for his laptop, almost as permanent as the kid seat in back. It's been a long time since Javier rode anyone shotgun in his personal car.

The house network tunes in automatically when he powers up the laptop. The system is based on motion detectors, so webcam four, one of a pair that covers the courtyard, picks up the subject immediately: Eva, towed on a diagonal line by Kristina, whose fist knotted in the flowing pants leg puts a hitch in Eva's stride. In fact she stumbles. The awkwardness is so unlikely that Javier finds himself holding his breath.

Eva shakes her head. A couple of braids come loose from her casual fichu. Gently she separates Kristina's hand from the fabric and holds it in her own slim palm. When they move again they are moving in time. Shit, thinks Javier, it can't be that I hired her for the way she walks. But somehow it seems reasonable that he did. They've moved to the edge of the camera's fish eye. Javier sees them kneel down beside of the pool. He clicks webcam six, knowing it doesn't cover this corner, and gets a view of the empty French windows from a point above the exit portal—a flicker of the big plasma TV inside. Webcam four: their activity at the edge of the lens is too distorted to be legible, but he is relieved, it seems wholesome enough.

He closes the laptop and starts his engine. As the car climbs the ramp, the transponder flashes and the steel panels of the garage door silently retract. A flight of small birds whirls and drops across the patch of empty sky as Javier drives toward it.

In fact there is not just one red clay jar above the lily pool, but three. The first is tilted just enough to spill its surplus into the mouth of the second, which overflows in turn, its excess channeled into a jagged hole in the rounded belly of the third jar, which lies on its side and gurgles water over its rolled clay lip into the pool.

It's intentional, then, the wound in the third jar. Eva, solemnly, regards it. But Kristina wants her attention on the pool.

She sees at first the shadow of her own reflection. Just the silhouette, containing a glimmer of sunlight on the greenish opaque surface of the water. On the green leaf flat against the water, a hovering blue dragonfly. Kristina's face reflected, still beside her own. Her eyes adjusting, Eva can begin to discern their features. The little girl holds a finger to her small pink lips for stillness. For a gringo child, Eva has noticed, Kristina has an unusual ability to be still.

A strand of her hair spills down toward the water,

split ends just dimpling the surface of the pool. Eva almost reaches to draw it back, thinks better of the notion. There is something beneath the surface Kristina is waiting for her to see. She watches as the ripples die, and then it rises, rolling upward from the dark silt on the bottom: framed in the shadow of Eva's own head is the wet translucent globe of the eye, the wavering feather-tipped fins, the gleaming armor of hammered gold scales. Within Eva's reflected head, the koi rolls, breaking the surface with a dorsal fin and the feathered tip of its tail, then drops away toward the bottom.

Eva sits back on her bare brown heels. Unconsciously Kristina slings that length of damp hair back over her shoulder. She smiles.

"Mucho bonito," Eva says, in a reverie, but the child's puzzled expression arouses her. "Kristina... very beautiful."

Kristina's stroller is serious business, beyond even the top-of-the line Graacos common at Morisco Park. Hers is a British make, the Rolls-Royce of strollers, or rather of *prams*. Eva looked it up on the internet and was... impressed, both by the price and the terminology. Not in the least impressed herself, Kristina won't be a passenger today, but prefers to install her doll in the elaborate carriage and push it to the park herself. To Eva it's a little unnerving at first, like a four-year-old driving an expensive car, but in fact

Kristina maneuvers the vehicle skillfully, though she can barely see over the handle. She knows her own way from house to park, better than Eva knows it.

Tuesdays and Thursdays, Kristina goes to a play school in the morning, but not today, and a lot of the kids from Jolly Toddlers have come to the park today. Kristina shows Eva off, then seems to forget her. Eva sits quietly, missal open on her knees. She watches. When other moms or nannies glance her way, she drops her eyes to the pale fold of the page.

After two hours plus, Kristina wants to go home- the park is emptying out for lunch. Though drooping a bit, Kristina still wants to push the pram herself and to lead the way. She's taking care of Eva, though it's up to Eva to punch in the special code Mister Connell gave her on the alarm system keypad, then unlock the heavy metal outer gate with her special key, then relock it behind her, before the inner door to the courtyard can be opened. Scrolled with iron vines, this outer gate looks decorative, but the lock on it is no joke at all. Mister Connell has told her two or three times that it costs over a hundred dollars US to replace either key so... she wears them round her neck on a long lanyard he gave her for the purpose. The skin above her navel shrinks away from the cold metal when the keys fall back into that place, but soon enough they warm to her.

Eva heats Spaghetti-Os in the microwave. She finishes what Kristina leaves, about half the bowl. The girl is still bouncing, but in slow motion. Mister Connell said a nap wasn't required but would probably happen. In the time it takes Eva to rinse bowl and can, and put one in the dishwasher and the other in the recycling bin, Kristina has fallen asleep on the couch, in front of the gabbling television, some cartoon.

Eva switches off the tube and wraps her arms around herself, a little chilled by the air-conditioning here. She doesn't see a thermostat and suspects she shouldn't tamper with it anyway. In Kristina's room she finds a fuzzy yellow blanket and drops it over the girl on the couch. She thinks of moving her, does not want to wake her. At the blanket's touch, Kristina stirs and murmurs, then she is still again, her breath even.

When Eva opens the French doors, the humid warmth pours in the courtyard. Her gooseflesh dies, her hands drop from her bare upper arms. Eva is free, and she likes the sensation. She likes the hacienda style of the house, the way it is a little fortress. She feels safe here. She doesn't feel trapped.

She stands in the doorway, tasting the feeling, her toes wrapping over the rails of the sill. She stands almost motionless, just slightly swaying, long enough to make Javier wonder just what she's looking at, something out of range of web camera six. In fact, though Eva's looking toward the three clay jars above the lily pool, though she is in earshot of the trickling water, it may well be that she's not seeing anything at all, unless it's the golden shimmering koi, dropping away and disappearing into the depths of her own mind.

Indoors, she moves to the black piano, strokes the long, glossily polished surface. She reaches in to pluck a high string of the harp, but because of the damper, there is no sound. Carefully she lifts the lid and depresses a cold ivory key. The brown note sounds, deep and sustained. Surprised at the volume, she draws back her hand. The note is muted.

Though Kristina has not stirred, Eva adjusts the blanket over her, so it covers completely the three slender yellowing marks on the underside of the girl's jaw. Mister Connell. She recognized him easily, that first time in the park. The double aspect of his face was the same as in the online photo. The amiable features of the fair-skinned face offset by the hard attention of his slate-gray eyes. Kristina's eyes are different, a deep brown that's sometimes almost black; they go a little strangely with the russet color of her wild hair.

"*Cómo está?*" she had tried to begin, but Mister Connell seemed to flush, just very slightly. "You can call me Javier," he said, with a crooked smile. "I'm sorry but I don't really speak Spanish. My mother liked to read romances. I think that's how I got the name."

"Meester Connle," Eva set, still registering the nuance of his expression, though her face was generally aimed at his knees.

"It's Connell," he told her, smiling somewhat more openly now. "I'm Boston Irish, actually. But you can call me Javier. Unless you prefer... Ms. Aguilar."

"No, Eva," she had said, her cheeks warming slightly. "Eva is fine."

Eva is more than fine. She drifts into the kitchen, pulls down a cookbook and opens it on the immaculate Corian countertop, but the instructions inside could just as well be Chinese to her. She closes the book and wanders toward Kristina's room. On the threshold she looks at the toys, the picture book, the striped shag rug with the kitty-kat head—all these things almost as incomprehensible to her as the cookbook. There's something funny about the door jamb—it's twice as wide as it needs to be to accommodate the door. In fact there's some kind of pocket door installed behind the hollow wooden one. Camouflaged under the same paint as the rest, but something altogether different, and when she touches it Eva feels the same hardened steel of the door that opens on the street.

Across the corridor, another sliding glass door gives onto the courtyard where the sunlight pours down. Eva gazes into that warm pool of light, fingertip still resting on the painted steel. She doesn't see a way to operate this hidden door, and doesn't suppose she needs to know how to do it. "Me?" Mister Connell had said in the park, "Well, I'm just a salesman really..." His eyes left her face to drift off somewhere in the clear blue sky.

"Cognobits," Mister Connell said.

"Cog.."

"Cognobits," he repeated. "It's a stupid name, I know. Marketing made it up—nobody gets it. It doesn't mean anything, that's why." He faked a cough and covered his mouth. "It's just a chip that goes in refrigerators, air-conditioners—a lot of appliances like that. Nothing exciting, but I do go to a lot of conferences, and sometimes I travel on short notice. To close a deal." His slate-colored eyes full on her now. "That's why I need a live-in. Reliable. You know."

"I understand," Eva said, acting the line with full conviction, forcing herself to meet his look, for a whole second before she lowered her head toward the ground.

"Okay," Mister Connell said, in the careless tone that didn't fit his eyes. "Then we understand each other."

The doorways to the connecting bathroom don't have the modification. The doorway from Mister Connell's room to the corridor does. Oh sure, Eva says to herself, tapping the steel edge. The voice in her head isn't quite her own. Like, there's really such a thing as Cognobits.

Mister Connell's bed is a king-sized futon, on a low blonde wooden frame, with long drawers underneath, like under a ship's bunk. Nearly as wide as it is long.

Two people could get lost from each other in there. It's covered with a patchwork quilt, a serpentine pattern, deep red, dark blue.

Eva is captured in the mirror above the bed, a huge pane of glass in an ornate gilt frame, at odds with the rest of the furniture, which is modern, the same blond wood as the bed. There are two bureaus, a vanity, a desk with a computer. All surfaces bare except for one bureau, which Mister Connell probably uses. Its mirror picks up the much larger gilded one, multiplying the reflections. Wherever Eva moves in the bedroom, her own eyes seem to follow her.

The closet is exactly half empty. Maybe two thirds. Mister Connell's stuff is compact, to the left, a couple of suits, dress shirts, and more casual garb, a lot of which seems to be army surplus. On the floor in the far corner, opposite a pair of Mister Connell's shoes, lies a wadded fishnet stocking and a silver disco purse. All right, Javier thinks, tracking Eva on one window of his laptop screen while he monitors Kristina's quiet sleep through another, It's ordinary curiosity, I'm sure I'd do the same if I were her.

She slides the door of the closet closed, turns back to face the room. On the flat screen of the computer spirals a screensaver, a city building, all by itself, collapsing into showers of glittering rubble, then slowly rebuilding itself again. She approaches the desk. Her hand hovers over the mouse. She doesn't quite touch it. Nonetheless, the city dissolves into sparkling sand.

She circles in front of Javier's bureau. On top a goose-neck lamp, a stack of pennies, brush and comb, a tube of chapstick and a ring of tarnished brass keys. An oval photo frame lies face down in a faint ring of pale dust. With her thumb she flips out the velvet brace and turns the picture upright. Then no she thinks it can't be her.

Hell. Not Hell. What are the odds? It can't be real; Eva must be dreaming the other woman's face in the oval frame echoing over and over again in the huge gilded mirror behind her. She stands so still for such a long time that webcam five shuts off.

Four

Eva didn't especially want days off but she got them anyway. Mister Connell seemed to press her to go out. Weekdays he was often late home, and he liked his weekends with Kristina... just the two of them.

Then too, Eva was supposed to be taking classes. To start taking classes at the Lake Reed community college branch, once her credits had transferred from downtown Miami, was the theory. Night classes, but these had not yet begun, she explained. In her leisure hours, Eva sometimes simply rode the bus. She took long, aimless walks on the beach.

The Lake Reed community college outpost was an architectural catastrophe from the mid-1970s, suggesting a flying saucer crash-landed half a mile inland from the dunes, or maybe a slowly collapsing layer cake. Outside the main door, candy wrappers and discarded flyers fluttered over a stark apron of pebbled concrete. A couple of gulls sorted pessimistically through the debris. Eva made a cautious approach, nervous of being intercepted, unconfident that she would know what to say or to present. A gang of boys in hip-hop track suits hung left of the door, smoking and talking, their eyes lingering on her ass as she passed them.

A receptionist's desk was empty, just inside the door. The hallway was a tilted corkscrew, something like the inner workings of a snail. Eva walked slowly up the gentle incline, the hard points of her heels snapping on the concrete. To her right the glass of the outer windows, though reinforced with wire, was dented in or broken through at fairly frequent intervals. To the left, the grimy beige was lined with stripes, apparently color-coded for different destinations.

Eva didn't know the code. Now and then, through open classroom doors, she glimpsed packs of students gaping up at Powerpoint presentations while voices of their teachers droned. Then a bell went off, so loud it made her jump. A rising tide of students poured around her. She choked up on her string bag, wrapping the cord handles around her wrist. A pair of pachucos had homed in behind her—psst! *Querida! Yo!* She wouldn't turn to look at them. She would annihilate them with her silence and averted eye. She knew their eyes were on her ass but wouldn't change the way she walked.

She turned left off the spiral corridor and slipped among a group of women. This new hall was like a spoke, leading to an inner hub, a light well. Distant now, the voices of the boys sounded merely silly. The cords of the bag made corrugated tracks on the back of her hand. The chatter of the women around her was as meaningless as birdsong. Her breath was catching, high in her throat. Among other women still, she turned into a classroom door. A moment's hesitation and she let her string bag down amidst a heap of multicolored backpacks on the floor. She followed others in the group and like them fished out a lump of dripping clay from a dark green plastic garbage can.

The two pachucos crossed the open doorway, glanced in, snickered, and moved on. Eva's heart and breathing slowed. She had merged with the class-full of women, most them close to her own age, prattling cheerfully in Spanglish. One of them got up from her potter's wheel and moved to shut the classroom door. A certain weariness in her authority made Eva realize she was older than the others, though her little white body seemed youthfully lithe beneath the blue coverall she wore. A few crows feet bracketed the corners of her mouth and eyes. The students seemed to call her Willow.

Eva sat on a low stool behind the potter's wheel, her wheel. Covertly she took clues from the girls on either side. She didn't want to look at Willow, lest Willow look at her. The wheel was turned by a foot-pedal. Soon enough Eva found an even groove.

Willow spoke in a calm, even voice, and as her own wheel revolved, her clay took form. Eva found her voice soothing but didn't bother picking out any words. The touch of her hand with the wheel's turning gave her chunk of clay a symmetrical grace. She pumped and modeled to a long shaft, then let it sink down, squatting into lower rondures—so rapt she never heard the bell go off a second time.

"Juanita Mores?"

With a thump of her heart Eva realized that Willow was addressing her and that she and the teacher were alone in the room.

"No? Maria Tedesco?" Willow was squinting at a large square of green and white computer paper in her left hand.

Eva let her wheel stop and stood up. Her clay, in long shaft mode, drooped from the tip like a wilting flower. The other students had all gone and Eva's string bag lay solitary, limp, just inside the door of the classroom.

"It's Eva," she said. "Eva Aguilar."

Willow glanced from the paper to Eva, then back at the printout. Her eyes were bright green, Eva had seen in the moment of contact. "Hmm," she said. "Are you registered for this course?"

"I'm... I'm a transfer," Eva said. "I just moved up from Miami Dade."

Willow shrugged. "Better check with the office if you want to get credit," she said. "You missed the first two but.." she glanced at Eva's collapsing clay rod and smiled "... your concentration seems good, anyway."

Eva tilted her face toward the floor and looked at the teacher from under her lashes. With a clay-streaked thumb, Willow hooked a lock of blonde hair from her face, then pulled down the zipper of her coverall, revealing a faded blue button-down shirt underneath.

"All right," she said, turning away as she stepped out of the coverall. "See you next Saturday then, Eva."

There were still many more hours of empty free time. That evening Mister Connell planned to take Kristina and two little friends out to Chuck E. Cheese's, but they wouldn't have left yet so Eva didn't want to go back there. She left the community college building, aware of the stripes of clay on her hands and the spatters drying on the skin of her face, and walked slowly for several blocks till she felt the wind coming off the sea. She took off her heels to cross the dunes, and once she reached the flat sand on the other side she pulled the T-shirt dress over her head and stood barefoot in the green one-piece bathing suit she wore underneath.

She waded knee deep in the warm water, low surf foaming around her shins, then crouched and washed the clay from her hands and her face, careful not to wet her hair, and trying her best to see under the water for sharks. Then she got out and collected her bag, stuffing the dress inside of it, and walked south on the beach, through the reddening afternoon sunlight, until the warm wind had dried her completely. In a pocket of dunes she changed into cargo pants and a shapeless, oversized T-shirt with a cartoon on the back of a slobbering dog. She slipped a pair of Chinese slippers on her feet and headed past Morisco Park toward the bus stop.

When darkness settled in she was still on the bus. On a Saturday evening it wasn't so crowded. People were already where they wanted to be. She unfastened her hair at the back and dropped her head so the braids snaked forward, cowling her face. Then she shook it back and turned to the window glass. The bus had stopped, and in the shadowy reflection a pair of distant streetlights filled the hollows of her eyes. She took a tube of glitter from her pants pocket and decorated the corners of her eye-sockets and the high edge of her cheekbones.

South of downtown Miami she got off the bus and went slowly strolling down Tamarind Way. On either side were small concrete bungalows, or sometimes just trailers on block foundations. Even the trailers had been there long enough to be snarled over with bougainvillea and other fast growing vines. It was not so hot tonight, but breathless, and the stench of the neighborhood meth labs was heavy on the air. In spite of the shapeless clothing she wore, the occasional low-rider slowed as it passed her, sleek heads thrusting out the window like the heads of seals breaking water.

"*Mmmmmxxnt! Da me un' beso..*"

"*Chinga su madre*," she told them, not bothering to turn her head. She wanted to adopt the foursquare graceless trudge of the regular American girl that should have been inside her clothes, but it was too much against her nature and she couldn't make herself do it.

The fourth car to slow was not a low-rider but one of those queer angular van-like things that had recently been forced into some sort of vogue by a huge onslaught of product placement. It look like a double-wide refrigerator being moved somewhere on a dolly. When the window came down, a pulse of house music throbbed into the street. Alfie was behind the wheel, ball cap backwards on his head. He'd grown a Vandyke since she last saw him, and had a new nine-millimeter cartridge casing clamped into the lobe of his ear.

"Babeee!" he said. "How's Trix?"

"Trix are for kids," she replied in a sugary tone. She shook her head slowly as she walked around the front end of the car, toward the passenger door he had popped open for her. The braids lashed around her chin. The car was two-tone—mint ice-cream and a darker shade.

"You bought this," she said. "I can't believe you

bought one of these."

"Partymobile, Trixie." Alfie rolled the volume knob and the superbass thrummed from a woofer buried somewhere in the back. "Gotcha sound system, gotcha teevee, gotcha fridge and ya wet bar... Check it out!"

She took a quick glance over her shoulder. "Where's the ring for the jello wrestling?"

They laughed together. Alfie slopped a kiss toward her; she turned her head quickly and caught it just beside her ear. When he settled back into his seat, she laid her hand on his bristly forearm.

"I can't believe you bought this," she said. "Don't they cost a bomb?"

"What the hey?" Alfie smiled on one side of his mouth only. "S'not like it was my money..." Again they laughed in perfect time. She didn't think she'd laughed so freely since whenever the last time was she saw Alfie.

He parked alongside Biscayne Bay where they could watch the headlights beading across the bridges toward South Beach while they made out. Alfie handled her like she was a big cat—friendly and furry and soft. There was no real intention to it. When she grew bored she ran her hand between his legs and as she expected found nothing much there. He pulled away and opened his mouth but before he could say he was too high, she snatched the giant pink pacifier he wore around his neck on an elastic cord and popped it into his mouth. He wiggled it at her with his thin lips, and bugged his eyes. Trix snickered, relieved that he wasn't offended. Alfie spat out the pacifier and let it rebound from his skinny chest on its string.

"Wanna run by the shop?" Alfie said.

Trix shook her head. "You know I'm retired."

"Straight life!" Alfie said brightly, and thumped her on the shoulder. "Living in the 'burbs, yet... Come on, just for a minute, my queen. Think how thrilled the kids will be."

Alfie pulled the mint-ice-cream minivan under a carport buried in vines beside one of the bungalows on Tamarind Way.

"Stinko," Trix said as she got down and slapped the door shut. "I mean, Alfie, the DEA can smell this shit from their helicopters practically."

"Not my problem," Alfie said. "S'not in my house."

"Oh no," said Trix. "Just next door. And the door after that. Just hope they don't kick down the wrong door when they come rolling down the block..."

Alfie, looking a little annoyed at last, pushed up his hat to scratch the brush cut under it and gave her a hard look.

"Don't worry," he said. "Be happy."

"*Claro*," said Trix. He put a hand in the small of her back to urge her inside, and Trix crossed the threshold with a cheerful little skip.

Lights were low in the living room, and Jerry Springer played on a projection screen that covered the wall. A grotesquely fat guy was talking a shower in a special glass booth on the Springer stage, touching himself lewdly while the audience booed. A couple of tweakers, do-rags on their heads, were stooped over a mirror and a small hillock of crystal, sparkling in the light from the TV.

The fat guy had left the booth, dripping. One of Springer's muscle-bound bouncers was hustling him off the stage. At ground level, the fat guy turned back and returned a shove. Though the movement looked flabby and ineffectual, the bouncer sat down hard on his ass and stayed there, a startled look on his face.

"Whoa, ho, look-it..." One of the tweakers sat up and looked at the screen. "Fat dudes is stronger than you think." He snickered. He himself was thin as a wire, his left eye twitching and his left foot jerking spasmodically against the floor. The other one elbowed him the ribs.

"Get off that geek."

"Who you shoving?" said the first one. "Check it out! Dude is sumo."

"Boys," said Alfie. "Have some respect. You don't know Trixie but she is *da bomb*."

The boys sat straighter and looked at her mutely. Alfie put one hand under Trix's elbow and gestured at the mirror with the other. *"Mi casa, su casa,"* he said. "Whatever you want.."

"Not that," she said. "You know me better."

"Oh yeah," Alfie looked at the ceiling. "Now what could I get you..."

"It's all right," Trix said, moving away from his touch.

"Twelve-stepping?" Alfie said. "But you're our guest!"

"*O Díos mio,*" Trixie said. "Bring me a beer already, then. Corona if you got it. With lime." She headed down the steps to the basement, where the action was. From behind her she heard Alfie say to the tweakers, *you boys make a dive?* And one of them: *Yeah, Buffy's got the bags downstairs.* And Alfie: *Get down there and help her then. We gotta get Trixie some traction.*

Buffy was even thinner now. Her kohl-drawn eyes looked like sockets in a skull. The Goth effect boosted by a cobwebby black scarf. She scurried up to Trix, the wind of her movement pouring through the holes. "Not go' kiss you," Buffy said blurrily. "Mouf too so'..." They hugged but with plenty of airspace between them. Trix held Buffy's boney shoulders and looked in her face. Her black lipstick was perforated with a couple of dozen small silver rings. Like what you'd put through a hog's nose to keep it from rooting under the fence, Trix thought, not knowing where that hard flash had come from. Several of the fresh piercings looked infected. As she dropped her hands from Buffy's shoulders she surreptitiously grazed her fingers over the Eva ID, securely snapped in her cargo-pants pocket. Alfie was coming down the steps with her beer, the pair of Dumpster-divers trailing him.

"Ugh, these fluorescents," Trix said, pushing the lime wedge down into her bottle. She turned on her flat heels, a full 360. "I feel like I locked myself in a freezer. Is this a class operation or what?"

In fact little had changed since she had last been here, though the hum of the light fixtures did make her teeth hurt. A dozen sleek laptops lined one side of the room, bound to the wall by phone cable spaghetti. Several land-line telephones were connected to the same snarl. Atop the file cabinets on the other side were as many cell phones, each marked with a scrawled sticky note. In the center was a bank of printers and the laminating machine, emitting a smell of toner and hot plastic. A couple of plastic garbage bags, stuffed with paper, leaned on a trio of colored milk crates. Buffy had been sorting through these when Trix came downstairs, now she sighed and went back to the work. The short wall opposite the stairs was completely closed off by a flat-panel TV screen where Snoop Doggy Dogg strutted through his latest video in a muted silence.

"Oo, Miz Stewart," Alfie simpered. "You wanted scented candlelight? Got to see what we're doing, you know..."

Trix sniffed.

"All right," Alfie said. "Let's say if you wanted to get on the *phone*, I'll do something about the lighting for you."

"I dunno," Trix said, as a matter of form.

"Ah, come on now. Give us a thrill. Y'know, it'll be good for the children."

"Oh..." said Trix, still revolving on her flat Chinese shoes. The movement made her a little giddy, though she hadn't yet even tasted her beer. She stopped. "Okay then."

Alfie clapped softly. "You wanna take one front to back? Show the boys how it's done."

"Nah," Trix said. "Buffy always does good prep work."

"Hey, yo," one of the tweakers said. "That's good shit there, like we triaged it already before we put it in the bag."

Buffy, smiling at the compliment, held up a crumpled credit card statement. Trix took it, squinted at the name. Lateesha Soames. Trix sat down in a swivel chair next to Buffy, pursing her lips as she set her beer aside on the countertop. A Visa, credit line of eight thousand dollars—six thousand and change available. Trix didn't bother to look at the charges. The home address was in Jacksonville. Trix spun her chair to one of the laptops and started a search for the phone number. Then she looked up at Alfie.

"Lights?"

Alfie smirked and killed the bank of fluorescents.

The room was now lit by laptop screen savers and dancing figures on the silenced MTV. Alfie circulated with a box of kitchen matches, lighting fat prayer candles in tall glass jars; soon their devotional aroma had smothered the smell of toner. One of the tweakers had clasped his hands in mock prayer. Trix was already dialing the credit card customer service number on a land-line.

"Yesss..." Looking up at candle-shadows wavering on the low ceiling. "Yes, please, it iss Mees Lateesha Soames... Yes, I have my credit card number hyeh. Ah am in Coral Gables, the Biltmore Hotel... Yes, you see..." Her island accent seemed to thicken with every word she spoke. "No, but de problem—dis nombah on the back of my cahd, it iss worn away—Dey do seh dey woan tek de cahd widdout daht..."

The customer service rep's voice whined like a grasshopper from Trix's receiver.

"What a mook," hissed one of the tweakers. "Put him on the speaker."

Trix glanced over at Alfie, who nodded. She hit the button.

"... well but Miss Soames, I'm really not authorized—"

"But dey do seh dey will mek me to liff de hotel... I doan hahv de cash moneh for to peh..."

"—I'm sorry, but Miss Soames, I—"

"—is okeh. Misstah, Misstah—"

"My name is Richard, Miss—"

"Oh Misstah Richahd, Ah know you help me if you could, but as you cannot," Trix's voice filled with an infinite, sexy, sadness. "—Ah muss den to go slip on de stritt…"

"Wait, Miss Soames—" The tinny voice strained. The tweakers snickered and covered their mouths.

"—this once—if I could just call back the hotel to confirm that you are a guest there—"

"Oh Misstah Richahd! Such kindness, a moment Ah find you daht numbeh, it is somewhere here.." Buffy popped a cell phone open in front of her and Trix read off the number from the display. "Yes, in room one-fo'teen. Oh Misstah Richahd! Surely, God will reward such kindness."

She hung up. The quivering tweakers took their hands off their mouths and let their laughter babble out.

"Shut up," Alfie said. He kicked the nearest one. A cell phone was ringing. Buffy picked it up and arched her eyebrows at Trix, pointing to her wounded lips. Trix snapped the phone open. The island accent was gone when she spoke.

"Coral Gables Biltmore Hotel… one moment please.." with her free hand, Trix rattled keys of a laptop, angling the phone to catch this sound effect. The tweakers doubled over, gutshot with strangled laughter.

"We have a Lateesha Soames, yes… let me see… Oh yes. Well, the CVC number on her card is illegible and we have a new security rule—Oh, you can fax it over?"

Buffy hung an index card in front of her face and Trix read off the number. "That will certainly ease the situation for our guest," she said. "Thank you so much." She hung up and leaned against her chair back with a faint smile.

"Go Buffy!" one of the tweakers said for no apparent reason. Then they began to chant in unison. "*Kill the vampire! Kill the vampire!*"

"You guys are soooo funny," Buffy said through her painful lips.

"Knock it off," Alfie told the tweakers. He was holding up ten fingers for a silent countdown, folding them down one by one. Four were still up when a fax line rang and a sheet of paper came crisping out. Trix took the first sip of her beer.

"Yes!" Alfie snatched the paper up. "Trix is still the queen."

"The queen of mean," said one of the tweakers.

"The queen of Trixiness," Alfie says, and shoved the fax in his direction. "Take that and order dinner."

"On her real card?" Trix said.

"Just one for love," Alfie said. "And a bang on the ear."

"Whatever." Trix said. "Now, let's get serious." She picked up a phone and dialed Lateesha Soames' Jacksonville number, sat back in the chair and studied the credit card statement till the phone was answered.

"I'm calling for Lateesha Soames... Yes, I'm calling from Bank of America Visa card Collection Center." Just a trace of the island accent had returned to her voice, but it was clipped now, and just a shade stern, with none of the melting sexiness of the first call. "Yes, your payment of seven hundred forty five dollars and fifty-three cents, due June fifth, has not been received... you sent it? Maybe it was lost in the mail—you have the cancelled check? In that case it must have been miscredited at our end—I'm so sorry! But if you could just give me the number of the check... Yes of course. Well. Do you have your card? Now if you look at the back you will see three numbers on the back of the card, just after the card number—nobody knows those three numbers but you and Bank of America—that should be six-four-two, yes? Exactly."

"Schmuckeroo!" crowed one of the tweakers. "Put her on the speaker!"

Trix swiveled toward them and glared for silence, then turned back to her laptop.

"Right, thanks. And the account number? Yes... and if you would just give me your social, that would speed things up—okay, bear with me..." Trix muted the phone and typed for a few seconds, then picked up the receiver. "Miss Soames? I *have* found your payment. It was miscredited, but we've taken care of the problem now. No, thank *you*. And sorry for the inconvenience."

She hung up. Buffy, Alfie and the two tweakers were clapping rhythmically. Trix dropped her head so that her braids shrouded her face.

"What should I get," she said, when the applause stopped. "American Express? She's already got one Visa."

"You can get her as many Visas as you want," one of the tweakers said.

"Let's get Diner's Club." Alfie said. "I kind of like Diner's Club. Let's start with that."

"Yeah," said one of the tweakers. "People don't take American Express like they useta."

Alfie turned on him. "So *you* go get it, big mouth. Anyone can do that. Once Trixie has done all the pre-texting for you..." He opened his arms and danced toward Trix, caroling, "Trixie is *my social engineer...*"

The caterer had rolled in and out by the time the Diner's Club application was done. The tweakers had ordered filet mignon, lobster, salads with caviar on hearts of palm. They didn't eat much of it though. The two of them wrestled over a four gallon magnum of Dom Perignon, struggling with the cork.

"Hey, yo—" Alfie said. "Aim that away from the television, wouldja?"

When the cork blew it only punched a hole in a ceiling tile.The top third of the Dom foamed out on the floor.

"You little *ratones*," Alfie said. "What is this, some freaking frat house? One of you go by Stanley Steamer. Before the next time you come to work, yo..."

The tweakers ignored him. "Welcome to Diner's Club," one of them said.

Buffy came floating upstairs like an emaciated bat. She vacuumed a good dose of meth up her nose, snorted, then cleared away the mirror and began to lay out the food. There were no glasses so they drank their Dom out of Styrofoam cups. Alfie raised his to toast Trix's accomplishments—*Queen of the Slipstream*. He'd tweaked hard while she was out of the room, it seemed and was no longer making good sense.

"*Oh Misstah Richahd!*" one of the tweakers mimed in falsetto, and the other one laughed. Even Buffy smiled with her ringed lips, and Trix raised her chin in acknowledgement.

"You should put some Neosporin on that," Trix said.

"You doan thing it look good?" Buffy touched a ring and winced.

"It's beautiful, *cara*. I think of your health. Alfie, make her take care of it?"

Alfie shrugged.

No one ate much. Buffy couldn't and the rest of the crew was too high. Trix wasn't hungry. Alfie's gang didn't have a lot of imagination about food, being that they really didn't eat much of it themselves. She forced down a lobster claw, a slice of steak and some of the salad. The waste upset her for some reason, tonight.

The champagne was going faster and after two cups her head felt fuzzy. Buffy's mutilated lips began to relax into something like a smile. Trix asked Alfie to call her a cab. He put the ride on the new credit card she had scored and they went out on the small crumbling patio to wait for it.

A previous tenant had been into gardening. Palmetto and banana fronds ran to the edge of the brick, and the damp air was full of heavy flower scents and a general odor of tropical rot, which muted the neighborhood's methedrine funk. Alfie lit two short black cigars, offered one to Trix and looked sad when she tried to wave it away.

"The Cubans? Baby you used to love these."

Trix took the cigar and sat down on a rusty iron chair. The overgrowth made the tiny backyard seem close and secure. Just a few stars visible at the top of the tube. Indeed when she took a cautious pull on the cigar the taste of tobacco gave her something of the feeling of sanctuary she wanted to remember about this place. So why ruin it? It was a tricksy impulse.

"See anything of Hell these days?"

"La bella Helena?" Alfie considered, comparing his orange cigar head to the pale pips of starlight. "Not in some time. I don't think I've seen her walk down the block, yet. It did seem like she was getting more into crack..."

Alfie's high had leveled off, Trix thought. Maybe the booze had tranqed him back into the range of rationality.

Hell on Wheels," Alfie mused, this being another of Hell's *sobriquets* as well as a description of the climate she tended to generate around her. "Ah... she must be getting her monkeys fed somewhere. Or she'd come knock-knocka-knocking on my door."

He tipped his ash over the edge of the bricks and squinted at Trix's dark silhouette. "Why do you ask?"

Then the cab horn blew at the front of the house.

"Babe!" Alfie said suddenly. "Don't leave me." But she was on her feet, kissing him quickly, darting her tongue between his teeth, her long fingers down the back of his pants. He tried to hold her, amorous now that she was leaving, and maybe even capable. She danced herself free, but he held on to her hand as they circled the house toward the honking cab.

"All right, already," Alfie muttered. "Gimme your phone?"

"I doan hahv a phone," Trix said, and kissed his cheek to distract him.

"Come on. You still on the same email?"

"No, really. I'm off the grid." She got into the cab.

"No smoking," the driver growled. She rolled down the window and passed Alfie the cigar.

"Hey, Trix," Alfie said, as the cab pulled from the curb. "You know you can't get off the grid." He had both cigars in one hand between two different fingers and he used them to draw a hash mark on the air between them. "The grid goes on and on and on..." He was still drawing checkerboards on the air when the cab made a corner and lost him.

Trix had given him a bogus address to call in. She changed it now, then shut down the conversation with the driver. It was a forty minute ride and she passed the time by sucking breath mints, which covered the cigar taste without removing it. The new address was also false but closer—a split-level opposite Morisco Park. She thrust a five at the driver for a tip as she bailed. He called after her—as she expected—she was supposed to present the physical card, and sign the ticket and so on. But in a moment she was across the dunes, in soft sand where the car couldn't follow. She listened for a door slam, nothing.

It was quite late and the beach was completely deserted. In the darkness she took off Trix's shirt and pulled on the T-shirt dress she had worn earlier. Under the long skirt she removed the cargo pants, folded them neatly and put them in her bag. She walked up the beach to the next access point and circled back through the empty streets to Mister Connell's house.

There she locked the outer gate before unlocking the inner one, as he had requested she be careful to do. Indeed, he had stepped into the doorway of the music room to greet her as she stepped out of the little Spanish archway with its decorative trimming of vine.

"Oh, Eva, it's you. Have a nice night?"

"Si. Yes thank you." She stepped aside from the inner gate and pulled on it to demonstrate that the lock had snapped properly shut.

"All set then," Javier Connell said, with a squared-away click of his tongue.

"And how was Chuckie Cheese?"

Mister Connell laughed and lowered his reddish blond head. "Chuckie Cheese is a reliable product," he said. "You can count on the same experience from coast to coast."

"And Kristina?"

"Oh, she's been asleep for three hours. That stuff tires her out." Mister Connell glanced at his wrist. "Me too, I think."

"Good night, then. Until tomorrow." She turned from the gate and rippled toward the door of her room, aware that he was always standing in the frame of the sliding glass door, though she didn't look.

Inside her room she bolted the door, and stripped to the green one-piece. She brushed her teeth and tongue for a long time and then sluiced Scope around her mouth till she really couldn't taste the cigar any more. Alfie had been good to her in his way. Better than almost anyone. But it had not been wise to go back there. She would have to think of new places to go.

She stood supplely erect before the mirror above the sink, staring into her own eyes until she was confident her retinas bore no impression of any person or object in the bungalow on Tamarind Way. Nothing no nothing no nothing at all. *Nada y pues nada nou pa gen anyen.* Her teeth were blazing and her eyes were clear and her ebony skin was taut and flawless—almost every inch of it. Life had left next to no mark on her surface, unless you really knew where to look.

But her eyes would not quite turn into Eva's eyes. She switched off the bathroom light, sat down on her bed, lit the white candle beside her blue-robed Madonna, and groped under the bed for something to cover them.

Javier pulled himself away from the sill of the sliding glass door as if from the edge of a whirlpool. He closed the door to keep in the central air and drew the white sheer curtain across it. At the piano bench he played about half an hour's worth from the Couperin score on the music stand, barely sounding the notes—it was a dolorous, crepuscular music. When he stood up and snapped off the light, some reflex hauled his attention to the glass door. Through the drifting sheer he seemed to see a white fox standing in Eva's doorway. White fox head and a dark woman's body and the nipples of two chocolate breasts looking right at him, while the eyes of the fox head seemed blind. You are not seeing this, Javier said to himself, you are dreaming.

He went into Kristina's room and listened to her sleeping breath until his heart rate slowed. On his way through the bath that divided their rooms he stopped to take a sedative. Having slung his clothes on a chair-back he lay on his back in his boxers, watching the vine shadow dance on the wall, waiting for the drug to take hold. As always he had left both doors open between himself and his daughter, so he could hear her murmur as she turned in bed and hear her breath regain a steady plane. That was real, the only real thing. Everything else was snare and delusion and he knew that the fantasies of his unserved need might sometimes take on a material appearance and present themselves, delusionally, to his senses, but he also knew that he damn well hadn't dreamed everything.

Five

"The fuck do all these bozos come from, think we sell spa equipment?" Enrique howled as he slammed down the phone.

Javier glanced toward him over the corner of his laptop screen—he had his laptop open and running, though at the moment he was actually typing on the keyboard of his desktop unit. Across the hall, Rico throbbed inside the taut fabric of his creamy linen suit.

"You're not supposed to deal with the public, *compañero*," Javier reminded him. "Let Alicia take those calls. It's what we pay her for."

"You think?" Rico raised a bushy black eyebrow. "Well, Alicia is MIA once again, off powdering her expensive little nose." Rico gave his own snout a twitch. "On the outside or the inside, I couldn't tell you."

Javier glanced at his watch; it was quarter to five. A shaft of the afternoon sun blazed over his shoulder and pooled in a brilliant oval on the surface of his desk.

"True party girls don't wear watches, yo," Rico informed him. "Ask her what time it is and see if she kn—" in mock alarm he clapped his hand over his mouth as Alicia cruised down the hall between their offices, gliding smoothly on her preposterously high heels, and trailing fumes of fresh nail polish. Today she wore a sequined T-shirt emblazoned with the logo of a *Pussycat Lounge* in Las Vegas, and silky black pants that looked painted on. They weren't hiring Alicia because she was one of his girlfriends, Harold had explained some months before, but because she was just the kind of receptionist that an enterprise such as theirs required. There was truth in this, Javier reflected, not because Alicia could type very fast or make sense on the phone, but because she looked like a piece of prize booty, in all the senses of the word.

"Look at me," Rico groaned, and tilted his desk chair so far and so brusquely that he almost flipped it over backward. "Flying a desk, *hijo de la puta*. Maybe I should have stayed in."

"Maybe," Javier said. "Right you could be getting blown up in Baghdad."

Rico righted his chair with a creak of its violated spring. "Could end up there yet if Harold starts slobbering after that easy contract money."

"Screw it!" With the slip of a finger Javier had deleted twenty lines of HTML code from the website he was working on, and the UNDO button wouldn't recover it. He pressed his fingers to his temples and scooted back from the desk, turning to face Enrique through the doorways.

"That money might look easy but it's not."

"Never boring, though," Rico said.

Javier snorted. "If you're bored like that, go wreck a car. Me, I'm a family man. I live in the realm of the reasonable.

"I hear you," Rico said, without conviction. "But Harold gets funny ideas sometimes. Like, you call your thing 'Essential Solutions' you get bozos wanting to know how to tan the Playboy bunny onto their butt cheek."

Javier laughed, in spite of himself. "Try hanging out a sign that says 'Soldier of Fortune' and see what kind of bozos you get." A movement on the laptop screen caught his eye but it was nothing, a bird taking off from a branch in the courtyard. "You mention Harold, seems like I didn't see him since lunch."

"Renée called," Rico said. "She has some bug up her *concha* which Harold must investigate right away."

"The mouth on you!" said Javier.

Rico got up and came around the corner of his desk. In spite of his bulk he moved lightly, rippling all over like a big jungle cat. It was merely a reflex for Javier to roll his chair a foot into the clear, and to poise the balls of his feet on the turquoise carpet. He had trusted Rico with his life for ten years or more.

Rico paused in the hallway to glance down to the reception area where Alicia was gazing at her elaborate telephone console with good-natured bemusement, perched on a tall, high-tech stool that afforded an excellent rear view from the back offices. Then he crossed over to Javier's desk and stopped to peer at the laptop.

"You spend a lot of time watching that baby-cam, bro."

"Yeah." Javier flicked a finger and tiled a dozen cameras on the screen. "I see the sparrow fall."

Rico squinted. The copper planes of his Indio face creased up and his black eyes sank deeper. He brought his long black braid over his shoulder and ran a thumb over the brush at the end it. Here and there the braid was threaded with white.

"Whoa... one in every room, huh?" Rico wrestled his collar open and probed the puckered scar on the side of his neck. "Your system would work in Paradise, you think?"

Javier shrugged. "In the Palace, maybe. With luck." He glanced up at Rico and snapped the laptop shut. Rico only played with his car when he was fretful about something. "You're not asking me that for a reason, are you?"

Trouble in Paradise. That was not only a joke but a code. Javier drove home, late, distracted. Late as it was, the downtown Miami traffic was still engorged.

He could move his sedan three feet at a time. He had spent two extra hours poring over the day's surprise commo, once Rico finally coughed it up. He hadn't looked in on Kristina when she woke from her nap and he hadn't called Eva to say he'd be late and he didn't much feel like doing it now.

"There's trouble in Paradise," Rico had said. "Harold thinks maybe you should go down."

"Since when? Why didn't you tell me? Before..."

"Cause you're like a freaking single parent now," Rico said, and ran his blunt forefinger all around the puckered purple center of his scar.

"I have a live-in," Javier said. "I can still travel. That was the deal. Why do I have to? I mean I looked at the intel this morning. What the hell could have happened since lunch?"

"Anytime you take your eye off the ball..."

Javier punched his desktop computer into a Listserv and messages began to tumble onto the screen. "Could you be a little more specific?" he said. "Or do I have to pitchfork through all this shit myself?"

"In twenty-five words, the Phantoms were frailing on the university protestors—"

"Right, they do that every other day." Javier scrolled and scanned messages, his lips pursed.

"Yeah, but today they broke into the national university compound and were hammering the students there. The university president, whatever they call him, came down to give them a lecture about it and they beat the whole fuck out of *him*—"

Javier spun away from his desk and looked up.

"—with iron rebar apparently. They broke both his legs and I don't know what else, so he's being flown out to Miami—"

Javier stood up and walked out to the glass wall behind his desk. The sun was sinking, a red disc with its edges crisp as it sliced at the downtown horizon. Three stories below, a Metromover train snaked by on its elevated track.

"I don't think you're gonna see the actual plane, *compañero*," Rico said. "But he'll be here. Or he is here. The *Herald*'s already on it. The whole hornet's nest is buzzing already. They're hanging the attack on his Holiness... or not. The usual people beating the usual drums.."

Javier turned from the window. "How's his Holiness taking it?"

"He's overflowing with pious indignation. What the hell did you expect?"

"You think he ordered this one?"

Rico shook his head. The braid switched behind him like a lion's tail. "Nothing in it for him but shit if he did. Of course that doesn't mean he didn't."

"Right. Where's Dayshon in all this?"

"He's freezing up, I think. He's fixing to hold his breath till he turns blue. You know, Dayshon is aces at protecting the asset in the field but liaison isn't his strongest suit. Not in Paradise, anyway. He can't handle that level of whatever the fuck it is that they do."

"You talked to him while I was out."

"Yeah."

"You didn't tell me you talked to him."

"Harold didn't tell you." Rico was sweating; he peeled off his creamy jacket and hurled it across the hall into his office. "The feeling was we didn't want to stick you with this one, maybe, with your personal situation and all. But I thought you might want to know for your information that the HNP liaison guys are pining for Chen Blan. He who speaks their savage lingo and understands their savage customs."

"Dayshon speaks the lingo."

"Not like you."

"So you talked to HNP. What's their read on it?"

"They seemed to think the Phantoms have slipped their leash."

"The Phantoms never had a leash," Javier said. "That's their whole problem."

The sun's disc cut into the horizon like the red hot blade of a table saw. Javier put his hand on the glass and felt the heat in the cup of his palm.

"What's your read on it?" he said.

"It's shaky but it's not irretrievable," Rico said. "An appearance from Chen Blan might cool it out."

Javier flexed his shoulders and let his arms swing free. "I could run down for a day or so."

"*Esta bien*," Rico said. "You want Alicia to book

you a ticket? Or no, you might end up in the wrong country."

By the time Javier turned onto his home block the tingle of anticipation of the trip was well worn off, and he was left with a residue of logistical worries. The stars were just coming out overhead. He punched the transponder and slid under the rising door into the underground garage. As soon as he cracked the car door he smelled smoke. He closed it, locked it, opened the laptop. Camera eleven. Eva was burning something in the kitchen, it seemed. Javier smiled and went up the steps two at a time.

The crackle of tension inside the kitchen soon dissipated his flush of relief. A burnt skillet of pancakes seemed to be the source of the smoke. Eva had laminated the batter to the metal, and then apparently run out of ideas. Javier fixed Kristina's location as he entered the room: next to the glass doors that led to the courtyard, her head rocking side to side like the weight on a metronome, long hair switching across her face.

"Don't be mad, Daddy," she called. "Don't be mad!"

Eva stood hunched in the center of the kitchen, sobbing into her cupped hands. Javier snatched the burning skillet into the sink, shut off the gas and snapped on the fan in the hood above the stove-top. He swung Kristina up to his hip and pushed open the sliding door to carry her outside. Kristina's head was still rocking.

"Stop a minute," Javier said. "Put your head on my shoulder." He turned around and around, T-stepping in a spiral toward the center of the courtyard, twirling her till her rhythm broke and she relaxed against him. When she lifted her head it was steady and she looked at him with clear eyes.

"Don't be mad at Eva, Daddy," she said soberly. "I don't want Eva to go."

"What?" He smoothed Kristina's hair back from either side of her face; the hair was loose and silky, the way Eva maintained it. "Who said? Eva's not going to leave."

"Don't get mad at her. Daddy?"

"I'm not mad at Eva." Javier peered toward the open glass door. Thanks to the cross-ventilation the smoke had mostly cleared from the kitchen and he could see Eva plainly. She was pacing up and down the kitchen like a dog in a run—the grace of her movement was lost and she paced in stuttering little jits. Then she crumpled onto a chair with her head and hands and hair in pool on the table before her.

Javier made his voice molasses-slow.

"Eva is mad at herself, old thing," he said. "You know how you get mad at yourself when you mess up? You draw the cat and it looks like a dog?"

Kristina smiled faintly.

"You draw the fish and it looks like a buffalo?"

Kristina giggled and put her finger on Javier's lower

lip.

"It makes you mad, right? So Eva tries to make pancakes and they come out looking like.."

"Burnt dirt!" Kristina cried.

"Sshh," said Javier. "Don't want to hurt her feelings. Come over here with me for a minute." He settled with her at the edge of the fish pool. "Are you hungry right this minute?"

Kristina shook her head. "I don't want Eva to go."

"Listen, old thing. Eva's not going anywhere. Because I'm going on a trip and Eva is going to stay with you. If Eva didn't stay, I couldn't go. Get it?"

Kristina nodded. "How long, Dad."

Javier calculated. The run to the island was supposed to take two days.

"A week at the most," he said. "You'll have fun with Eva. I'll tell her to order lots of take-out. You can get coconut shrimp and all that."

Kristina nodded. Her attention shifted to the pool, where a speckled koi drifted just below the surface of the water. Javier took a granola bar out of his pocket and pressed it into her hand.

"Chomp on that," he said. "Supper might be a little late. Watch the fish a minute, while I go talk to Eva, cause I think Eva is maybe a little upset."

Halfway to the kitchen door he turned back. "Don't feed that to the fish, all right? It's not fish food. It's not good for them." Kristina laughed and waved him on.

Javier's prior experience with hysterical women had not been very positive. He went to the sink and ran water into the skillet before trying an approach on Eva. The pan hissed and steam shot up and Eva burbled into louder sobs.

"It's all right," Javier said. "It's okay." He wished he knew how to say it in Spanish. Eva kept crying into the tabletop. Her lack of posture struck him as strange; she was dropped there like an unstrung marionette. She was leaning so far into the table that her shirt had gapped from the waistband of her pants, revealing three knobs of her spine and what looked like the top edge of a tattoo, a smudge barely visible against the black velvet of her skin. Unlike practically all other women in South Florida, Eva didn't dress to expose this part of herself.

Javier looked away from it. He laid the flat of his hand between her heaving shoulder blades, the spot where he used to pat Kristina, rhythmically, soothingly, when she was small enough to cry through long nights in her crib. Eva's distress spread into his palm and thrilled all through him, pouring down his spine to his feet and shooting back up his legs to his belly. What kind of a sick puppy are you, he thought, getting off on somebody's pain this way?

He took his hand away and rapped his knuckles on the table. "Get a hold of yourself," he said. Too loud. Eva shot upright as though she'd been struck with a cattle prod. With an effort, he made his voice low and smooth. "There's no harm," he said. "No damage done. Everybody makes mistakes."

Standing a full body's length away from her, he delivered a clinically therapeutic touch to the sharp bone of her shoulder. Eva straightened and looked at him through her tears. The sobs had subsided into hard breathing, and the rise and fall of her sternum brought her breasts hard against the flimsy cloth of her shirt. Look at her face, Javier told himself, and narrowed the focus of his sight into her eyes, which were red from crying, and maybe also from all the smoke.

"I said I could cook." The smooth darkness of Eva's voice had gone ragged.

"Well, you *can* cook," Javier told her, thinking. "You can cook scrambled eggs and rice and beans. I've seen you bake a chicken." He forced a smile. "So far you never blew up the microwave."

Eva looked down because she was smiling, but her chest was still heaving hysterically fast.

"Pancakes are tricky," Javier said. "You burn a batch of pancakes, it's not a capital offense. You hear me?"

Eva's shoulders were still heaving. He sat down at the table across from her. "You don't lose your job over burnt pancakes, all right? So you can calm down now. Give me your hand."

He didn't know why he had said that, but Eva seemed to understand. She let her hand slip across the table to him, and Javier took it in both of his own.

He turned it palm up and then palm down. There was no resistance in her body; the whole arm was like a strand of seaweed floating in the ocean. The hand was delicate, with long slender fingers, rich velvety black on the back and a surprising warm pink on the palm. He rubbed the muscle at the base of her thumb and felt her breathing begin to relax. Javier felt more in control now; he had been here before, finding a route to deliver comfort to a crying child, and he was comfortable with where he was.

"Come on," he said. "I'll show you."

He got up and went to the sink to wash the skillet, but Eva soon nudged him aside and took over the task herself. She did it thoroughly, using scouring power to wear away the last dot of burn. When she had finished, the stainless steel gleamed like a star.

"Okay," Javier said. He raised a spoon from the crockery bowl and watched the batter spool down. "You put in the eggs? You put in the oil?"

Eva nodded. "I put everything it say on the box."

"The oil's important," Javier said. "Now here's the trick." He put the skillet on a burner and snapped on the gas.

Eva made a quick jittery moment toward the stove. Her bottom lip was caught in her top teeth.

"Easy," Javier said, trying not to get himself involved in the plumpness of that lip. "Not quite yet." He wet his finger at the sink and shook a few drops of water into the skillet; they splattered and sizzled away.

"Another minute." He held his palm above the hot metal. Eva watched him, curious now, a finger on her chin. Javier shook droplets into the skillet and this time they rolled and scurried over the surface like tiny beads of mercury. Eva swallowed a giggle and covered her mouth with both hands.

"*That's* how you know it's just hot enough." Javier kept up the molasses voice. "Got to be *just* right..." Quickly he dropped half a dozen spoons of batter into the skillet and then planted one the middle. Eva was closing in with a spatula raised high.

"Not yet." He fended her off, and took the spatula from her. "Wait till the bubbles come through on top and it gets a little brown around the edge, see? *Then* you can turn them." He demonstrated. "All right." He passed her the spatula. "You can do the rest."

Gingerly, Eva turned the other six cakes. She was smiling into the skillet now.

"That's the way," Javier said. "Another minute, you can take them out."

Kristina was coming in through the glass doors from the courtyard. Javier grinned, and spread his arms wide, the wooden spoon held high in his right hand.

"Behold the Pancake King!" he said. Kristina laughed and he glanced at Eva. "*And* the Pancake Queen." He pushed the bowl and spoon toward Eva. "Go on, you can do the next batch."

"And the pancake princess!" Kristina shrieked.

"Oh yeah," Javier reached under the sink and pulled out a small fire extinguisher. "Next time when the Pancake Queen makes pancakes, the Pancake Princess will stand guard with this."

Kristina dissolved into giggles, and Eva doubled over laughing, though she was careful not to overturn the skillet.

Javier rinsed the batter bowl and beat four eggs into it while Eva levered the second batch of pancakes onto a plate.

"Put those in the oven to stay warm," he said. He took the spatula from her and scraped a few crumbs of pancake of the skillet, and judged it clean enough.

"Now the omelet," he said. "The principle is similar. Not quite the same..." He poured a little olive on the hot metal and tilted the pan to coat the surface. Eva was watching closely. "Pass me those eggs if you would." Javier tilted the bowl and poured the eggs into the center of the pool of oil and shivered the pan so the egg mixture ran to the edges.

"Now," he said. "You just do nothing for a minute or so. Sometimes nothing is the hardest thing to do but... if you leave it alone, it's not going to stick. See, it's starting to cook through to the top... I just throw on a little cheese like so." Javier demonstrated, slinging a handful of slivered Parmesan into the pan; the cheese settled into the uncooked egg on top of the hardening yellow disc.

"A shake of pepper maybe... and we just cover her

up, so she cooks from the top."

Javier put the lid on the skillet, stood back and clasped his hands. "Now we pray to the saints. Just a minute or so."

Eva, uncertain, imitated the mock reverence. Kristina sat at the table now, swinging her bare legs and giggling over her clasped hands.

"Now," said Javier. "The unveiling!" He lifted the lid. "See, cheese all melted, egg is all cooked, and you can just—" He lifted an edge of the omelet with the spatula, then let it drop.

"All right, you can do this." He thrust the spatula toward Eva, who ducked and backed away.

"Come on, you can do it. Just fold it in half—it's a no-brainer."

Cautiously Eva accepted the spatula. She crept to the stove, took hold of the skillet handle, and teeth clenched, folded the omelet.

"That's it," Javier said. "You made an omelet. Which many excellent cooks can't do."

"I didn't." Eva said. "You made it."

"You did the hard part," Javier said. "Turning it, that's the moment of danger. That's where careless people go wrong."

Eva looked at him and then away. She had recovered her composure to the point that he had no idea what was going on in her well-shaped head.

"So there we are," Javier took the platter of pancakes out of the oven. "Let's eat."

They ate pancakes with syrup and the omelet cut in three, while Kristina told them about the morning at the beach, where they had seen dolphins swimming in close to shore, and a big stingray washed up on the strand, and some jellyfish too, but she didn't get stung. In the afternoon at Morisco Park there had been a bad boy that bumped girls' legs with his big metal toy Hummer. But Eva said something to the boy that made him leave Kristina alone.

"Oh really," Javier looked from Kristina to Eva, inscrutable, and back. "What did Eva say?"

"I don't know Spanish words, Daddy. But that boy went all the way on the other side of the swings and he didn't come back where we were all day."

"Well," Javier said. "Maybe I ought to learn these Spanish words." Eva was standing up to clear the table. "Or maybe not." He smiled into his hand.

"Where are you going, Daddy?"

Eva was behind him, at the sink, but Javier was pretty sure he could feel her eyes on the back of his head.

"Got to go to Paradise, old thing," he said. "Just for a little while."

"I wanna go to Paradise," said Kristina.

Javier pushed his chair back and looked up at the ceiling. "Not this time, kid. I'll take some pictures for you, though."

"Isn't it safe there yet, Dad?"

"For me it is," Javier said. "For little girls, not quite.

We're working on fixing it up for you still."

Kristina yawned. "When do I get to go to Paradise?"

Javier sighed. "Wait till the moon is full."

"You always say that, Dad."

"Yeah," said Javier. "I always do." He stood up and moved around the table toward her. "Come on, sleepy girl," he said, opening his arms for her. "Let's get you started on the path."

"What path, daddy?" Kristina molded to him as he picked her up.

"To the Big Rock Candy Mountain," he told her. "That's the path that goes through your bath and into your bed."

"Then where, Daddy." Kristina nuzzled his neck as he carried her into her bedroom and set her down to start the bath water running.

"Then you float up out of your bed and you're on the Big Rock Candy Mountain in your dream. And in the morning you climb back down the Big Rock Candy Mountain and you'll wake up in your bed."

"And you'll be in Paradise then, Daddy."

"So I will," said Javier. "And you'll be here with Eva. I'll send you a picture on the computer too."

He stayed with her in the bath until Eva came in and then he went to his bedroom and set up an email account for Eva on the desktop computer there, and printed her out a note with some phone numbers. When she had finished brushing Eva's hair, he called for her and she came through the bathroom door and stood on the threshold, waiting. Javier rolled his chair away from the screen.

"Come take a look at this," he said. "You know your way around a computer?"

"A little," Eva said, and stayed where she was.

"Email and that kind of thing?"

Eva nodded.

"Okay, you're *evaaguilar007@earthlink.net*," he told her, standing up from the chair. "I made you an identity on the computer so—look, let's restart it and take from the top."

Eva flowed toward him, her slender hands swimming around her hips. At his gesture she sat down and he swiveled her toward the computer, his hands on the chair back, not touching her anywhere.

The screen swam into resolution and three icons floated up—a snap of Kristina, smiling into the camera, a snap of the back Javier's head, and a full-length picture of Eva, standing straight and still and gazing at the fish pond in the courtyard. She turned her head three quarters, still not quite enough to see him where he was standing directly behind the chair.

"You have my picture?"

"It's magic," Javier said, and kicked himself for thinking that was a cute thing to do. He was glad she couldn't see the flush he felt rising in his cheeks until he realized she was looking at the big mirror over the bed and could see anything she wanted of him there. He set his teeth and thought of something he'd once seen on the road outside Kandahar until his blood reversed its flow and his face went pale.

"Just click and you're in," he said. "Okay? There you go. You can use this email program. I made the password be the same as your address but you can change it if you want. And look, you already have a message."

Eva looked confident enough as she clicked her way into her mail.

From: perroblanco@earthlink.net
BOO!

"So that's me," Javier said.

"*Perro blanco?*" She was looking at him in the mirror again and seemed to be suppressing a smile.

"Whatever," Javier said. "No one else had it. I have to go on one of my sales trips tomorrow. You know, I told you I would.."

"Yes," Eva said slowly. "To sell... Cognobits. No?"

Now Javier caught her openly smiling in the mirror. "You have a good memory."

"No," Eva said. She closed her smile and dropped her head. "Not really."

"So look," he said. "If you could email me once a day, maybe. In the evening, let me know how things are going. And I may send Kristina a picture or something like that. If she has a message for me she can send it this way too. Okay?"

"Yes," said Eva. "I understand."

"And of course you can use the computer to surf the internet or whatever you want."

"Yes. Thank you. Mister Con*nell*." Without prompting she hit the sequence of buttons to shut down the computer.

"I shouldn't be gone more than a week. It might be shorter. The cell phone number should find me anywhere... if something comes up. But if I don't answer, call the office number and they'll find me for you."

"Yes," Eva stood up. "I should sleep—"

"Yeah, you're right," Javier said. "Better you should stay in this room while I'm away." He looked at the doors and started to say something more and didn't. Now both of them were looking across the wide expanse of the king-sized bed, to their own reflected images in the mirror behind it, awkwardly balanced in the glass. Again he could feel that annoying flush rising up his throat.

"Well, you can clean the sheets, I guess..."

"*Claro*," Eva said. "I do it every week."

"Of course," Javier said. But somehow he was still impaled on the moment, till Kristina called from the bedroom. Javier went in and kissed her on the forehead.

"I want Eva to read," Kristina said.

"You should be with your father," Eva said. "You won't see him for a week, maybe."

"I want Eva," Kristina said, reaching toward her with a Beatrix Potter book in one hand.

"Hey," Javier said. "It's a good thing." Eva took the book and settled on the bed and Javier went out and sat down before the piano. Eva's soft accent made the familiar words of "The Roly-Poly Pudding" seem perfumed and exotic. After a moment he opened a score and began to play one of Hiraki Oe's short melodies that he thought worked well for a lullaby. Kristina's last words had allayed his sense that the whole situation was a little shaky. It was a good thing that the child could still give her love and trust so easily. He felt calm, and even happy, and the music soothed him further. He wasn't sure how much time had passed when Eva came gliding silently into the room.

"You play so nice," Eva said. "Nice music. It sounds like birds."

"Well," said Javier. "You've got ears. Oe took a lot of these tunes from bird songs. So they say."

Eva pushed back a clump of her tight braids and touched her small dark ear, as if surprised to find that it was a good one.

"How did you learn to play like that?"

"Oh," said Javier, and shifted on the bench. "Both my parents were classical pianists. My brothers, my sisters, they all play professionally. All of us had lessons from jump."

"How many you have?" Eva asked. "Brothers, sisters?"

"Two each," Javier said. "Yeah. I'm the last one."

"But you don't... you don't go in a..." Eva seemed to

be stuck for a word.

"In an orchestra? No." Javier spread his hands and looked at his fingers, slightly crooked. "Too much of a good thing maybe, six pro musicians in one family already—I couldn't quite push it through to lucky seven." He dropped his hands to his knees. "I was in my first year at Peabody and I cracked, I guess. I just wanted to do something different, and I went and joined—um. Well. I signed up with Essential Solutions, I mean."

"To sell Cognobits."

"Right." Javier looked up at her sharply, wondering if she was on to him, but Eva stood in her nun-like pose, her face turned demurely down.

"It's a living," Javier said. "There's not a lot of work for concert pianists really." He pointed at the couch behind her. "Sit down a minute."

Eva obeyed, closing her body as she settled, knees close together and her hands folded on her knees, her back supply straight but her face lowered, eyes closed on her folded hands.

"Listen," he said. He would have liked to make eye contact somehow but he felt it would be a violation. There were ten feet of bare carpet between them and he didn't dare to close the distance.

"Anybody can burn a batch of pancakes," he said. "Say you exaggerated your housekeeping skills a bit—so what? You've been doing the job we need done." He wished he could feel less like he was programming a robot or hypnotizing someone against her will.

"You're safe here," he said. "I mean, your job's safe. I mean anybody could cook and clean but not anybody could take of Kristina the way you do. She's fond of you. And I think you really care for her."

"*Es verdad*." Eva looked up. Her eyes were warm and brown and for once there seemed to be something in them besides her perfect submission.

"*Gracias*," Javier said. "Well. I speak that much Spanish, but that's about it."

"*De nada*," Eva said, but now she was talking to her hands folded on her knees.

Javier relaxed on the bench, leaning his back against the edge of the keyboard. *Mission accomplished*, he thought. Eva remained exactly as she was. She would stay that way, he realized, till he told her to do something else. Probably she would do anything he told her to.

"Okay," he said, shifting on the bench. "I'll be out of here before you two wake up, most likely, and I think I better pack and—"

"*Buenas noches*," Eva said. She was up and gliding smoothly through the glass doors into the courtyard, looking back once obscurely through the shadowed glass as she closed the door behind her.

Javier kept a small duffel ready-packed for such excursions, so all he had to do was make a five-minute inventory of the contents. He zipped the bag and set it by the door. The AC shut off and the house was silent, except for the light sound of Kristina's breathing on the other side of the bathroom doors. He turned off the light and walked through to watch her from her doorway for a moment, then went back to his room and slipped out of his clothes in the dark.

For half an hour or so he lay on his back under the thin sheet and watched the vine shadows flickering on the wall. Somehow his eyes didn't want to close. Maybe it was mission nerves, but he hadn't had that since before Afghanistan. He was sure everything was squared away here and really he was looking forward to a quick run back to Paradise. So what? A few minutes later he stood up and padded into the living room in his shorts. He snapped on a light and scanned his CDs until he found a Mingus record, then turned out the light when the music started.

"Myself When I Am Real." He kept the volume low so as not to wake Kristina, though nothing much would wake her when she was well asleep. When the last lingering notes of the piano solo had faded he shut off the machine and turned to his own keyboard, hands hovering over the keys, unable to punch into them. He had the chops to play the tune, but it was all Mingus and could never be him.

That thought saddened and confused him. He closed the lid on the piano, thinking maybe he would drug himself to sleep. Then something stirred on the edge of his peripheral vision and he turned his head and saw, through the glass, that Eva's door was open across the courtyard; there was a warm orangey glow of candlelight inside.

He stood up and moved to the glass door. It seemed that he could see her shadow moving inside the lighted room. When his breath began to fog the glass he opened the door, cautiously, silently, then stepped out and closed it behind him just as carefully, hands working behind his back so that his eyes could always be fixed on the light of the door across the courtyard. All that craftiness must have some intention behind it, though he would not admit to himself what the intention was.

Presently Eva's silhouette appeared in the doorway. He saw the swing of her long skirt as she moved, but it seemed to him that her torso was bare. He couldn't be sure, with the light behind her. She stood perfectly still, and he saw nothing but her outline. The night was overcast, heavy and still and completely dark, and he had been sweating but didn't realize it till a rivulet of sweat ran into the corner of his mouth with a taste of blood.

There was no light whatsoever on his side of the courtyard, so since she had come out of a lighted room she shouldn't have been able to see him at all. Except he was wearing a pair of white boxers, and she had been standing there long enough for her eyes to adjust, and once she picked out the boxers she would probably be able to make out the rest of his form against whatever ambient light was captured by the plate of glass behind him. She saw him, Javier was sure of it, and she was seeing the intention in his mind more clearly than he could see it himself.

The ripple of water from the courtyard fountain seemed suddenly, surprisingly loud. Eva turned, and he saw the lift of her bare breast against the lighted doorway. She was still looking back at him over her shoulder as her hands went to her waist and her hips undulated and the skirt dropped away and pooled on the doorsill as she stepped out of it, out of sight into the room, whose door was still hanging open.

A cricket sound high up in Javier's head kept chirping *you're not gonna do this you're not doing this* but it had no more influence than a cricket would have had. A martial arts teacher had once told his squad that before the brain got into the head there had been another more primitive brain situated in the *dantyen* area between the navel and the genitalia. Javier's body was taking orders from this brain now. The one in his cranium had signed out for the night. As he lurched across the courtyard toward the lighted door, he tucked the tip of his erection under the elastic waistband of his shorts so the thing wouldn't keep wagging so awkwardly in front of him.

The statuette of Our Lady of Sorrows was shrouded in the red bandanna like before. The candle had burned halfway down the jar. Its light came glittering through the glass and danced along the wall.

Javier shut the door with a click that struck him like a gunshot; at the sound, the woman's body stirred under the white sheet. She had moved her narrow bed, pulling it out at an angle from the wall so the foot of it was aimed at the door, directly toward him. He took a step toward her and she reached with her right hand and pulled the sheet clear of her raised knees. As her legs opened, her head rolled to the side, turning her face hard to the wall, so Javier could see nothing of her features, but maybe that was meant to make it easier for him. The flower of her cunt bloomed open, showing him a glistening red smile. Just before they joined at the hood of her clit, the lips were joined by a fine gold chain, with a translucent red bead fixed at the center. The surprise of that! His eyes locked there, his breath caught at the top of his throat, and a rush of blood flowed into his groin.

He snatched at the waistband of his shorts; a snap popped loose and the cloth slithered down his legs and disappeared. He was kneeling between her legs. She had set her pillow beneath her slim haunches. His brain-cricket chirped that it still might be possible for him to turn back from the act and then it shriveled and blew away, a dry husk. He couldn't tell whether he wanted more to look or touch, and there was some faraway fluttering idea that he should try not to go too fast. He rocked forward till the underside of his glans just touched the red bead on the chain, and the cool shock of the contact made his whole body tremble, and her thighs quivered, as if she were responding. Then with a sudden impatience she hooked an arm around the back of his neck, though her face was still turned hard away, and pulled him down. He fell and caught himself with his hands flat on the mattress on either side of her head, and as he fell she made a cunning move of her hips to take him in, all the way to the hilt in the hot velvet sheath. For a moment he remained absolutely still, astonished to find himself where he was, her slick heat swelling and closing around his cock, and then the thrusting began of itself, uncontrollable. He searched for her mouth but she would not give him that—her head was thrown back very far, so his lips and tongue worked frantically along the raised tendons and strained curve of her neck. They slipped against each other in a slick of sweat; the room was so hot and close he imagined that his whole body was inside hers. He twisted his back and found her small round breast; the nipple swelled into his mouth, long as a finger, and she made a sound, some ambiguous gasp, it might have been annoyance but still it encouraged him, so that he slowed his blind doglike hunching and tried to find a rhythm that would please her, bring her into the movement of his desire, drawing his cock back till the head lay twitching just at the very edge of her lower lips, then pressing it home again, but gently this time, slowly, once, twice, and then another dalliance on the brink, and then he lost control and drove down and in, pulling her up with his hands cupped under her small taut buttocks. Her breath came whistling through her teeth, but still her face was turned away. He came kissing along the bottom of her jaw line, which somehow was as far as he could reach, and this time she hid her face from him by locking it into his shoulder, wrapping her arms around him hard and snapping her heels to the small of his back, rocking him with a long serpentine movement of her spine that ended at the bottom with a buck so explosive that he had to free a hand and reach down and squeeze it hard around the base of his cock to stop himself from coming too soon. With every ripple of her hips the red bead on her piercing punched a dent in the soft skin above the shaft, and the image of it, more than the sensation, excited him immeasurably. Surely there must be a way to bring her with him. His other hand drifted to the cleft of her ass, and he recalled the edge of the tattoo he'd seen that evening, in some other world, only it seemed to be more substantial than just ink, raised like a welt, a sign his fingertip might read if he knew how to read it. He counted down the round bones to her coccyx and let one finger slide a little further in the damp until it touched the pucker of her rectum. She made another inscrutable sound and set her teeth into the skin of his collarbone, but delicately, like a dog lifting a puppy by its scruff. The same snakelike movement of her spine drove her pelvic bone into him so hard he felt the red bead of her piercing punch a little round dent in the flesh above his root. Now she held it, her lower back arched, lifting his weight so he was unable to withdraw from her if he had wanted to. Her breath came hard, and rasped a little, but it was a controlled, athletic effort, and the hot red clasp of her cunt was closing on him, rippling with the same snake motion that had started in her spine, milking it slowly from the base to the tip, once, twice—the third time he had to give it up and burst into a flash of white light behind his eyes.

His head went around and around in a peppermint swirl. He had collapsed, almost sobbing, into the clump of sweat-soaked sheet above her shoulder. The candle had gone out, he didn't know why, and in the close dark he could hear the slow drone of her breathing and could feel her heart, if it wasn't his, beating somewhere in the space between them. Otherwise she was as still and slack as a wild animal shot with a tranquilizer gun.

He sat back on his heels, withdrawing limply from her. Her face was still turned away, he knew, though it was invisible in the dark.

"*Gracias*," he breathed, just before he stood up. She didn't say *de nada* this time, but still he knew it was nothing to her.

Six

When the man has left my girl, lying limp and absent, as if dead, just barely breathing, her lower lips still open to the cooling, shrinking space where the man has been, then *Brise* flies up and out the low mouth of the cave, rising above the triple candles flickering in their jars inside, across the trickle of the spring where the red-trimmed leaves of aloe grow, rising high above the mountain on the warm spiraling currents of air... *Brise* rises dark-winged and invisible, higher still until below the plain curves to the edge of the bay, and the ocean curves to the edge of the world—I meet her good little angel there in the place where it has fled. O Eve O Eve O Eve... now Eve and *Brise* can be together, warm and strong on the easy wind.

"She needs to eat," Eduardo is saying. "*Claro que si...* a little meat on this bone." He prods a finger into her skinny thigh. But he isn't really talking to her, and she isn't listening at all. She sits on his lap where he has placed her, but stiffly, her breath shallow, her arms and legs brittle under the loose white shift in which he has dressed her. They are uneasily posed together on one of the two fish-fighting chairs in the stern of the long black cigarette boat.

"*A ver*," Eduardo murmurs. "I want her hungry too, you see..." Red Mickey is not listening to him either. Eduardo's words smoke up, into the blank sky above the empty sea, where the boat rocks slowly over the long waves. Jorge and Jésus don't listen either. They are oily up to their armpits, muttering to themselves in Spanish as they labor over the hatch of the engine compartment, exchanging chunks of twisted, blackened metal, struggling to make the motor purr again, like a big black sleepy cat. Red Mickey mutters to himself as well, American words, curses mostly—she does not really understand them. They are impatient, all three of Eduardo's men, though they keep the feeling bottled up. Eduardo is in no hurry. Eduardo is happy to be adrift so, because he needs some slow time with his girl.

Although her empty stomach is knotted, the pitch and roll of the powerless boat makes her a little nauseous. Inside the cavern of her head, black thoughts flutter through shadows like bats. Somehow they don't bump into each other. There is hardly any connection between them.

As often as Eduardo talks about feeding her up, he

doesn't really give her much. Sometimes a handful of crackers out of the square tin can. The men eat a thing called MRE, which doesn't seems like food to her, though she tries to swallow what they give her from it. Sometimes Red Mickey catches a fish and Jésus grills it on the deck. The smell of the fish makes her stomach wrinkle but Eduardo gives her little but the bones. Red Mickey is cutting a fish up now, but Jésus isn't going to cook it. Still mumbling his American curses, Red Mickey is threading bloody chunks of fish onto a steel hook as big as the crook of her arm.

At one of the little islands where they docked and refueled there was a restaurant where Eduardo bought her an ice cream cone. Then all the bat thoughts flew out of her ears because there was no room anywhere in her being for anything but the milky smooth sweet taste. How many days ago that was she can't remember. She can't remember how many days since the mountains of the big island sank and disappeared into the ocean.

A bat banks, chittering, to follow the inner curve of her skull's wall. Hunger, the doubled fist of an empty gut, is nothing new to her. When she was smaller her belly swelled with its own emptiness and her black hair turned red for the same reason.

See her standing among her brothers and sisters on the packed dirt of the yard, gaping at the giant white

Jeep Cherokee that had just rumbled to a stop outside the waist-high cactus fence. All morning her father has been sitting on the sill of the clay house, staring at his blood-stained bandage. He has been sitting so every day since the stone crushed his foot, because he is too lame to climb to the rock mine until it heals, if it ever does. But now he stands, with the help of a crooked stick, and hobbles grinning and simpering to meet Monsieur Duclos, who has just climbed down from the passenger seat of the big white Jeep where the chauffeur still sits, gazing vacantly in the other direction across a sweep of desiccated grass, and the guard still cradles his shotgun in back.

One of her bigger brothers catches the little starveling dog by the hank of string around its neck, holding it so it will not snap at Monsieur Duclos's ankles as he moves among the other children, now and then touching one of them lightly with the tip of his gold-headed cane. Though her toes are gray and bare in the dust, Eva is wearing a clean blue dress, and her braids are tied with shreds of gaily colored plastic bag, and she smiles cheerfully up at Monsieur Duclos when he stops in front of her, because she hopes she may be chosen to ride in the big white Jeep. Monsieur Duclos has a bald shiny head and a round face that seems jolly enough. He is covered all over with nice firm fat, so there must be plenty to eat where he comes from. Yes she will be given plenty to eat herself and yes they will certainly send her to school and to the church, the big cathedral in town indeed, and her father is agreeing to everything, smiling and bobbing his head like a coconut hull floating in the bay as Monsieur Duclos opens his large leather wallet and chooses from it the most worn-out bills, so grimy and frayed that the images of the heroes are no longer visible upon them... and not too many of them either.

She sits shyly on the edge of the back seat, feet together, knees together. Sometimes she looks quickly at the pistol-grip shotgun across the thighs of the guard beside her, and then still more quickly away. Never before has she ridden in a vehicle so grand or sat so high above the world where barefoot peasants trudge behind their donkeys through the clouds of dust the big tires of the Jeep kick up. When the Jeep begins climbing the road to Bel Air she glimpses, through the odd rent in the foliage, the calm blue water of the port, with a foundered freighter melting slowly into it.

Excitement is a great distraction. Also there is a lot of work in the Duclos compound for her to do. Not till that night, when she lies on the straw mat on the concrete floor beside Man Brigitte (still a snoring stranger) does she think of her mother, who was far away that morning, climbing the ravine to find water at the spring below the cave of *Brise.*

The bat folds its wings and drops into darkness. Red

Mickey has hurled his hook into the water. Cursing in his usual monotone, he stirs a bucket of blood and entrails. The day-old blood is thick and sour and it has drawn flies even here in the middle of all emptiness, no land in sight—she wonders where they came from. The blood-smell reminds her queerly of Marie-Angelique. It was she who washed the underthings, thoroughly in cold, cold water, each month when Marie-Angelique suffered her *règles*. She did not suffer *règles* herself, though scarcely a year younger than Marie-Angelique—that was because she never got enough to eat, though she never understood that was the reason. She did not go to school either, and rarely to church; she did not see her mother again and only Man Brigitte was good to her. Once when a chocolate cake sat unguarded on the table she could not restrain herself from taking a bite, and Marie-Angelique whipped her legs then, using her braided leather riding crop with the mean little loop at the end. She won't see Marie-Angelique any more, but in her mind's eye she does see the blood running over the white steps of the Duclos house.

Red Mickey stirs the blood, still muttering *what a fucked-up run why don't we just fucking drift all over the fucking ocean till the fucking Coast Guard picks us up with all this fucking dope* and Jésus and Jorge have closed the hatch of the engine compartment and they are ready to give it a try only Red Mickey chops a hand at them for them to wait until he has dumped the bucket of blood off of the stern, and then there is not long to wait. The nylon rope tied to the sunken hook snaps taut, thrumming from the base of the other fish-fighting chair where Red Mickey tied it, and he pulls it in, snubbing it around a stanchion, then turns the rope over to Jorgé and Jésus to haul, while he himself picks up a gaff. Eduardo pulls her tighter to him, rocking the two of them back on the spring of their fish-fighting chair, an embrace which might be meant to reassure, though he is hardening against her lean buttocks, sliding one hand under her garment to hover over the slack skin below her navel. The slick of chum behind the boat is lashed by several steel-gray fins. There are more sharks than the one on the line, all thrashing together in the narrow patch of water, then one, the one with the steel hook piercing its inverted smile, breaks the surface, and Jorge hauls him tighter to the boat, then Red Mickey jams the gaff in his gills and hauls the whole shuddering six feet of him aboard. A whip of his tail dashes stinging scales of salt water across her face— she is shaking with excitement and fear, so Eduardo pulls her closer, molds himself to her, drops his heavy jaw on her narrow shoulder so near that she can feel the first burst of beard through the skin he shaved that morning and smell the sickly sweetness of the scent he wears.

The three men are struggling with the shark on the boards just below the fighting chairs, the shark whipping and snapping, jaws closing on empty air, until finally Jorge and Jésus, tightening the rope turn by turn around the stanchion, manage to get the bullet head wedged into a corner. The rest of the body still twists and bucks and slams into the deck but now she can clearly see the fretted white teeth, row on row in the slit mouth of the imprisoned head. Some of them are bloody. Her heart is pounding, and Eduardo encloses a part of her ribcage, spreading and cupping his big hand so that her whole frantic heartbeat pours into his palm; he says nothing but she feels a smile in his scented cheek which is pressed against hers. She doesn't pull away or stiffen because certainly it is safer with Eduardo than the shark. Red Mickey snaps out his K-Bar knife with the Day-Glo plastic handle and as he rips the shark's belly up from the anus to the gills, Eduardo traces the same line from her belly to the flat bone between her nipples, with a slow horrible gentleness. The horny edge of his fingernail leaves a red line of sensation where it has been. Now the men flip the shark back over the rail, an arc of his entrails spilling out from its belly and other sharks thrusting up to snatch their portion of those guts before the wounded shark has even hit the water. The bloody ocean boils. There are more sharks now, at least a dozen, and *motherfuckers*, Red Mickey is screaming as he sprays a burst from his AK-47 into the finny stew, *come on motherfuckers let's see you all eat each other alive.* Red Mickey's hips are bucking and thrusting as his machine-gun spurts lead into the bloody water and torn flesh; he is still shouting, who knows what, with a white slobber gathering at the corners of his mouth. Jorge and Jésus are careful to stay behind Red Mickey, though they are very excited too, shouting *Chocha! Maricon! Tu puta madre me la chupa!* almost as if they have particular grievances against particular sharks.

Now Red Mickey's clip must be empty, but he is still jabbing the barrel this way and that, making the sputtering sound with his lips, and the white slobber flies. Jorgé and Jésus have calmed down, and finally Red Mickey's shoulders slump and he stares blankly into the calming water, the blood-cloud diffusing in the blue.

"*Si, muchachos,*" Eduardo says. "You have some fon, no? When you sail with Eduardo, is time for work, is time for fon *tambien.*"

"*Claro,*" says Jésus; it seems clear to him that the fun is over now, at least for him.

"The engine?" Eduardo says. He has relaxed his grip on her to a loose cradle.

"*Si, enseguida,*" says Jorge. He goes forward with the key.

Eduardo turns to Red Mickey. "Have your fon, Mick," he says. "But doan spend *all* your bullets on the sharks."

Red Mickey looks not at him but at her. "Jesus," he says, with an air of distaste. "Look at her, she's all eyeballs." He turns away and spits over the rail. "Ask me, we ought to drop her in the soup."

Eduardo rises, letting her slide to the deck, now holding her only by her hand. "Doan disrespect my girl," he says. But the threat is soft, lazy, he lets Red Mickey pretend not to have heard it, as the motor begins to thrum in the boards beneath their feet.

In the narrow forward cabin the engine throbs harder, vibrating from the sloping walls. The cabin is the shape of the shark's head, she now realizes, and the bumps in the oil-smelling eggshell foam mattress are where the teeth would be.

"Doan let another man do this," Eduardo says, as he parts her lips with his meaty tongue. "This is only for your *corazon*."

And at the same time his hand dips between her legs, hesitates as if it means to count the sparse hairs there, before an oiled finger curls into her bòbòt, far enough to test the membrane there, as it has done before.

"This.." his sour breath rasps in her ear, "This too we save, for the special won..."

The greasy finger shifts and rises, circles and teases her *languet*, until it swells and lifts itself from its shroud of skin (regardless of *her* wishes), a naked pearl. A moment before her breath had stopped but now the attack of invasive sensation pumps the air in and out of her lungs, and Eduardo is listening, studying this forced rhythm of her breath. She knows what she is supposed to do next so scarcely needs his grip on her wrist to guide her hand into his crotch. When she opens his trousers, the *zozo* blooms up from the mat of hair like seaweed floating underwater. Now the probing finger hovers on the puckered rim of her *bounda*, where it has also been before... but all of it has already happened before—she knows how to put the lubricant on him, exactly where and how to touch... yet on the edge of the next step she hesitates still. Resists, if only a little, in her stiffness and her halted breath.

"Doan be stubborn," Eduardo reminds her. "Remember the sharks? We doan wan' a stubborn girl."

But there is no possibility of her ever forgetting the sharks, and she understands very well what Red Mickey meant, if she didn't understand the words he meant it in, so she turns over, kneels and bows, her head trapped in the airless pocket where the walls of the forward cabin curve together and the engine throbs in time to the slow rhythm of his strokes and the men on deck turn up the boom-box to cover the noise of her cries, which Eduardo doesn't mind at all, but rather encourages, stroking the nape of her neck with the same grisly delicacy as before, and she doesn't hear herself at all. She is gone into darkness, then into light—her good little angel rocketing up into the vacant sky, where she and *Brise* are searching for each other.

Afterward she washes him docilely, as she has been

taught, and examines him carefully as she has been taught, and of course the *zozo* revives and fattens under the movements of the wet rag. He puts the molasses on it himself, from the dark sticky bottle. "*Venga*," he tells her. "*Dulces! Provecho.*" For this, of course, he needs her to be hungry.

Days later (though she does not count days) they come in view of a different string of islands, threaded together by a long ribbon of highway. For most of the afternoon they run north along the beaches, some of them lined with high-rise hotels, the like of which she has never seen. The cigarette boat cruises just beyond the surf, so near that she can see the pale-skinned people roasting themselves on the white sand. When the boat passes under a bridge of the highway, she gazes up, wondering, at the huge concrete stanchions.

On the lee shore is a harbor, full of large white power boats. Eduardo has let go her hand, a rare thing when she is out on deck. But she stays far from the rails, remembering the sharks, and always feeling the hard beads of Red Mickey's eyes. Eduardo checks the plastic bag of white powder in one of the button-flap pockets of his khaki shirt, then lifts up the shirt tail to be sure the flat pistol is snug in his waistband. He speaks into his cell phone, then snaps it shut.

Jésus has to stay with the boat. Red Mickey and Jorge come with Eduardo and her, to meet the squat woman who drives the powder-blue Cadillac.

"Gloria!" Eduardo kisses both her cheeks. She pulls her mouth away from his each time.

"I got shotgun," Red Mickey grunts, and gets into the front. Eduardo hands her into the back of the car, where she sits between him and Jorge, peering past them as best she can. The road beneath the wheels of the car is smooth as butter. But her head is still rocking with the movement of the waves.

The wall around the bungalow where they arrive is high as the wall around the Duclos house, and topped with broken bottles set in the cement, in the same way. In the Duclos compound there were places where rusting rebar still sprouted from the blocks, and there was a spot where she could climb, with Man Brigitte and look down through the leaves of flamboyant and mango to see the blue water so far below, and to breathe the salt air, ten times deeply, as Man Brigitte taught her do each day before their work began. But here the wall is smooth and featureless and she doesn't see any place to climb up, though of course she has not yet walked all the way around the inside of it.

As the gate shuts behind them, and the two security men set their backs against the gate, a handful of girls comes tumbling out of a long building with many doors behind the peeling pink cottage. They are older than she is, or maybe just better fed, but all of them have a woman's shape. They wear

clothes like the girls on the American television programs that Marie-Angelique always liked to watch,
though she did not understand the American words
in these programs. Most look Spanish; a couple are
white. Not a one so black as she. They stand with
their hips swaying slightly, all of them, though all of
them look uneasily down at the sandy ground. Each
girl dangles a numbered tag from her hand.

"I guess I'll go with Jail Bait here," Red Mickey
snickers after a moment.

"You have to say the number," the squat woman
tells him.

"Fuck you, Gloria," snaps Red Mickey. "Six."

The white girl in the tight T-shirt labeled Jail Bait
beckons with her key tag, though without looking up,
and Red Mickey follows her toward the door in the
long building numbered 6. The squat woman looks
at Jorge. Her cheekbones are high and her nose sharp
like Eduardo's, but her eyes more slanted... Chinese
eyes.

Jorge shrugs. "*Cuatro.*" A girl breaks from the line
and leads him toward the door marked with a 4.

"*Está bien,*" Eduardo said, glancing toward the squat
woman. "Let's go inside."

As they move toward the kitchen door, she looks
once over her shoulder at the security men sitting
on metal chairs on either side of the solid iron gate,
their eyes invisible behind tear-drop mirror glasses.
Then Eduardo is holding the screen door toward her,

urging her in ahead of him. The dim square room smells of Chinese food. She swallows.

"Anything she can eat?" Eduardo inquires.

Gloria grunts, transfers a paper carton from the fridge to the microwave. She snaps on the bare bulb above the table. Beside the bulb a curl of sticky paper dangles, sticky with black flies.

Eduardo pulls the Ziploc bag from his shirt pocket, glances at it, puts it back. She feels the Gloria's attention come to a point—no particular look or gesture but something she can feel. The microwave dings, and her attention points the same way at the odor of the food.

Eduardo's hand is heavy on her shoulder, and Gloria's eyes are sharp on his fat shirt pocket. "Take special care of this won , hmmm?" he says. "This won, this won is special to me."

Gloria shrugs, taking the steaming carton out of the microwave and pushing it across the table toward her. With it there is a white plastic spoon. The first taste, both sweet and salty, explodes along her jawline almost painfully.

"Too dark," Gloria says.

"She is my chocolate *baby*," Eduardo gives her back a thump, then removes his hand. More at her ease, she plies her spoon, forcing herself to eat slowly so she won't burn her mouth or choke.

"And she's French." Eduardo smiles.

"I know what she is." Gloria snorts. "So, you give

her a name?"

"Solange," Eduardo pronounces it voluptuously.

"Solange," Gloria repeats, pursing her lips and nodding. "She speak any English?"

"Ah, but she's young!" says Eduardo. "Besides, I taught her other things."

"I'm sure." Gloria's snaky plucked eyebrows arch.

"Listen to me," Eduardo raises his meaty palm. "*En la boca, está bien. En el culo, está bien.* But you will be sure to keep her jewel safe. Tell me that you understand."

"*Suerte,*" Gloria says. "Well, I have another one I can put her with. Nadya."

Now it's Eduardo's eyebrows that rise.

"The Russians brought her," Gloria explains.

"All right then." He turns his shit-brown eyes on Solange as she scrapes the last grain of oily rice from the corner of the carton.

"You see?" he tells her. "You're going to have a little friend here."

Solange looks at him, with no expression. She is waiting, because she feels he will go.

"*Hasta la vista, mi corazon.*" For a moment she fears he will kiss her but instead he turns, drops the bag on the table, and goes out. Before the screen has creaked back into the frame on its rusty spring, Gloria has made the bag disappear and darted through an inner door.

"Don't move," she calls back to Solange, her voice

oddly muffled. "Stay where you are."

In a moment Gloria returns, with a spring in her step and a new glitter in her slightly crossed eyes.

"*Ai, Dios,*" she breathes, and massages her temples. "That's better, no?"

Solange hears the question without understanding all of the words. She nods, just slightly, not knowing if an answer is expected.

Gloria beckons. From a patch pocket of her dress she hauls out a ring of keys as big as the one Madame Duclos used to have for all the locks of the house in Bel Air. Solange follows her down the basement stairs. At the bottom, Gloria unlocks a metal door and urges her in.

There is a red light bulb in the ceiling and a blue light from a tube plugged into the wall—the light from the tube makes her white dress glow so eerily that Solange half-wants to tear it off. There are two wide beds with a beaded curtain between them. A small television throws shadows on the walls, which are papered with pictures of half-naked models, cut out from magazines. The white girl stretched on the nearest bed doesn't look up when they enter. Her face is inches from the television screen.

Gloria claps her hands sharply. "Nadya!"

Slowly the white girl turns her head from the box.

"This is Solange. Solange, understand? Teach her the rules."

Nadya's lipsticked mouth hangs open, slack. Her

long hair is a beautiful corn-shuck color that makes Solange want to touch it, though of course she is far too shy. But perhaps, if she is to serve this Nadya as she once served Marie-Angelique, she will brush her hair one hundred strokes before Nadya goes to bed.

When Nadya finally nods her head, Gloria goes out and shuts the door behind her.

"God," says Nadya, as Gloria's key grates in the lock. "God, you should see your teeth in the black light."

Her accent is peculiar, and Solange doesn't have enough English to know what she means. But something makes her close her mouth all the same. Cautiously she creeps to the edge of the other bed and sits down. From here she can see most the TV screen, though parts of it are blocked by Nadya's stringy hair. Out from the box come American words. It is the same sort of program Marie Angelique once liked, with expensively dressed and made-up white people standing in richly furnished rooms, talking fervently to one another about their personal problems. She remembers the hotels along the beaches this morning, and the vast bridge they passed under in the cigarette boat, and the butter-smooth road that brought them here... for the first time it dawns on her where she must be. A place that people make the most terrible sacrifices to be able to reach.

"America?" she says. But she has to say it two more times before Nadya turns and gives her a lazy look over her shoulder.

Solange waves her arms all around the windowless basement room. "Is America?"

"Yeah, so what?" Nadya says, and drops her sulky face back into the lurid glow of the TV. "At least, that's where they *told* me I was going."

Seven

Javier left town on a Monday morning, and on Tuesday Eva delivered Kristina to her playgroup and was free for four hours. She didn't know what to do with this freedom. There was no shopping to be done for the house, which Javier had left fully stocked with idiot-proof instant food and a wide fan of take-out menus. She went back there, carefully following Javier's security procedures as she let herself in and locked up behind her. For ten minutes she lay on the bed in her room, eyes lightly closed, listening to the chatter of birds outside the wall. In Javier's room, which she'd occupied the night before to be nearer to Kristina, she had slept poorly. Now, however, she could not sleep. Soon she grew restless and got up.

In the courtyard she sat cross-legged on the tiles before the pool and listened to the water purling out of the broken jar and watched the golden, red-tinged koi swirling among the lily pads. The clematis on the trellised wall was blooming; now and then a hummingbird hovered before a blossom There was something about the gash in the jar that troubled her, though. Like a wound in her own belly. It had been broken deliberately to become part of the fountain, and that distressed her, even though it was only an ordinary red clay jar, one of a million that would never be missed, and had probably been made to be broken anyway.

She shook her head, sending her long braids winding over her shoulders, and got up. In Javier's bedroom, the computer screen dissolved and recomposed the shining, collapsing city. That shifting light had played over her all night, and maybe had disturbed her sleep. Tonight she'd shut the computer down, or cover the screen with a towel.

But now she sat down in the swivel chair, watched the shattering city for a minute or more, then joggled the mouse to bring the desktop up. She checked mail on the address Javier had given her. There was an innocuous message from him, telling her all was well at his destination, and that he had sent a picture to Kristina. She typed out an equally bland message to him, letting him know that all was well here, then closed the browser.

Google Earth was on the desktop, and Eva clicked to open it. Alf had introduced her to the program, and she and the tweakers had spent a lot of time playing with it. She could feel the mind of Trix beginning to stir behind her eyes. Though she didn't want that, she thought perhaps she could enjoy the program as Eva.

The program started as usual, zooming in on the turquoise jewel of planet Earth until the continents filled the screen, but it didn't stop there as it usually did—instead it kept zooming onto what must have been one of Javier's bookmarks. The coast of Florida whirled off the top left corner of the screen and the zoom plunged into the island so fast that Eva could barely register its contours. When it stopped she was looking at a satellite picture of the white oblong of the Presidential Palace and the intricate parquet squares of the Champ de Mars. Though she had never been to this place herself she could recognize it from a photograph she had once seen... a long time ago, in a world she believed no longer existed.

The jolt unsettled her, so that neither Trix nor Eva fully occupied the space inside her head. She put her right hand on the bone of her sternum and her left hand on her belly below her navel, and breathed into the palm of her left hand until she felt calm enough to look further. When she touched the tilt button the program displayed the sparse trees of the Champ de Mars, squashed into bulbs like broccoli, and the distorted façade of the white palace came into view. She caught her breath, zoomed out a bit, and began to scroll north slowly.

With Alf's crew she had practiced relating the streets she'd traveled in Miami to the streams of bird's-eye-view on the screen. Though she'd never seen a map of this country, it was still somehow sufficiently familiar. When she reached the mountains of the north it was though she were flying among the beaks in a small plane or on the invisible wings of a *loupgarou*. She followed the road to the gate of the town, where the harbor spread blue-green to the right... and surely those red roofs on the peak to the left lined the high road into Bel Air. She couldn't tell which house it was, but in one of them the photograph of the Champ de Mars and the Palace had hung. Weekly either she or Man Brigitte had taken it down and carefully, delicately cleaned the thin skein of plastic stretched over the frame to protect the photo paper from dust.

Her hand slipped away from the mouse and fell to her knee. She closed her eyes. There was a whole lagoon of vanished memory shining up at her but she was terrified of the shadows that moved beneath its surface. This world she had thought to be lost was still there. She didn't want to move further toward it but she was unable to move away.

Finally a chirp from the alarm system roused her, and when her eyes popped open, there was a message crawling over the very bottom of her screen.

!intrusion! Front Door !intrusion! Front Door !instrusion! Front Door !instrusion! Front Door !intrusion!

Eva broke out of her paralysis, plucked one of the alarm system remotes from the bracket by the bedroom door and crossed the courtyard to investigate. The inner door had an observation hatch in it, secured with a scrolled iron bolt. She shot back the bolt and pulled the hatch open. Through the square aperture she could see Hell, her black hair cinched so tight to the back her head it pulled her eyes wide open. A ring of white showed all around the irises. Hell was stabbing a key at the outer gate. The key looked much the same as the ones Javier had given Eva, but it didn't seem to fit the lock, maybe because Hell was shaky... She was wearing a tight black sequined tube-top over a pair of dirty streaked jeans, and she looked as if she probably had been up all night.

"Son of a bitch!" A thrust of the key bounced off the lock plate, and made a bright gash on one of the iron vines of the gate. Hell brought her knuckle to her thin lips, looked through the gate, and caught Eva's eye.

"Who the hell are *you!* What're *you* doing here?"

"I take care of the girl," Eva said, and immediately wished she hadn't.

Hell licked her knuckle thoughtfully; she had scraped it in her struggle with the lock. "Son of a bitch," she said. "He told me there wasn't anyone else. That lying bastard."

Eva pulled her face to one side of the hatch. "I only

take care of the girl," she breathed.

Hell stepped sideways, to regain her view. "Oh yeah. I bet that's all you do. You lying *cunt!*" She looked at the useless key in her palm, then raised her eyes to Eva again, studying. "Hey. Wait a minute. You look like Trix."

Eva banged the hatch door shut and stood, leaning her whole weight into her hand against it. Beyond, the gate was rattling in its frame.

"Goddammit!"

Eva could hear the voice plainly enough, in spite of the closed door between them. The gate clattered angrily. Most houses on this street were set well back and screened by shrubbery but this tantrum was extravagant enough to be heard from a long way off.

"He got no right to lock me out! I only want what's mine!"

Eva opened the hatch. "Wait," she said. "Be quiet. I'll get you something." These could be magic words, she knew. Alf had used them to good effect sometimes, when Hell came raving to the house on Tamarind Way, where this kind of commotion on the street was much more problematic than here. As if by magic, Hell calmed down. She looked at Eva cannily, her tongue rasping on a cold sore at the corner of her mouth.

"You are Trix. Aren't you? Why, you *crafty little bitch.* How did you ever weasel your way in here?"

"I don't know what you're talking about," Eva said.

"I never saw you before in my life."

"Just let me fucking in already." Hell raised her voice, gave the gate another shake, breaking off one of her long black nails against the tangled iron. "I only want what's mine."

"Mister Connell is not at home," Eva said. "I'm not allowed to let anyone in."

Hell raised one hand to her face and noticed the broken nail. Her face twisted tight. "She banged her palm against the gate, winced and grew calmer. "Listen, Trixie... I don't want to mess with your game. I don't even need to know what it is. Just *let me in a minute*. I only want what's mine."

"I'm not allowed," Eva said. "I'm sorry. I don't know you. But wait. Be quiet. I'll get you something."

She closed the hatch. The banging on the gate did not resume, but she was sure that Hell was still out there, clinging to it like a bat. In two and half hours she would have to go out those doors to collect Kristina from Jolly Toddlers. The thought of calling the police never entered her mind and she thought of Javier's emergency number even less.

What's mine. I want what's mine. When Hell threw these fits on Tamarind Way, she was after dope, or something she could sell for dope. In the end, Alf always said, it was cheaper to give her something to get rid of her. But Alf liked Hell well enough on a good day. Alf called her the girl with the strawberry curl, for Hell sometimes dyed a red streak into her snarly black locks. When she was good she was very very good and when she was bad she was horrid.

In the Javier's bedroom, Google Earth had given way to the screen saver. Eva slid open the closet door and found the silver disco purse in the back corner. *What's mine.* She felt oppressed by the gleam of the big mirror at her back. What if Hell thought everything in this house was hers? What if it really was? Eva had never owned anything herself but her body and a few sets of clothes to cover it. If that. She took two twenties from the housekeeping money Javier had left her, zipped the money into the purse and started back.

There was no noise of cursing or rattling now beyond the barriers. Maybe Hell had given up and gone away? Eve unlocked the inner door and pulled it open. Hell was there, silent and attentive, her hands with their black nails curled slack through the iron vines of the gate. Eva sucked in a breath and walked toward her.

"Here." She had to fold the purse to begin poking it through one of the gaps in the ironwork, for none of them were very big at all. But somehow Hell got her narrow hand through it and clamped it onto Eva's wrist.

"You *cunt!*—you think I came for *this?*"

Solange went limp whenever anyone touched her anywhere. Trix was generally too prickly to be touched at all. Eva hadn't had time to learn what Eva did in such situations. Hell's bony hand was like a handcuff locking her to the gate.

"I don't know what you came for," she said.

Hell's grip tightened. "So. You're fucking him." Her breath was sour: cigarette smoke and crack fumes and a deep internal rot. "So good for you. *I* never liked it."

"I don't know what you're talking about." With her free hand, Eva shoved the folded purse a little further through the gate. "Just take the money and go."

At the word *money*, Hell's eyes flickered and her grip went a little slack. Without extraordinary effort, Eva twisted herself free.

"Ow!—goddamn!" Hell pulled her hand back, flexed the wrist, and cradled it for a moment with her other hand. Eva had stepped back, out of her reach. With a quick pecking movement she snatched the folded purse free of the iron, then pulled the zipper open.

"Forty bucks? You think you can buy me off like I was some crack ho? I ought to have half this fucking house!"

So drop the money, Eva thought. Drop it on the ground and turn your back. She didn't say it. She could more or less see the wheels ratcheting in Hell's brain—something she had seen before. Hell was seldom in the mood for crystal when she came to Alf's, but she would take whatever crystal she could get and trade it up for something she wanted more.

Money was even more negotiable. Forty bucks would buy a monkey his next meal.

Hell closed the purse and moved its rolled leather strap to her shoulder. "Don't think it's over," she said. "This doesn't begin to touch what I'm owed."

A whistling hole opened up in the back of Eva's head and words came through it from a long way behind—she heard them as if she were a bystander listening.

"You know, you're lucky he's not here. He'd probably kill you, after what you did."

Maybe Hell turned pale at that. Eva herself was frightened. But Hell was practically always pale. She pushed her chin up boldly. The weary skin pulled tight along her cheekbones. Eva saw the good looks Hell might still recover if her monkey didn't ride her so hard. Hell sniffed and turned her back. Her gait was only slightly rickety. The hard little heels of her disco boots still clacked on the sidewalk after she was out of Eva's view.

Eva sat on the bed in her room, staring at the driver's license, her picture framed by the name and the numbers and the various codes. Eva Aguilar. Eva Aguilar. I am Eva Aguilar.

Today is the First Day of the Rest of Your Life.

The door to her little bathroom was open and the

medicine cabinet mirror showed her bending over the laminated card like a wild dog crouching over a bone. She picked up one of the cloths from the feet of the blue-robed Mary on her night stand and held in front her face as she approached the mirror and covered it.

That was better.

Inside the house she covered all the mirrors with dishtowels or pillowcases, according to size. The big mirror in the bedroom required a bed sheet. When she had finished this work she returned to the computer, zooming out on Google Earth till she saw the Florida panhandle thrusting out into the blue sea among dots of indistinguishable islands. She typed in Javier's address and watched the program close upon it. There was the hacienda-style enclosure, the red tile of the roofs and the rose tile of the courtyard. She could see the green blurs of the shrubs in the courtyard and a faint gleam reflected from the fish-pool. She knew that she was there herself, although she was invisible.

That was better too.

At the usual hour she went out to pick Kristina up from her playschool, pushing the elaborate pram ahead of her. In one of the pram's utility pockets she had set a large kitchen knife, disguised in a wash-rag, its handle an inch or two from her hand. But she didn't see Hell anywhere on her way. Hell would have had to go a long way from here to score, and once she had done that she would have no pressing reason to return. Also Eva believed that the last words out of her own mouth had a real power to repulse Hell and fend her away. On the streets of this quiet neighborhood she saw no one but dog-walkers and other au pairs or stay-at-home moms. Most of them knew her by sight by this time and would wave in return of Eva's shy smile.

Kristina wanted to go to the park, and though Eva tried to talk her into to going home to play Rook or Cootie Bugs or watch TV or take her nap, Kristina couldn't be persuaded. She knew she didn't *have* to take a nap, and she wasn't sleepy, and her friends were going to the park from the playschool—Robin and Maria. Eva gave way. In Morisco Park, however, she wouldn't be drawn into play with the little girls, but stayed on her bench near the pram and the masked handle of the knife. In case... what? Kristina herself was something Hell might claim as hers, and if she appeared beside the swing-sets to make the claim, Eva could hardly picture herself whipping out the knife and plunging the long triangular blade into Hell's skinny thorax, but then she could hardly picture herself doing anything... that was a larger problem. She held her missal on her knee, not looking at the pages. Robin and Maria and Kristina had all brought Jewel-Rider figurines into the sandbox and were arguing, though not unpleasantly, about the story line in which these actors played.

Her body grew cold, and her heart shrank, as though a shadow had passed over the sun. There was no shadow, only a lean figure groping at the latch of the gate. Not Hell at all, but a skinny Anglo boy, dark-haired, pale and hollow-eyed. She looked at the knife, without moving toward it. He wasn't there for her, though she could feel the pattern of his frustrated need printed all over her reflexes.

He locked his brown eyes with Annika's ice-blue ones, then finally let his own eyes weaken and fall away, but still he came fumbling in through the gate, faltering his under-confident way toward her. Annika had been hired by another family in the neighborhood, to look after Robin, which meant she had some contact with Eva because Robin and Kristina often played together. Passed over by Javier in Eva's favor, Annika would never look at Eva if she had to speak to her, but Eva was well past the point of being wounded by disregard.

Brigitta, another of the German au pairs as like to Annika as two ducklings were alike, lounged beside her friend on the bench, fixing the dark-haired boy with the double-barreled blue chill of their stare. He faltered as he came nearer, and stopped on the sandy tiles before he reached them.

"I am vorking, James," Annika said. "You know, you must not come vhen I am vorking."

James spread his hands. Long fingers. Delicate.

The slender body was a ghost inside the billowing loose white shirt "I know, but Annika, I had to come. After.." He glanced at Brigitta, whose hard eyes scrolled up and down his figure from his sandaled feet to his tousled hair. "Couldn't we just.." he glanced at the gate he had just come through. "Can't we just... go over there and talk?"

"I don't haff time vor you vhen I am vorking," Annika said. She stretched then, deliciously, arching her back against the bench, so that the pendant of her navel piercing sparkled under the hem of her spaghetti strapped top, and the nipples of her little breasts thrust up through the satiny fabric. His desire swirled over her like sunlight, and she basked. She dropped her head back over the top rail of the bench, exposing her white throat, then raised it with a wicked smile. "Anyway, it is not talk you vant."

Eva looked down at the cover of her missal. It was strange to her how neither Annika nor James seemed to know that he might simply throw her down and take whatever he wanted from her. Perhaps not here, in the park before witnesses, but later somewhere else where no one would see. At his pleasure and not hers. Almost any man could do this, to almost any woman, and most would. How was it that these two didn't know it?

"When you get off work?" James was saying. "When do you?"

This ignorance weakened him and strengthened

her, Eva realized. Annika gained power not by sur-
render, but refusal. The force of her refusal was
blowing the boy out of the park like a strong wind,
slumped inside the cloak of this need that he had no
idea how to satisfy.

"Maybe I have time tomorrow, James." Annika said
to his back. "If you call, leave a message on my voice
mail."

When the boy had gone, both Brigitta and Annika
turned their gaze on Eva, almost as if they could see
through to the mystification in her mind.

Eva made macaroni and cheese for their supper, scru-
pulously following the instructions on the box. She
sliced carrots and green pepper rings and she and
Kristina dipped them in a saucer of ranch dressing
to go along with the macaroni. For Kristina, an ice
cream sandwich after.

While the girl was in her bath, Eva remembered
that Javier had sent her a picture via email. She started the computer under Kristina's identity, but left it
for the girl to open her own email account, once she
had toweled off and slipped into her nightgown. In
fact there were two messages from Javier—one an an-
imated greeting card that sent Woody Woodpecker
chittering across the screen and the other a photograph of Javier standing next to a heavy-set black
man with his hair in tight cornrows. In the background were a couple of palms and a white archway

framing an iron gate.

Hi Kristina! A big hello from Dayshon and love from Dad. I'll be home before you know it.

"Dad's in Paradise," Kristina clapped her hands and wriggled in the desk chair. "With Dayshon."

"Is that Dayshon in the picture, the other man ?"

"Yep. Dayshon is *strong*. I saw him bend a horseshoe once. Just with his hands."

"He must be strong, then," Eva murmured. She stood behind Kristina, beginning almost surreptitiously to work tangles out of her damp hair with the big comb. "Stronger than your Dad, you think?"

"Dayshon's bigger, yeah. But stronger? I don't know. Dad's different."

Eva combed and studied the picture. Dayshon had thrown a big arm over Javier's shoulder. Though distinctly smaller, Javier didn't seem dominated by the pose. He was balanced on his own hard center, like a thunderstone.

"Where is this Paradise?" she asked.

"In the ocean. I get to go but only when I'm bigger."

"Why?" Eva paused with her combing.

"It's not safe now for little girls. Later will be better. And I'll be bigger too."

"Of course you will." Eva smiled, raising her head toward the big mirror behind Javier's bed. Sheeted, it returned only shadows of their two reflections.

"How come you covered all the mirrors?"

"So ghosts won't look at us from the other side."

Kristina seemed to accept this answer. Eva laid the comb aside, and lightly massaged her scalp. Kristina liked this, curved into it like a cat. Eva caught sight of the photo face-down on the dresser and heard herself say, "What happened to your mother?

"She died."

"I'm sorry," Eva said, regretting the question as soon as she asked it—what *had* she asked it for? But Kristina had stopped responding on all levels. Her whole body had gone cool and stiff under Eva's hands.

"Kristina? Kris?" Eva swirled the stool around, and knelt to peer into the girl's face, but Kristina's eyes shot through her head and into the sheeted mirror beyond. One might say they were no longer Kristina's eyes at all. A pair of black wormholes into nowhere at all. Eva was dismayed but not astonished. She had seen these zombi stares before. On Nadya's face, for one—under the black-light in the basement room, when Nadya had a visitor, and for an hour or so after the visitor left—

Stop it.

She picked Kristina up, her arms and legs dangling limp as wet dishrags, carried her to her bed and crawled in beside her. She held her in a cocoon of warm harmless contact until in twenty minutes or so the child's body softened and her eyes slipped shut and presently she breathed against Eva's cheek in ordinary sleep.

Eva slept too, but dream caught her up in a set of iron claws and cast her back down into Gloria's basement, where Solange and Nadya both had their visitors, sometimes for one, sometimes the other—sometimes for both at the same time, and sometimes two men or more just for one of them. Sometimes they wanted Solange and Nadya to do things to each other while they watched and took pictures, or Gloria would take pictures while the men did things to Solange or Nadya. There was nothing the men could not do to them, except one thing, Gloria always told them if they were Anglos, shaking her finger archly, the long cracked claw curving—*una cosa solamente no puede hacer* if they were Latin. Once a visitor tried to do it anyway, the thing that Eduardo had forbidden, but Gloria called one of the guards from the gate and he ran down the stairs and broke the visitor's nose with the butt of his gun and dragged that visitor away, leaving Solange and Nadya to clean up for once someone else's blood instead of their own. For Nadya it was a Russian named Timon who did the forbidding. Timon sometimes visited Nadya himself, for a long time, while Solange watched, since there was nowhere to go but the bathroom and the bathroom had no door, and Timon wanted her to watch besides. Eduardo didn't visit. They didn't see daylight for weeks in the basement room. Gloria brought them their food. There was no clock but they could tell time from the TV when there were no visitors and they learned English that way too, from looking at the television. Home Shopping Network was good for learning English words for things and sometimes the visitors also liked to have the TV on.

Then one day Gloria brought down to them new dresses, white sun dresses and little white socks with a ruffle and little shiny black shoes with a strap, and ordered them to wash carefully and put on these clothes, then finally they were called up into the kitchen above, blinking and squinting in the dreadful glare of the sun. Eduardo gave them each a pair of red heart-shaped sunglasses, which helped a little when they went outside, and the windows of the black car where Timon was waiting were tinted, and that helped too. They drove up the Keys for an hour or two, and by the time they turned into the Disney World parking lot Solange's eyes had stopped hurting so much.

Solange knew it was Disney World, because of the television. She looked at Nadya but Nadya's face was as blank as a cartoon character's behind the silly sunglasses. The men bought them tickets, but once they passed through the gate they stayed just on the other side, waiting and shifting their weight from one foot to the other in the painful sunlight, with Timon and Eduardo holding their hands, and no one speaking. A visitor came for Nadya first, a wrinkly tan Anglo in golf clothes, his face hidden by the long snout of his cap. He snickered and said the sunglasses were a nice touch as he slipped a small envelope from his hand to Timon's, and he took Nadya's arm and led her away; Solange never saw Nadya again. Alone with Eduardo, Solange peered around herself for a few minutes more—the outsize Disney characters were capering among the throngs of arriving families and she noticed that a lot of the smaller children seemed to frightened of them. She felt a little frightened herself, and then from behind a big bobbing Mickey Mouse appeared her Anglo visitor, older than the other one, in bright red pants with a potbelly under the waistband, a plaid shirt and white hair on his arms, and his eyes were watery and his breath smelled like the dead mice in the corners of Gloria's basement and Eduardo was whispering in her ear that this was what he had saved her for—pushing her in the small of the back into the hands of the Anglo visitor and she knew somehow that what was coming would be worse than anything that had happened before.

Then darkness, Solange was ripped away and Eva fell down a great black suffocating chute, hemmed in by a hideous screaming, only she must not have screamed out loud because when she jolted awake Kristina was still quietly sleeping beside her, *Agradezco a Dios*. Eva was covered in a cold stinging sweat and her heart was pounding as if it wanted to crack her ribs, but Kristina was breathing a sweet sleep breath on her throat, thank God thank God. She took hold of the child's wrist and found a pulse and gradually her own heart slowed to match it. Moonlight cast shadows of the vines across the girl's small sleeping face, bougainvillea with its flowers and thorns—the thorns against robbers and the vine against the intangible threats. Eva made Kristina a number of silent promises as she watched. Javier, who thanks to a Starlite scope fitted onto webcam eighteen was able to capture this image of the sleeping child with the black Madonna, let his own heart loosen and give way, thinking, *we got ourselves a damn lucky draw.*

Presently Eva got up from the bed and left the room, but Javier stayed with the sleeping Kristina, satisfied, stretching out under the mosquito net he'd strung in an upper gallery of the Palace, letting his eyes drift shut as the laptop screen power-saved itself into darkness. In the kitchen Eva forced herself to drink a tall glass of water, gagging a little at the cold hard contact on her throat, but she stopped that reflex and swallowed it all down. A minute later she began to feel better as the moisture began to reach into her flesh. She walked to the fountain and crouched, trailing her finger in the pool, then dabbing that dampness against the nape of her neck as she rose upright; that cool wet contact seemed to brighten her mind and tighten her focus.

Before the computer she punched Javier's identity. A password prompt popped onto the screen. She typed Javier and Connell and JavierConnell and all three words backwards but none of it worked. She typed Dayshon, Hell, Helena. Invalid all three. The Trix mind was rising from the stem of her brain and flowering into the top of her skull. She logged on under her own identity and entered a Chat Room called the Crystal Cave.

> **Tryxmystrys: trixrfrkidz!**
>
> **Bulbunscrewd: Salutations my queen. Where have you been!**
>
> **Tryxmystrys: walking in the world and going up and down in it. What else!**
>
> **Klean Machine: RU sticking widda program tryx?**

Crystal Cave was, ostensibly, a recovery room and support group for meth addicts on the mend, but was also equally a pretty good place to score, which made the atmosphere sometimes confusing.

> **Tryxmystrys: you know it mista KLEAN and thanx 4 axing.**

BRYTERLATER: 12-STEPPIN ALL THE WAY
HOME RIGHT TRIX

Tryxmystrys: never doubt it

Bulbunscrewed: I need a meeting. Numba 10.
comp me a tryxy tip.

A meeting was rehab, number 10 was a score. Or
so it had been the last time Trix was in here. She
hadn't been here recently. Rules and codes were ever
changing.

Tryxmystrys: better ask Apteryx where is
he anyhow?

BRYTERLATER: LURKING. HIDING HIS FACE
IN HIS HAIRY FEATHERS

Apteryx: U Rang? BuS Meering 4 U, numba ten,
corner of Desdemona and Vine, South Beach.

Bulbunscreweds: Kool Beans..

Klean Machine: Forgot what happened last time,
Bulbus?—your six months good right down the
drain.

{Buulbunscrewed has left the Crystal Cave}

Klean Machine: Apteryx, you prehistoric shitbird, get your hairy feather ass outa our safe space.

Apteryx: Or ?

Klean Machine: I guess u think nobody knows how 2 find ur skinny ass in realtime.

Apteryx: Don't you see I'm walking with my QUEEN ? Trixy baby it's been too long. When did you get in?

Tryxmystrys: Awww! U noticed.

Apteryx: U R the light of my life. Come see me FTF awri! I need

Tryxmystrys: A I'm looking for a logger quick, state of the art—can u help me out

Apteryx: Whoa Tryx U R axing little old moi?

Tryxmystrys: well I

BRYTERLATER: WOULD YOU TWO CUNTS STOP SELLING DOPE AND SCHEMING CRIMES IN OUR SAFE SPACE GODDAMMIT???

Apteryx: Watch your language in fronta my girl.

Klean Machine: I know we are all committed to

nonviolent conflict resolution so Bryte if you have any beef with Apteryx that cant be settled her you can always check him out at 2235 Tam

Apteryx: I'm outa here! Tryx, check your hotmail address I hope u still have it

{Apteryx has left the Crystal Cave}

Tryxmystrys: U guyz r kinda crossing the line

BRYTERLATER: US? US?

Tryxmystrys: Whatever. Sayonara. See you never.

{Tryxmystrys has left the Crystal Cave}

She closed the chat room window and opened her Hotmail account on the browser. The message from Alf was already there at the top, with an .exe file attachment: Big Dipper.

"My hero," she typed in the reply line. "Hope I didn't get you in trouble."

"No biggie," Alf came right back. "I know where both of their asses live too. When you coming to the house again? We miss you. We miss your... magic fingers."

"I'm sure," she typed. "My best to the family! And Alfie, thanks for the bot."

She closed Hotmail before he could answer. With a couple of strokes she opened Big Dipper and stashed it in a hidden folder under her own identity. Then she logged off and made a another pass at Javier's identity—typing <<Apteryx>> for the password this time, just for laughs. The log-on failed as she expected it would. But when she returned to Big Dipper, the <<Apteryx>> keystrokes had been faithfully captured. As whatever Javier's real password would be, whenever he next logged onto this machine.

The catch was that whenever Javier next logged onto this machine he would be back in town and back in the house and then she would have less access and then... what was it exactly she wanted to know? Maybe she ought to go and see Alf. Alf had been good to her. He had taught her lots. If not for Alf she never could have... but being around Alf was only going to make her mind fill up more with Trixyness than it already was right now. Now when Eva wanted Trix to leave her alone in her own head. In whosever head it was anyway. It would be better to sweep away every trace that Trix had ever existed, so no drop-by to see Alf and the crew on Tamarind Way and no more visits to the Crystal Cave, but the problem was that Hell had followed Trix all the way to this door and to get rid of that trace Eva would have to start all over somewhere else. But she had just made Kristina a lot of secret promises she didn't mean to break. Those were Eva's promises.

Eva Aguilar.

The trouble with Trix is she never slept because she was always too busy, hacking and phishing and scheming. But Eva, Eva wanted to sleep. Without dreams. So *Adios, Trixy*. She had sat long enough without touching a key that the computer screensaver had begun to rebuild and destroy the shining city. She woke it up to shut it down.

Salga lejos, Trix. Eva dropped a towel over the monitor, took off her clothes and got into bed.

When Jolly Toddlers reconvened on Thursday morning, Eva pushed the empty stroller briskly home, carefully locked herself in, and picked up the phone. Her finger was on the last digit of the work number Javier had given her when she remembered caller ID. Strollerless now, she left the house, locked up carefully and set the alarm, and walked twenty minutes to the small shopping center where she had been picking up milk and a few other perishables during Javier's absence. She dropped coins into a payphone outside the Chuck E. Cheese's and dialed the same number again. A woman answered, with a slight Latin accent, voice so sultry Eva imagined she could smell the haze of perfume that had to go with it.

"Essential Solutions!? How may I direct your call?!"

Eva coughed. "I'd like to order some Cognobits."

"I beg your pardon?!"

"I'd like to order some Cognobits, please—for refrigerators."

"For refrigerators?! Gog... Cogn?! *Just* one moment please?!"

The hold music was a lethargic *merengue*. Eva turned her back to the booth and peered through her vague reflection in Chuck E. Cheese's plate glass window at the drink cooler inside, next to the cash register. In less than a minute, a man's voice came on the line.

"Essential Solutions. What was your question?"

"Cognobits."

"Cognowhats?" This voice also had a Latin tinge but no sultriness, rather a grating edge.

"Yes, I'm calling from the, ah—" she could just read the name on the handle of the Chuck E. Cheese's cooler inside the glass—"ah, the *Whirlpool* factory in, in Evanston, Illinois, ah, to order more Cognobits. For refrigerators. Whirlpool refrigerators."

"Okay." The man's voice had taken on a weighty calm. "You're calling from a Whirlpool factory. For Cogno... Cognobits. For refrigerators."

"Yes, that's right. Our local distributor ran out, ran out of Cognobits, you see, and suggested we call Essential Solutions directly—"

"Right. Just one moment—please stay on the line."

The *merengue* trickled to its end and was replaced by a brisker *compas*. The quicker tempo made Eva jumpy but before she could make up her mind to hang up and bolt, the man's voice returned to the phone.

"Miss?"

"Um yes?"

"If you could just clear up one thing for me?"

"Yes?"

"If you're representing a Whirlpool factory in Evanston, Illinois, why is it that you're calling from a pay phone in Boynton Beach?"

Eva's heart lurched.

"See, we're having a little bit of a problem here understanding exactly what it is you're after, but if you just want to step into that Chuck E. Cheese's right behind you and order yourself a Slurpee and a slice, I think I can have a car over there by the time you're done, and somebody to answer all your questions, and maybe share a big laugh with you too, in case this is your idea of some kind of *fucking joke*—"

When he realized that he was now talking to a dial tone, Rico aimed the receiver at the cradle with enough force to smash the whole apparatus through his desktop, but at the very last second pulled the power out of the movement, and replaced the handset softly, almost without a sound. Almost without a sound he rose and padded down the hall to the receptionist's desk. Alicia had opened a little silver compact and seemed submerged in the study of the pores of her left cheek. Was she ignoring him? Or was it possible that she was really so oblivious that she just didn't realize he was standing right in front of her, elbows propped on the rosewood ledge of her desk, near enough that with one quick motion he could snap her elegant neck?

She showed no surprise when he crooked a finger under her chin and raised her face to look at him.

"Next time anyone calls about *Cognobits*...'"

"*Si?*" Alicia's eyes were empty, disinterested, above the compact's silver rim.

"Don't put them through."

Eva sat in front of Javier's computer, her legs twitching from the strain of walking home at a normal pace, without breaking into a panicked run. A Google Search brought up the Essential Solutions official web site on the first try. There was no mention of Cognobits or refrigeration of any kind, although the contact number was the same as the one that Javier had given her, the same number she had just called. Essential Solutions seemed to offer services rather than a material product: Risk Management, Crisis Avoidance, and Executive Protection. Eva sifted through clouds of euphemism until her head began to hurt. By the time she stood up from the machine she had a coalescing idea that Essential Solutions sold security for highflying businesspeople in risky spots around the world and that the company prided itself on being one of the few private enterprises to have successfully sold its services to foreign heads of state.

No mention of any place called "Paradise." Nor of any other particular place. Or person.

Eva drifted to the bedroom door and ran her finger along the steely edge of that mysterious pocket door behind the wooden one. If that was what it really was. Thus far she had never seen it used and hadn't found a handle for it. She stooped and lifted the hem of Javier's batik bedspread. There was a long drawer in the teak frame under the mattress, locked. Eva twirled the brass combination wheels at random. She dropped the bedspread back into place and straightened up. The movement sent a shower of golden sparks across her field of vision, and she had to brace herself against the wall for a moment till the dizziness passed.

After all she had not slept so well last night. She hadn't eaten this morning either, because she was all nervous with her tricksy social engineering plan for Javier's company. That had been stupid. Why did she need to find out what she already knew? She went into the kitchen and shook some Rice Krispies into a bowl, mixed in a fruit yoghurt and ate, mechanically. The hum of the refrigerator was very loud in the room. Cognobits my ass. That was Trix's voice again. But she had learned something new. Now she knew that Javier's company was very quick and efficient at what it did. *Bastantes. Pare el pensar.*

The refrigerator stopped its humming and now she could hear the tick of the kitchen clock. The steel face of the refrigerator door was covered with multi-colored alphabet magnets with which Kristina had misspelled her name. Above, at adult eye level, was a calendar with Kristina's birthday circled in red, the third Saturday in August, still a few weeks off.

She rinsed her bowl and put it in the dishwasher, then went out to feed the fish, lingering to watch the koi rising, kissing their rubbery lips at the flecks of floating meal. In the kitchen again, she put the fish food back on its shelf. The calendar, with its circled date, caught her eye, and she stepped quickly back into the bedroom with the computer and typed Kristina's birth date, in words, in the box for Javier's password.

No.

She typed the date as a string of numbers. Javier's desktop opened on the screen.

Javier had used different passwords for his financial program and for most of his word-processing files. He must be acutely *security-conscious*. Eva had acquired that phrase today, from the Essential Solutions website. To be *security-conscious* was a virtue in that world. Big Dipper would crack those other codes, in time. Meanwhile Eva paged through Javier's photo files. The usual occasions. Christmas. Kristina's birthdays, one two three and four. In this sequence, Helena appeared to age ten years. With a little fullness in her face, a year or so back, she looked not only prettier but calmer. More recent was the face Trix had known better, the one with the bones pushing through the skin. Helena going to Hell over time and the sawing of a need that could be appeased but not satisfied. The monkey craving out through her eyeholes.

In one folder Helena wore the same outfit as in the framed close-up that Javier had turned face down on his dresser. Eva was curious enough to get up from the desk-chair and lift the photo out of its ring of dust to confirm it. Yes, it was the same café au lait-colored silk, with the oddly demure little round collar and the modest string of turquoise beads. The framed photo shared a streak of the same sunset with the group shot on the computer screen, the one with Javier and Hell lightly holding hands, flanked by a couple of women Eva didn't know, and the black guy with the cornrows, Dayshon, and a similarly heavy-set Latin man with a long braid going gray slung forward over his shoulder—both of them looking uncomfortable in the matching suits they were stuffed into. Javier wore his suit more easily.

She was looking at their wedding, Eva realized. She clicked Properties and read the date. Just three years back. But Kristina was four.

She went up a level in the file tree, resorted the folders by date and opened the most recent one. Just one picture, Kristina in her bathtub, splashing, a bright curve of water rising toward the camera. After a moment Eva realized this wasn't a still but a video, and after a little fumbling got it started in a media player.

Kristina was laughing, though without sound, as the silver sheet of water slopped over onto the bathroom floor. The door popped open, knob smacking the wall, without sound, and here was Hell screaming in a herky-jerky silence as she yanked Kristina out of the tub and cracked her across the jaw one-two, whipping her head from left to right, the long wet tangled hair flying, and shook her, screaming silently into her churning face and then let her fall to the tile floor where Kristina lay, apparently too stunned to cry.

The video stopped.

Eva clicked Properties and read the date. She couldn't be certain, she hadn't kept track, but the video had been uploaded no more than a week or ten days before her first meeting with Javier and Kristina in Morisco Park. She wasn't going to watch that video again but it seemed easy enough to match the marks on Kristina's body—faded to a jaundice yellow by the time Eva gave her her first bath—to the events the camera had captured. Eva had watched the bruises fade and watched, maybe without knowing she was watching, for new ones to appear. None had.

The camera! Solange had known plenty of those, seldom troubling to disguise themselves, but shoving their chrome snouts boldly between the bodies of girls and their visitors. Eduardo himself had painstakingly recorded a memento of Solange and the palsied visitor who'd bought her maidenhead at Disney World; he sold a copy to the visitor and kept a secret copy for himself. Unique in its particulars, it was not the first in which she had costarred. Sometimes there were surveillance cameras in the rooms where she was kept, but no one bothered to conceal them; they crouched like ugly metal spiders in the eaves.

It came to her that this would be one of the services veiled in the vapors of the Essential Solutions website parlance. She went into the bathroom and washed her hands fastidiously, then dried them on the towel while she searched the mirror above the basin, considering the angle of the video she'd just seen, but the mirror's frame stopped too short. She adjusted the towel on its rack and turned, carelessly—there was something like a little mirrored capsule in a high corner of the molding opposite the tub, but she didn't mean to look at it too hard or too long. She stole her one glance by raising her eyes only, not her whole head. Still Javier felt the quick shock of eye contact, a flash of adrenalin as he thought, *she knows! She knows!* But then Eva walked out of the shot with no second look, no hitch in her step and no hint of awareness, so he could still think, *maybe she doesn't know...*

Every day Eva sent a vacuous message assuring Javier that all was well and typed a little note at Kristina's dictation, and every day Javier sent an innocuous photo of himself against some Paradisal backdrop, a beach or pool or a casino, saying he'd be home before Kristina knew it. On Saturday morning he had not yet returned and Eva decided to take Kristina to the pottery class at the community college. She put the child on the floor by her wheel and gave her a lump of clay to occupy her. Kristina made a trio of stumpy doglike creatures and played with them quietly or else sat still and watched the vortex of Eva's spinning wheel.

"That's a well-behaved kid," Willow said, as the other students trooped out of the room. "Ninety minutes without a peep—I guess I don't mind if you bring her again. Normally I don't allow it."

Eva looked at the floor. "Her father's out of town. I'm sorry."

"It's okay," Willow said. For a moment she looked at Eva in the odd piercing way she looked at things before she modeled them in clay. Then she turned to hang her coverall on a peg behind her.

"Let's talk," she said. "I'll buy you coffee."

"I..." Eva's eyes were still on her shoes. Kristina came and clutched the loose coarse fabric of her pants leg.

"What's your name?" Willow crouched on her heels, easily, bringing her clear blue eyes to the child's level.

"Kris-Kristina."

Willow offered her hand, and Kristina disengaged hers from Eva's pants and took it with a giggle.

There was a coffee stand just inside the main entrance, and on the apron of pebbled concrete outside, a half dozen iron tables with chairs. Willow and Eva sat down with their coffees. Kristina had a chocolate milk, which she drank quickly. Eva wiped away her mustache with a tissue, then blew up a yellow balloon from her bag and gave it to her. Kristina began patting the balloon across the courtyard, following the breeze from the sea.

"Charming child," Willow said. "Not yours."

"No," said Eva. "I work for her fa- for the family."

A couple of pachucos sat down at the next table from them, staring. One of them stuck his tongue a long way out and made pointed licking motions while the other grinned. With her head lowered to the mesh of the table, Eva found Kristina with the corner of her eye, and held her breath. Willow looked straight at the two men, fixing them—her eyes become the color of blowtorch flame. The tongue slithered back into its mouth and the grin vanished. Presently the two stood up and walked away.

"How did you do that?" Eva said.

"Focus." Willow softened her gaze. "Looking is a two-way street, you know. You never have to be a victim of anyone else's eyes. Not unless you want to be."

"I didn't know that," Eva said, humbly. She wasn't sure that she believed it either, though Willow

seemed to able to make it be true. Something reminded her of the episode she'd witnessed between
Annika and James in the park on Tuesday. Willow
leaned back and laughed at the description.

"They don't have pussy-whipping where you come
from?" Willow said, and then, looking at Eva's puzzled face. "Okay, I guess they don't."

"Kristina!" Eva called, looking over her shoulder.
"Don't go out of here, okay?"

Willow looked with her, toward the edge of the
concrete where Kristina was keeping her balloon
alive and aloft with quick little pats, wandering
among the scraps of blowing paper, which a couple
of gulls were foraging for crumbs.

"She's all right," Willow said. "I'm a little worried
about you."

Eva looked up at her with blank alarm.

"Look," Willow said. "This is a pottery class. You
come in every week and you make this kind of phallic
stalk that gets longer and skinnier until it falls over
and then you do it all over again. And I guess it satis-
fies you! Because you look like you're way deep down
in a trance the whole time. The only thing is, I would
have to fail you for this... only you're not in the class."

"I'm not in the class?" Eva said.

"On paper, no. There's no Eva Aguilar enrolled at
Lake Reed Community College. Officially, you don't
exist."

"I want to make a jar," Eva said. "But I don't know

how."

Willow looked at her. "What kind of jar?"

"A whole one." Eva shaped it with her hands.

"I've been teaching that since you first showed up," Willow said. "Maybe you need some extra help, mmm? I'm usually there an hour or so before class—I have stuff to do with the kiln, but I'd have some time for you before the others show up."

Eva still had the same blank expression.

"You can bring the girl if you need to. Kristina."

Eva didn't answer this. Willow leaned forward and covered Eva's hand with hers. "Word's out around here that I'm a dyke," she said. "That's what those punks at the next table think they know. But I don't go after children or students and I'm not after you. I thought you might need some help is all. I thought maybe you might even need a friend."

Confusion was swimming in Eva's eyes. Willow let go her hand and sat back.

"Do they not have friends where you come from?" she said. "Or is that just a real stupid question?"

Then Eva snatched Willow's hand in both of hers and stooped as though she would kiss it, but instead only squeezed it as she hissed, "*Gracias, Muchas Gracias*—Thank you." Then she was up, collecting her bag, capturing Kristina's hand as she walked away.

Willow watched the back of her beautifully balanced head receding—and *Brise* was there too right behind her head, always always even if Eva had forgotten that she knew it. That power she'd seen in Willow was there for her, there though she had forgotten how to call it to herself. She didn't know she knew that *Brise* was there. It was her decision, all alone, to live all by herself.

Eight

Return to Paradise still brought Javier a touch of the old euphoria—the heat rushing up from the tarmac, dazzling shimmer of the light, the pervasive odor of slightly rotten fruit, all somehow combined to give him a rush of excitement, tempered by the slightest edge of fear. Stepping down from the plane, he knotted a camo bandanna around his head as a sweat-catcher, and to help his canvas jungle hat stay on his head in the gusts that cut across the airstrip. A five-piece band struck up an unusually lugubrious *compas* as he and the other passengers entered the airless low building.

Dayshon was waiting for him just outside what passed for security here. When they hugged, Javier felt Dayshon's hand slip a Glock nine into his waistband, under the loose tail of his Hawaiian shirt.

"That bad?" he said.

"You know it, white boy." Dayshon grinned and shook his corn-rowed head as he led Javier toward a Montero four-by-four, refitted with one-way glass and steel plates in the doors. The back hatch was open and a lean black man in a black jumpsuit sat on the backward facing seat, cradling a pistol-grip pump shotgun. Javier didn't recognize him. He reached under his shirt to scratch and check the grip of the pistol Dayshon had put there for him as he passed. Fan-Fan was at the wheel and Javier greeted him with a touch on the forearm as he and Dayshon slid into the back.

"I hate those Annie Oakley guns," he muttered, as Fan-Fan pulled out into traffic. "Who is that guy, anyway? What do they think's gonna happen when they fire it—the barrel flies up and hits them in the nose and maybe it puts another crater on the moon..."

"HNP loaned him to us," Dayshon said. "He's all right. Take it easy, will you—he might speak some English."

Mildly embarrassed, Javier shut up. Arrival jitters were making him jabbery. Fan-Fan made a turn up the hill from the airport and joined a long turgid line of traffic, climbing toward the backbone of the ridge that divided the capital. Hawkers strolled down the line of stopped cars, offering batteries, newspapers, plastic sachets of water.

The sweat Javier had broken when he left the plane was gelling in the air-conditioning of the truck. He touched the button to lower the smoked window. A rich swirl of odors rose from the gully beside the roadway, where a trio of long-eared black swine rooted in a garbage dump. Charcoal smoke rose from braziers where yellow corn was roasting. Javier's eye tracked the smooth swinging glide of a young woman walking down the hill with a huge enameled pot of avocados balanced on her head. An old Toyota pickup, its bed refitted with a sort of iron trellis to which some twenty-five passengers clung, lurched past them.

"*Chen Blan!*" One of the young men perched high on the truck-trellis flashed a brilliant smile and jerked Javier a thumbs-up as he went by.

Dayshon nudged him in the ribs. "Uh," he said, "Look. The next one who knows you may not be actually be a member of your fan club."

Javier put the window up. "Eh," he said. "I guess times have changed."

Essential Solutions kept a suite of rooms at the Holiday Inn which stood at the top of the Champ de Mars. Two years before, Javier had supervised some strategic improvements to that little block of real estate—the rooms were more or less bullet-proof now and had recessed steel gates that could quickly seal off the doors and windows. A satellite dish on the roof belonged exclusively to the company and it was an easy walk, when times were good, across the dilapidated park and parade ground to work in the National Palace.

But at the moment times weren't good and Fan-Fan drove their blinded vehicle straight to the palace gate. The iron fences enclosing the palace grounds had been sandbagged and the snout of a 50-caliber machine gun protruded from a wooden tower to the left of the gate.

"Why the sandbags?" Javier grumbled, as the gate swung open and the truck bumped over the threshold. "You're making it look like a siege situation."

"Not me, bro," Dayshon said. "HNP sandbagged the joint."

"Essentials is supposed to be calling the shots inside this perimeter," Javier said. "We don't want HNP that close to our asset anyway."

"Huh," Dayshon said. "I guess you can try explaining that to the asset yourself."

"Well," Javier said. "You'd think he'd understand it already. Because if he could actually trust his own people he wouldn't need to be paying for us."

The heat boomed at him from the concrete when he opened the door of the car. Fan-Fan drove the vehicle to a hangar along the back wall of the compound. The HNP shot-gunner stayed with the car. Dayshon walked Javier toward one of the rear entries to the palace. A couple of HNP guards were playing dominos in the shade of a flamboyant tree near the back door in question. They glanced up briefly at Dayshon and Javier, though with no particular interest or animation. Javier snorted as they went in. The high-ceilinged hallways were shady but hardly any cooler than outside. The air-conditioning units that grumbled on the upper balconies could only cool a few selected areas.

"His Holiness commuting from the mountain?" Javier asked.

"Not since the latest," Dayshon said. "He's staying here at night. Our guys are on it."

As they climbed to the second-floor hallway, two men in sunglasses and headwraps overtook them and swung down the hall toward the big mahogany doors to the Presidential Offices. A couple of Essentials personnel nodded to them and stepped aside to let them in.

"What's up, Doc?" Javier said. The man on the left offered his hand. Javier's own palm felt clammy in the clasp. "Eugene," he said to the other man.

"His Holiness is in a meeting," Eugene said.

"Right," Javier said. "I can see that."

With Dayshon he circled the residential suite on the floor above. The Essentials detail, some twenty strong, was camped in empty offices at either end of the hall. The palace was incompletely restored since the looting that had followed the last change of government and the off-duty men lounged on camp mats in rooms that were mostly unfurnished. There were pale patches on the walls and floors where carpets and pictures had been abruptly removed. Javier greeted a few people, and passed on.

"It's fucked up," he said to Dayshon as they climbed the next staircase. "Sorry, but I just don't like it. We don't even have a clean perimeter around his apartment down there. HNP is all higgledy-piggledy with our guys and the Phantoms are walking in and out of here at will—"

"I know," Dayshon said, massaging the back of his corn-rowed head. "I know. It's *political* is what everybody keeps telling me. They gotta have access, His Holiness says."

"Yeah?" said Javier. "He gives enough people enough access somebody's gonna take him out. And the best we can do is whack the guy while he's leaving. Is that what he wants?"

"I'm not all that sure he knows what he wants," Dayshon said. "He's a man on a mission from God."

Javier looked at him for a moment and nodded. They stepped out onto the top floor gallery. At the corner an M-107 sniper rifle had been set up on its bipod to command a view out over the palace fence to the blue roofs of the old army barracks beyond—which since the dissolution of the army had been reconstituted as the Museum of Peace and Freedom, though part of the complex was now used by the police. Jared, a long-legged ex-Ranger from Milwaukee, reclined on a mat beside the gun, scanning the rooftops with a Swarovski spotter scope. He jumped and ran to bump knuckles with Javier.

"Nice," Javier said. His eyes wouldn't leave the rifle.

"Thought you'd like that," Dayshon said. "I set up six of these posts up here so we cover the compound inside and out. There's radio contact between them and the rooms downstairs and the hotel too."

"What's the deployment?"

"We got forty-two total, counting me. Well, you know that. Forty-three as long as you're here. I'm running three watches with twenty-eight men somewhere in this building and the rest at the hotel. The guys at the hotel have got two vehicles with mounted machine guns they can come down with if something breaks."

"Yeah," Javier said. "So if there was an attack from outside like the one in two thousand..."

"We'd take it from the rear and be done with it."

Javier stroked the stubble on his jaw-line. "That doesn't really cover you for an inside job."

"No," said Dayshon. "But what does?" He waved an arm along the gallery. "And with these posts up here we cover everything inside the compound too—I mean right to the doors of the building."

"Right," said Javier, and let down a little. "I think I'd like to do my watch up here."

He reached into his pocket for a small silver camera which he passed to Jared. "Here," he said, moving shoulder to shoulder with Dayshon, tight enough to block the camera's view of the gun. "Take us a picture for the girls back home."

By the afternoon he was on his way to Capetown on the north Atlantic coast—a commercial flight on a little prop plane. Flying coffins, the locals liked to call them for a joke. Security was so next to non-existent that Javier got on board the aircraft with the nine Dayshon had given him still tucked in the back of his waistband. Two or three other men came onto the plane with the cylinders of their revolvers rolled out to show they were unloaded. One of them Javier recognized as an out of uniform HNP officer—he had no idea about the others.

They lumbered through the heavy air for less than an hour, over-flying mountain tops with their slopes denuded of trees by the charcoal burners, now clawed with raw red gullies on all sides. The land route, which Javier had driven many a time, was pot-holed to resemble a video game for the driver, and plagued by bandits even by day. They might have deployed a couple of their Rat Patrol vehicles but Dayshon didn't want to spare them from the capital now and anyway it hardly seemed worth the trouble. Despite the jokes, the commercial flights were reputed to be reasonably safe.

The tropical funk rose up to meet them as they homed in on their landing; ground crew chivvied soccer players and a few grazing cows hastily off the airstrip.

Though the second largest city in Paradise, Capetown was much smaller than the capital—you could walk from one end to the other of the colonial part in no more than an hour. They had a car and driver to meet them, but Javier wanted to walk from the Cathedral to the Carenage at least, over Dayshon's objections, but Dayshon got down and walked with him. In the square before the Cathedral, the youth of the town had come out to stroll, *pou flane kò yo* in the cooling red light of the setting sun. Javier was still a celebrity here, so there were several calls of *Chen Blan!* when he passed, and the older girls let their wide eyes linger after him. There was something in the floating way they moved... It cost him an effort not to engage their eyes. Just a hint of invitation and he'd have one or a couple of them in his hip pocket for the rest of the night.

Dayshon's gaze wandered, Javier walked on. Soon they had entered the deep shade of the old palms in the courtyard of the commissariat—it was twilight now, and the roosting crows were chittering in the leaves. The commissariat compound was closed for the night and Javier stopped on the ancient cobblestones and stared at the blue and white gateway.

"They painted it out," Dayshon said. "Come on, yo, we'll check them out tomorrow. They're done for the day, and since you ditched our transport we have a good hill to hump up, which I want to get it over with ASAP."

Javier chuckled. Before, the A-teams had bivouacked in the commissariat—once they had wrested control from the army and the paras—but Essential Solutions took rooms in the fancy mountain hotel which catered to foreigners. "At least you'll sweat off a pound or two on the climb. People are starting to call you *gwo nèg* around here, you know that?"

"Mofo!" Dayshon snapped. "I'll see you whenever you drag yourself up there." He broke away in a long easy lope, and Javier jogged along after him—Dayshon had much longer legs, and much more weight to carry. He left Dayshon the lead for the next three blocks—the women who sold grilled corn and fried plantain from their caldrons on the street clapped at their passage. The hotel drive was some seventy yards of near-vertical corrugated pavement. Halfway up, Dayshon's running pace broke and wound down into a stagger. Javier passed him and pushed briskly ahead, stopping at the first patch of level ground to blow and turn his face and body to the breeze so as to cool the river of sweat that ran from him. The chauffeurs and guides and hustlers hanging around the driveway laughed and capered. *Gade-o! Chen Blan k'ap monte kon sa! Pi vite pase mwen!* one cried. Javier smiled finally. He didn't actually have wind enough yet to hold up his end of the repartee. Dayshon arrived, trudging the last steps—his dark face smoldering.

"Forget about it," Javier said. "I'll buy you a beer."

They started with two tall glasses of water, though—Son-Son had set them on the bar as soon as he saw them appear. With those drained, a couple of beers were uncorked. Dayshon pulled out a pack of Comme Il Fauts, and Javier, after a moment's hesitation, accepted a cigarette. The hotel looked busier than he expected. Some white missionary types were cavorting in the kidney-shaped pool below the open bar and its patio, along with a couple of jet black children, and in the pool-side restaurant several different sets of local movers and shakers were murmuring fervently to their foreign counterparts. Beyond was a panoramic view of the mountains and the port.

By the time Javier had pushed his first empty bottle to the inside of the rail, two marvelously lovely girls had appeared, with bright eyes, hot smiles, long black ringlets purling over their bare shoulders. One wore a bikini still damp from the pool—the other a spangled tube top that left most of her long lithe torso on view. Dominicaines, was the local term. Javier's heart dropped a little. Son-Son had made them appear out of nowhere... more likely by some occult power he shared with them than with a button under the bar. It would be taxing to deflect the offer without offending anyone. He turned to the barman.

"*Ba'm youn coup d'rhum,*" he said. "*Ak glaçons tannpri.*"

Son-Son raised his eyebrows a little, for Javier normally confined himself to beer, then poured a shot of the amber rum sufficient for a whole patrol. Javier sipped cautiously. The flavor was more like a fine brandy than rum. When he turned back, Dayshon was kissing the girl in the bikini, but respectfully, on both cheeks.

"You remember Myrième?" and the girl tossed her hair back, lifting her breasts prettily: "*O! nou konnen nou déja...*"

"*Kote Raisha? Kote Mike?*"

"*Nan piscine-a.*"

« What, by themselves?" Dayshon said.

"No, Cheri." Myrième broke into a sort of English. "Wiss ma cousine."

Dayshon pointed at the other girl, who had sidled near enough to Javier that he could smell her skin, but was looking pointedly away from him, across the bar to white caps on the darkening harbor, sipping some fruit concoction Son-Son had given her, through a straw. Dominicaines of the north didn't jump right in your lap or grab you by the crotch as they did in other countries or even in the capital sometimes, and Javier was grateful for that.

"*Sa se cousine mwen ki rele Mimette,*" Both Myrième and Mimette now smiled at Javier most expectantly. "Down dar, by zee pool ees ma cousine *ki rele Manilise*. She watching *ti moun yo*—they doan drown!"

Javier moved to the rail and looked more comprehensively at the area around the pool. Manilise was perusing empty water now—the missionaries had gone to dress for dinner and Raisha and Mike were racing up the stairs to wrap their arms around the pillars of Dayshon's legs. They were good-looking children—just the very thing that Javier's dedicated celibacy in these missions was intended to avoid. He turned from the group, took a long draw of his rum and raised his eyes up to the moon.

"*Chen Blan!*" Son-Son was telling his story to the girls, though Myrième probably already knew it. Javier had heard it often enough it seemed like a story about someone else.

On their first mission into Cape Town, the A-teams had given an ultimatum to the soldiers in the commissariat to lay down their arms and come out in an hour's time or face all-out assault. The soldiers had spent that hour playing dominoes with the paramilitaries there. When the A-teams went into position around the gate, one of the soldiers produced an antique .38 five-shooter and managed to pop Jared in the foot. Dayshon pulled the trigger on the belt-fed M-50 machine gun and turned the enemy soldier into a bloody silhouette of himself splashed onto the commissariat gatepost—an instructional image which the Capetown populace would study soberly for days and weeks to come.

"Hold your fire!" Javier rapped out. He thumped Dayshon on the shoulder to make his point. There were going to be a lot of people killed if something didn't happen, and some of them probably on his side. "*Depoze zam-w!*" he called. They'd given them all a crash course in the language in the weeks before the intervention but Javier had picked it up quicker than most. *"Nou pa vle la guerre! Nou la pou la paix."*

Lay down your arms! We don't want war! We are here for peace...

But the answer came in broken English from one of the paras who stood deep in the courtyard, cradling a nasty little gangsta machine-gun—the ever-popular Uzi. He looked a true *gwo nèg,* tall, muscular, his neck at least as wide as his shaved head—eyes masked in wraparound black sunglasses. "White dog," he called to Javier or to all of them. "Go away from our house while you have your legs or we will shoot you down like the dogs that you are."

"And it was then," Son Son chanted to the two girls and the round-eyed children. "Then Ogou-Feray the war god mounted Chen Blan's head—*li te gegne mouchwa rouj sou têt li deja* and then—"

Javier kept his distance, chuckled at the rising moon. But it was true that something had come over him then, something strange and unfamiliar.

He knew rage and had surprised people with it before now. Normally his rage was red, but this was blue and steely. "The fuck you think you're doing," Rico said and put a hand on Javier's shoulder to stop him and then snatched the hand away as though it had been stung. He had crossed his own lines now, and was entering the gate of the commissariat at an ordinary walking pace.

"Wi, se Chen Blan mwen ye!" It was a growling voice

Javier scarcely recognized, coming out of his own mouth. *"W gen zafè ak Chen Blan, vre—Pinga! Mete ba zam w!"*

Javier's hands were empty and he had not increased his pace as he approached the para, who stood as if immobilized, turned perhaps to stone, though his arms were trembled a little and the barrel of the Uzi shook. The flak jacket Javier was wearing struck him as miserably hot enough, so he had switched his helmet for a red bandanna tied over his head—a coincidence that somehow formed a nexus for the local superstitions afterward. Meanwhile Javier had come so close that it would have been easy enough for the para to have put a burst right between his eyes, close enough that when the para did make a move or a click or something Javier could side-step, knock the barrel aside and hit the para with an elbow shot that knocked him to the ground and also broke his jaw.

The rest of them surrendered after that. Javier got a commendation for avoiding more casualties. Chen Blan became the biggest baddest dog on the walk, the strongest warlord and most coveted fixer.

Oh, and most desirable lover too. The women in these parts were easily enamored of power—they were pragmatists in that way.

Son-Son had finished his narrative and Mimette was wending her way toward Javier now, where he stood at the rail with the moon behind him. What did that liquid swimming walk say to him? Surely she was a lovely flower. But. He took her hand and used it to hold her at a distance from him.

"*Dezolé,*" he said "*Pa kab touché fanm – m'ap mache ak lespri mwen.*"

Once he'd learned this line, it never failed. She retreated to the bar, looking back over her shoulder wistfully but with no resentment. That movement pulled at the pit of his stomach. Dayshon came out to carry him another rum.

"What dya tell'm?" he said. "I know you're not gay."

"That wouldn't fly here, even if I was," Javier said. "I say I'm forbidden to touch a woman because I'm walking with my spirit."

Dayshon laughed but softly, it couldn't be heard from the bar. "The great Chen Blan," he said. "Well. That makes all the more for me."

The man they'd come to Capetown to see did not turn up, or answer the phone, so Javier turned in early. He didn't drink such a lot in Paradise. A beer or so, one glass of rum after and that was it. Dayshon took his women dancing at a club in the Carenage— straight down the bluff from the hotel swimming pool. Javier went to his room, ascertained that the ragged window screens had not been repaired, and strung his mosquito net over the bed.

The bass line from the club came thundering up from the chasm. Now and then came a man's shout or a woman's excited squeal, but these were all good-time noises, Javier was sure—never hitting the special pitches of real violence or real fear. Javier loved a mosquito net; there was nothing more soothing than the sound of a mosquito whining in frustration when it couldn't actually bite you.

Sleep soon covered him, thick as black tar. He woke to the sound of a palm leaf broom pushing past his door, got up, went barefoot down the outdoor steps and ordered a cup of coffee. Dawn light was glassy on the sheet of calm harbor, beyond the breakwater containing the Boulevard de Mer down below. Fisherman were putting out in wooden boats which gathered speed as the lines hauled patchy sails into position.

Dayshon stalked the outer rim of the pool, stabbing his fingers at a satellite phone. When he saw Javier he flipped the phone shut with a snap like a firecracker and walked over toward his table.

Javier pushed the metal coffee pot his way. "What's eating you."

Dayshon clicked his tongue, looking out at the harbor. "Voltaire's down at the capital, so they say."

"What?" Voltaire was the regional HNP commissioner they had flown up to Capetown to confer with. "Harold set up the meet with him here."

"Right," Dayshon said. "Somebody didn't get the memo." He peered down at Javier's feet. "Might want to get your shoes on, bro. I got us on the morning plane back down there."

In the capital a few more phone calls established that Commissioner Voltaire was not there after all but had instead gone to Provo, or possibly Havana. Now it was Javier staring balefully at the satellite phone.

"He left the country? I don't like this at all."

Dayshon wagged his head. "Ain't right."

"You know it." Javier rattled his fingers on the table top. They were making their calls from an open air pizza place on the second floor of a concrete bunker a few doors over from the Holiday Inn. On the scaling wall opposite was graffiti so fresh it looked still wet.

Aba lapolis
Aba HNP
Tout moun kap fe travay la polis

"Harold wants you back in Mee-ah-mee," Dayshon said.

"How's that?" Javier squinted. "We don't have our business fixed here yet."

"No," Dayshon said. "But I see his point. I mean they ask for you and then they don't show so hey you don't sit around and wait."

A woman had appeared, next to the graffiti. Seeing the foreigners on the balcony above, she held up an extremely listless-looking baby in the crook of one elbow. Her other hand stretched out, palm up, empty. Something was wrong with that baby, Javier thought. She must hope they would throw coins down to her but that would be too—he'd give her something hand to hand if she was still there when they descended.

An unfindable HNP higher-up did not improve his sense of the general shakiness of the situation. Guys like that skipped the country when they knew bad things were fixing to happen.

Down with the police
Down with HNP
Anybody can do the work of the police

"Harold wants to, you know, re-teach them the priorities."

"Oh," Javier said. "So I just piss away three days down here for nothing." That woman had vanished from the sidewalk, so absolutely he wondered if she'd ever been there at all. "And go home and then turn around and come back."

"That's about it, yeah," Dayshon said. "We still got, what, a few weeks before the balloon goes up."

"And you think things are gonna improve in that time."

"Not necessarily," Dayshon said. "But hey—you get paid either way, and I know you don't like to be gone from Kristina. Ms. Alicia has you on the first flight out tomorrow."

Internet was functioning at the palace. Javier sent a snapshot to Kristina, then quickly checked his cameras, and was startled to the pit of his stomach when he thought that Eva had briefly, consciously, met his gaze. And what the hell was the idea of veiling all the mirrors? But wherever Kristina crossed a camera's memory she looked clean and cheerful and composed. He never saw her chewing her hair. He pushed his doubts out of his mind.

That night he ate with the crew at a restaurant they all knew across the Champ de Mars from the Palace—it was calm enough for that, at least for this one night. They had a Caribbean feast with all the trimmings. Departing from his usual Paradise practices, Javier drank more of the local rum than he should have, but left the party when the whores showed up—identifiable on sight by their bright miniskirts and hot-pants. Respectable women in Paradise wore their skirts down to their ankles, a system which kept things appealingly simple.

He had rights to a clammy room in the hotel, flavored by air-conditioner mildew, but by preference had strung his mosquito net over a mat on the gallery near the sniper post that Fan-Fan manned tonight. When the rum wore off he woke with a jolt. Perhaps he had made some sort of sound, for Fan-Fan lowered his Starlite scope and looked at him curiously. Indeed it seemed that Fan-Fan didn't recognize him straight-away and Javier spent a moment longer wondering just exactly who in the here and now he was supposed to be.

The silvery light of the Wolf Moon made his net-ting glisten like a cobweb. He smoothed it away and stretched out behind the M-107, tucking the stubby stock against his shoulder and fitting the eyepiece of the Swarovski scope to his socket. The rum here was so pure he didn't even have a headache, and his head felt clean and empty as a church bell. None of his own personality was left in it. He was free. The gun-sight simplified everything wonderfully. So long as his vision was expressed in that crystal orb he might have been anybody he had ever been anywhere, here in Paradise or on some Mogadishu rooftop or in am-bush above a crossroad outside Kabul.

"There," Fan-Fan breathed. "By the pedestal—you see?"

The restaurants and clubs across the square were shuttered and dark and all the park was empty but for this one target—who wore a backwards cap and the loose and baggy hip-hop garb that local bad boys imi-tated from their colleagues in the States. Certainly he must be a criminal or wouldn't have dared be there alone at this hour in these times, hovering by the pedestal of the statue called the Rebel Slave.

"He's yours," said Fan-Fan, who had spotted other targets for Javier up north, back in the day. The para Javier had disarmed so brusquely in the Capetown commissariat had somehow managed to remain at large, hissing threats through his wired-shut jaw, and actually managing to stir up a fair amount of trouble.

But even after everything that had gone down in Mogadishu, where he'd been a nineteen-year-old Ranger scared out of his ever-loving mind, Javier drew a line just short of raw assassination—that is until the para engineered an ambush a mile outside the Capetown gate where Javier took a crease on his left shoulder from an Uzi round and some scratches along the cheekbone from the windshield exploding his face—if not for the sunglasses he'd been wearing he might well have lost an eye.

But Fan-Fan knew the para's routes, and he found Javier a place to post the M-107 overlooking his house gate. The para had a habit of sneaking his lovers out of the house near dawn... and it was just a matter of breathe and squeeze. The girl ran screaming to spread the tale of what happened to anyone who dared to mess with Chen Blan.

Javier adjusted a ring on the scope and brought the backward cap crisp into the crosshairs. Another notch on Chen Blan's gun. The optics were so good and moon so bright that he could see the target's jaw muscle pulsing—probably he was chewing gum. A fifty-caliber round from this weapon could cut a body right in half, or explode a head like rotten melon. According to the local beliefs it might well be told that some stray spirit had entered his skull and used his hands to pull the trigger. He could hear Fan-Fan holding his breath.

With a great effort he called himself back into his

head and let go of the rifle and sat up, away from the stock and the trigger guard. You wouldn't just shoot somebody for no reason just like you wouldn't fuck somebody for no reason. Fan-Fan was giving him such a funny look that Javier wondered if he might have stated this aphorism out loud. His head did hurt a little now and his fingertips were trembling a little.

The target got up from where he'd been sitting and sauntered away in his outsized shorts, as if he too understood the encounter was over. Javier didn't know why the second part the statement seemed to follow inevitably from the first, but it did. He usually tried to observe the principle—a pity he didn't always succeed.

He took a late flight back to Miami and after a whole bouquet of delays it was after midnight when the transponder opened the door for him and let his sedan slip quietly down into the garage below his house. He sat there quietly in the dark, listening to the cooling engine tick. Before climbing the stairs he took of his shoes, with the idea of not waking Kristina. Softly he laid his cases on the carpet by the piano, then sock-footed cautiously into her room— the girl slept peacefully in the orangey glow of a night light Eva must have put in there. Javier wondered if Kristina might have asked to have it.

He slipped into the bathroom and pushed the door shut, flinching slightly at the tiny click of the catch.

When he glanced automatically at the mirror his view of himself was blocked by a towel. A muted light leaked under the door from the bedroom. Of course he had only been pretending not to remember that Eva Aguilar was sleeping in his bed. He could go back the way he had come and stretch out on the floor by Kristina's bed, or he could go and sleep on the couch.

When he opened the door to the bedroom the woman was sitting up bare-breasted in the bed, her hips caught up in a swirl of the sheet, her eyes alert in the holes of the white fox mask. He looked for her rear view in the mirror behind the bed but this one was shrouded in another sheet. He stumbled toward her, tripping over his dropped pants, and she cupped him delicately under the scrotum and directed his movement so deftly that he went deliciously all the way into her as she rolled backward onto the bed to receive him. Her heels were locked around his spine and her nails raked across the cheeks of his ass and she bucked up into him like a wild horse. The mask was made of some velvety fabric, with puffs of faux-fur around the eyeholes, but the white-fox teeth were sharp and pointed on the muscle of his shoulder, so that somewhere off in the distance where his consciousness had fled he wondered if she might be drawing blood.

When she flicked his coccyx with the ball of her finger he came like a bomb and rolled off of her, wet and breathless, a little nauseous, sick at the thought that he had done it at all and hadn't been able to last longer. The vixen was up and prowling the room, prancing high on her toes like a real wild fox. She had put the lamp on the floor, he saw now, and draped it with some peach colored garment to soften the light. Below the muff between her legs he saw the red bead winking as she turned, and her dark chocolate nipples were taut and still erect. She stopped for a moment, closing her legs, and lifted the photo of Helena where it lay face down on the top of the bureau and showed it to him silently.

"She's dead to me," Javier said, and cleared his throat. "She's dead because I wanted her to be."

The white fox dropped the picture where she'd found it and bent to the floor, the dark globes of her buttocks parting as she leaned. The vixen was still in her rut, he realized. Or he was. She came up holding a silky black bag in one hand. As she approached him he sat up and she slipped the bag over his head as if he'd been expecting it.

After the first shock he realized the weave of the thing was loose enough he could still see almost clearly. She crawled past him on her hands and knees and pulled the sheet down from the mirror, revealing the hooded executioner poised behind her where she knelt, his cock so hugely swollen he thought it might explode and spray blood all over the room like a fire hose. But there was no Javier no Chen Blan nobody no human partner at all in the ruthless movement of the figure looming in the silvered glass... and which she had after all invited with her pose, her gesture, the encouraging hand groping up to between her own legs, to capture and guide him in again. Her head was twisted to one side, mouth lasciviously smiling under the blank eyeholes of the mask. He fed himself inch by inch up her ass, moving slowly so as not to tear the delicate lining, watching the mouth moan and implore him in Spanish, controlling himself with the picture of a fifty-caliber slug tumbling through wet red viscera. You wouldn't just fuck someone for no reason, like you wouldn't just kill someone for no reason. Except of course for the times when you would.

Nine

"What about these blankets over the mirrors?" Javier asked Kristina in a teasing voice. "Do you know what's up with that?"

Kristina was flirting, squirting chocolate sauce on French toast. "Eva knows, you can ask Eva—there she is!"

When Javier turned toward where Kristina was indicating, Eva felt his glance shoot over her shoulder somehow. Or rather, she understood that he knew where her hands and her feet were and where they might move, but he was making no contact with her eyes and her face.

"Kristina can tell you," she said softly. "Tell your father, about our mirror game." She moved around the table where father and daughter sit, in the direction of the coffee pot, feeling how Javier's eyes knew exactly where she was without exactly following her.

"A game!" Kristina's eyes went round with shock— she tossed her head of unkempt curls. "It's real,"

"What kind of real?" Javier said, then to Eva, "There's more French toast in the oven, help yourself."

"For the ghosts, Daddy," Kristina explained. "So the ghosts don't see us."

"Ah, the ghosts," said Javier, "Of course."

"Because of, when the ghosts look at us.." Kristina fidgeted, rolling her head and looking at the ceiling. "Maybe they want what we have maybe..."

"You mean our Jewel Riders?" Javier said. "Our Barbie dolls?"

"More like our breath," Kristina said. "They want our breath and our blood because they're cold."

"Really?" Javier said. "The ghosts behind the mirrors, they want that? But what about the ones that live under the water? Like in the fish pond maybe?"

A cold bolt ran down Eva's spine. Her back was to them. She clutched her coffee mug, then set it down, carefully, without spilling.

"Sometimes if a child cannot sleep," she said. "I tell a story."

"Of course," said Javier. Kristina was eating her French toast. A chocolate smudge grew around her mouth.

"I take the cloth down from the mirrors, now you are home," Eva said. She was putting a single piece of French toast on a plate, which she placed on the table. Then she sat down behind it. Javier recalled in a flash just how the mirror in the bedroom had been unveiled the night before, but that seemed to have nothing to do with the girl who sat before him, eyes downcast, not touching her food.

"I don't know," Javier said, looking at Kristina. "I don't guess I want ghosts looking at us, wanting what we got."

Eva chopped off the corner of her toast and moved it away from the main slice with the tines of her fork.

"Maybe in the bathroom though," Javier said. "It's easier, for shaving."

Kristina giggled.

"Why don't you take the day off?" Javier said, looking past Eva, through glass doors onto the terrace. "I'll be with Kristina. It feels like I've been gone a long time. And you've been working twenty-four-seven." He saw that Eva didn't understand this expression, but it didn't seem like it would improve things to explain it.

"Yes," Eva said. "I go now?"

Javier thought about urging her to eat but didn't.

Eva walked for a long time on the beach, swinging her bag and singing into the wind. She waded, holding her long skirt high, looking past the low breakers that foamed around her shinbones. Today she was not thinking of sharks so much, but of the golden fish that turned ceaselessly below the surface of the fish pond at Mister Connell's house. *Anba dlo. Anba dlo. Anba dlo m'ap tande...*

Hunger overtook her in the afternoon. She walked

inland to a different shopping strip, further away from the Connell house, and bought an order of fries and a Coke. When she had eaten she carried the bag into the bathroom and bolted herself into a stall to change into Trix's clothes. With her long dress in the bag on her shoulder she went out and caught a bus downtown to Tamarind Way.

Alf's boxy little van was parked in the carport beside the bungalow, but no one came when she rang and knocked at the door. The shades were all drawn, though that wasn't unusual. Yet somehow the house seemed uncannily still. She walked around the back, looking. The settling brick of the small patio was littered with squashed cigarette butts, but it looked like they had all been rained on and it had been two days since it had rained. The back door wasn't pushed all the way into the jamb and when she tapped above the knob it swung open into the interior dim.

She glanced down the basement steps: darkness. Alfie's bedroom door was open and he lay with his head hanging off the foot of the bed, looking at her upside down.

"Trixie," he said, happy but slack. "It's been so long."

"Looks like nobody's humming in the hive," she said. "Where's Buffy?" It was Trix's vocabulary and Trix's sardonic smile, but she didn't feel like Trix had the usual hundred-percent occupancy of her head.

"Trombone holiday," Alfie said. It was what he called it, she had no idea why. She knew the bag and works would be there on the bedside table before she saw them. The sight reminded her of how sore she was inside from the bout of unaccustomed fucking the night before.

"God I'm glad to see you," Alfie said. "You'd have been here yesterday if I knew where to call. Can I get a little assist? I got backwards somehow—can't see the TV."

"Just a minute," she said. "You left the back door open, Alf."

"See?" Alfie said. "I need you. Baby. What would I do without you?"

She could hear him still singing those words from the bedroom as she turned the deadbolt on the back door and then made a quick patrol of the other points of entry. When she returned, Alf had wormed his way up so that his head lay on the mattress. She helped him turn around and settle on a mound of pillows. His arm unrolled limply into her lap, and she counted off the fresh needle stings along the vein.

"I need a bump, too," he said. "As long as you're here."

"Alfie, for real. How much have you had?"

"Too much ain't enough, Trixie." Alfie cackled, but without real glee. "Help yourself to a snort. There's plenty."

Trix cradled the slack arm, stroking it gently from the inside of the elbow to the heel of the palm, looking at the dance of colored shadow on the muted TV beyond the foot of the bed. Alfie sighed.

"Come on, baby. Let's us spend some quality time."

She turned her head toward the night-stand. Alfie had luxurious works—Bunsen burner with a proper tripod and a small glass beaker, red rubber tubing, like what a doctor might use to tie off. New disposable syringes in their properly sealed packaging A little jar of distilled water stood beside it all, and a gag lighter in the form of a Pez dispenser that spat fire. The heroin, though, lay in an ordinary Ziploc bag.

Alfie liked her to prepare with a ritual solemnity, like a geisha making tea or serving sake. In time she had come to enjoy that herself. There was something in the decorum of the motions and the sense of the purpose served that seemed to carry her back to some other life before. She measured, mixed, cooked up and drew the shot up through the needle. Alfie held his breath when his blood surged in the syringe, releasing it in a long sigh when she pushed the plunger. He was soon dreaming.

She disengaged from his slumped body for long enough to cut herself a small line on the glass top of the nightstand. Not so much as to leave her in black despair on the morning after, but enough to let her stand outside and above her pain.

Afterward she held him, drifting pleasantly. She had been careful not to form a habit. His habit was the island that they shared. She had first met Alfie a few months after Eduardo began to send Solange on calls. There had been three girls the first time on Tamarind Way; Trinka was one, another Russian or Pole with a made-up name. She didn't really remember the third. A VIP party with a dozen men—a couple of women too but the women mostly watched. Alfie had taken no piece of that action, except to take pictures which he gave to his guests when it was all over. A pair of Eduardo's runners dropped the girls off in the evening and picked them up six hours later.

The next time Alfie called Eduardo he wanted Solange only, and it was their first Trombone Holiday. Their friendship had first grown out of the fact that Alfie didn't really want to fuck. But Alfie was willing and able to purchase extraordinary amounts of her time, and Eduardo was willing, at first, to take the money. The house on Tamarind Way became a regular date for Solange. If it was a Trombone Holiday, the date might go on for three days. Eduardo's runners would do no more than pass by every twenty-four hours or so to make certain that she was still in the house.

Other times there was no Trombone Holiday; instead Alfie would be tweaking with the kids, as he called them, and running manically up and down stairs from the basement. At the end of those days he might take them all clubbing—he'd had a larger van before his current boxy vehicle, into which a rough dozen tweakers could be stuffed—or they would go to house parties or raves. The first elements of the

Trix wardrobe had been put together for the first of those excursions, Buffy and the kids all helping to makeover Solange, as a joke, sort of. She could tell from Alfie's appraising eye that he had some purpose beyond the gag but she couldn't make out what it was until the day Eduardo came over and looked straight at Trix and then beyond her, altogether failing to recognize Solange...

If it wasn't a Trombone Holiday, she spent time with the kids in the basement, which was where Trixie's remarkable talent for pretexting, *hacking the person* as Alfie would say, had first emerged. Seeing her gift, Alfie had taught her the essentials of navigating the internet—and if it was a Trombone Holiday, when he'd chased everyone else away for a couple of days, she had loads of time with the computers, when Alfie went out on the nod, for almost always she declined to take the drug herself.

Happy days, in their weird way. It began to end when Eduardo first saw Trix, and thought nothing of her. It wasn't the first time he had come. His drop-ins were casual, and didn't last long. He appeared to pay no attention to Solange, or hardly any. Sometimes he came down Tamarind Way for crystal—he didn't take the drug himself but occasionally offered it at parties, and if he didn't want to go to one of the labs on the street, Alfie would toss him a bag for cost. Solange had had misgivings, from the moment Eduardo missed seeing her in Trix.

He was waiting for her in the house when his runners brought her back, and as soon as she came in he sent the other girls out of the tawdry little parlor where they paraded for the johns that came to them.

Solange, Solange, mi corazon, he murmured, turning up her chin with one hand while he ran the other down the back of her tight shorts, tracing the outline of the tattoo he'd inscribed there, a few months after the trip to Disney World. He made a show of sniffing her all over as he held her close to him. *I doan know... he iss paying to fock you, Alfie, but I doan know iss he really focking you?* The thick finger probed lower, exploring between her buttocks, testing, as he peered closely into her eyes. *He gives me to his friends* she said, though it hadn't happened since the first time. She wanted to twist away from him but she didn't try. *I go by the house today he said, but I doan see you.*

With that it came to her that Alfie hadn't wanted her to be recognizable the nights that they went out and that in fact she wasn't. *I was in the bedroom* she said, and he grinned at her unpleasantly: *where your little ass belong...* He took hold of her hair at the nape of her neck and pulled her head back. *I giff your ass to my frens*, he said. *But Alfie giff your ass to his? I doan know...* He shook his head. *He's paying for it, isn't he?* she told him then.

Eduardo sniffed her one more time and let her go, his focus slackening, but he was still suspicious. She went on two or three more calls to Tamarind Way before he put a stop to it, but that gave her time to smuggle a couple of changes of Trix's clothes back to the house where he was keeping her, and by then she had already learned how to sweep up the footprints of someone else's passage through the world and gather them into her own store. She had what she needed to go on. She waited several weeks from the last time she saw Alfie, and when she skipped she was on a call on the other side of town from Tamarind Way.

Alfie had taught her how to know a good one when she saw one. *The dead ones are the best,* he always said.

He stirred and murmured now, and she pulled him closer. Sometimes, snuggling Alf this way, she felt a warm glad feeling all through her body, a sensation she'd otherwise long ago lost. Fucking would have scattered it, she knew. The colored lights of the silent TV played over his face like firelight. His eyes opened and stayed that way, calm, just barely processing the images. She was coming out of her own drift as well, but painlessly. She hadn't taken too much after all, but she was a little alarmed when she noticed the time.

"Gotta go," she said, disentangling her arm. The windows had been dark, she realized, for a couple of hours or so.

"Ah come on," he said, stroking her vaguely with his rubbery limbs. "Stay a little."

"I can't stay over, Alfie," she said. "Work. I gotta go."

Alf pushed himself up on the pillows, and came a little further into focus. "Okay," he said. "Don't tell me where you're going."

A cool shadow glided over her heart. "What are you saying?"

Alf was looking at the TV, where a cartoon program played in silence. "Eduardo's been slinking around," he said. "You know? Flashing a picture of Solange."

"Who's that?" she said.

Alfie laughed, but none too easily. "I dunno what got him excited about it again. I didn't know anything to tell him before. That was a good thing. And Hell. You asked about Hell? She's been around, the last few days. Got some bug up her nose about Trix."

"Hijo de la puta!" she blurted. "Are they talking to each other?"

Alfie hooked his thumb under the pacifier on its pink string around his neck and lifted it as though presenting a cross to a vampire. "Kinda sorta maybe yeah, but what're the odds they'd put it together they're actually talking about the same person?"

She let that hang.

Alfie was looking at her now. "See," he said. "Eduardo is not totally a nice guy, we know. But if he was to ask me straight up where you were I wouldn't know what to tell him. And that's a good thing. You follow?"

"I do." She nodded, and gave him a last quick

squeeze before she slipped away.

"It's all good," Alfie murmured, sinking lower into the pillows as she went out at the door.

Javier had spent a happy day between the beach and the playground with Kristina, but when supper and bath time passed with no sign of Eva, the girl became a little fretful. He had to struggle, washing her hair—Kristina thought that Eva did it better.

"How do you know she's coming back?"

"Just do," Javier said.

"But how do you *know?* How do you *know?*"

She was about to lock onto the phrase and start chanting it. The bathroom could be stressful for her, he recalled. He wrapped her in a towel and carried her to her room.

"Put on your jimjams," he said. "I'll comb your hair."

Kristina didn't ask about Eva again until the hair was done. Javier, however, caught himself straining his ears for the sound of the door. It didn't come. He tucked Kristina into bed and read her a story and turned out the light.

"But how do you know?" she said, as he got up to go to his own bedroom. Javier turned to look back at her, her eyes dark in the moonlight where she lay on the white pillow. It was a question, not a semi-autistic mantra. She had only asked it once and she was waiting for an answer.

"She loves you," he said, but how did he know that?

He came back and sat down on the floor, leaning his back against her mattress. "She wouldn't go off and leave you any more than I would."

Kristina rolled toward him and dropped an arm over his shoulder. Her small hand dipped into the hollow of his collarbone. There was a thoughtfulness in the touch that moved him, as if she meant to reassure him. He remembered the morning, when he'd sent Eva away—she felt nothing at leaving him, that was clear, but when she parted from Kristina he had felt a thousand threads of attachment pulling tight, and when Eva looked at Kristina (just once on her way to the door) her eyes had been completely alive.

Kristina's sleeping breath warmed the back of his neck. He folded her arm back under the sheet, softly rose and made his way out. He circled the front room, looking at the piano, but somehow he didn't want any sound. When he stepped onto the terrace he heard nothing but insects ticking, wind in the leaves, the slow purling of the fountain into the pool.

He went to the bedroom, swept the screensaver from the face of the computer, and checked his email—there was nothing much. Still listening, he browsed the webcam recordings. And really, why should he have been so startled by what fumed out of webcam seven?

The single fixed angle made it look like the cheapest of cheap porn. Black-hooded dog-fox hunching into the white-faced vixen from behind... the costumery and the echoing of the jerky movements from the mirror behind the bed made it all seem sleazier still, but God he was grateful he didn't have to see his own face. His stomach turned, and still the picture held him. How long could the goddamn thing possibly go on? It was still happening when he heard a sound at the gateway behind him. Webcam one popped up in a window and he saw Eva in her long demure skirt, turning dutifully to lock the gate behind her before she opened the inner door to the courtyard. Shuddering, he shut the computer off.

With the screen extinguished the whole room was dark. The glass doors onto the terrace were open, so he should have been able to hear the light tap of Eva entering her room, but instead the slow swish of her skirt was coming toward him. Or no. She was going to check on Kristina, he realized. Silence marked her pause in the child's room. As a rule Eva moved very quietly, but her heels did click a bit on the tiles of the bathroom floor.

When she came into the bedroom Javier turned on the bedside lamp. Both of them flinched from the light, then recovered.

"Uh," he said. "I'm home now." With one hand he made half a gesture toward the courtyard and her room on the other side of it.

"I know."

Was that the trace of a smile on her heavy lips? No. The mouth had the weight and shape of a leaf-blade spear. She was coming toward him with her chin high and her back straight as a lance, but supple; the extraordinary undulant movement. *Glissando.*

"Stop," he said. "We can't keep doing this."

She did stop. He looked over his shoulder, noticing for the first time that she must have covered the mirror again before leaving the house that morning. It was a relief not to see the two of them together on that screen.

"But you want it," she said. "You want my *ti minou. Epi...*" There ought to have been a smile here but there wasn't. "*El mio culo.*"

Javier focused on a memory of lying in ambush in the low ground south of Mogadishu, holding himself stone-still while a three-foot-long viper crawled over his thigh. It seemed to help a little. "Well maybe I do," he said. "But none of that is mine to take." A queer insight struck him. "And it's not yours to give either, is it?"

Eva turned from him then, and sat down on the foot of the bed. Her long hands were folded in her lap. "I have to be near her," she said.

This statement somehow seemed irrefutable. It was just what he always felt himself. He squatted down, dialed the combination on the long drawer beneath the mattress, and stood up cradling the M-16.

"It's all right," he said to her widening eyes. "Nobody's planning to shoot you. It won't go off if you follow the rules."

He pulled down the bedclothes and positioned the rifle straight up and down in the middle of the bottom sheet.

"Here's the rules," he told her, pointing to the spot nearest the wall. "You sleep on that side, I sleep on this one. Understand?"

"Yes." Her eyes contracted and she lowered her head.

"All right then." Javier switched out the light and stretched out, pulling the top sheet over him. He closed his eyes. But then she could approach him unaware. But when he opened them he could see her undressing in the moonlight.

Jesus. He closed his eyes and concentrated on ambush mode and the slow scaly pull of snake across his leg. Presently he felt her small weight settling cautiously on the other side of the M-16. When the movement stopped, he opened his eyes to the shadows on the ceiling and got ready to lie rigidly awake until morning. Thirty seconds later the room was full of sunlight and he was alone in bed with the rifle, though he could hear Eva and Kristina singing some silly song together in the kitchen.

Ten

Dayshon and Javier stood on the little stone bridge that traversed the ravine bordering the left of the commissariat compound. The ravine ran all the way down from a cleft in the mountaintop behind Capetown, and was, traditionally, a way to infiltrate the place. It also served as an open dump, cleaned out occasionally by the rains. During Javier's first tour of Paradise, his A-team had secured the ravine, above and below at points parallel to the compound wall, using three rolls of razor ribbon at each point and driving the metal stakes in deep to hold them in place.

But now the wire had all rusted out, and the stakes had been stolen, for use in construction. At this point the ravine was shallow, no more than a ditch, mounded with rags and plantain peels, through which a handful of pigs were rooting, in the company of a pair of spotted goats.

Dayshon looked at his huge diver's watch, then up

at the filigreed iron gate of the commissariat, secured by a rusty chain padlocked through the rails.

"What the hell?" he said. "We could just walk in with the livestock."

Javier squinted over the knee high parapet of the bridge. "Looks kinda soggy to me," he said. "And who's in such a big hurry?"

It was an hour after dawn, and they stood in the shade of the tall palms in the ancient square outside the station. The sun leaking through the long bladed leaves was warming the back of Javier's neck already. In another half hour it would be downright hot and—

A barefoot scarecrow in a loose pair of HNP uniform pants appeared on the inside of the gate and began to struggle with the padlock. When at last it clanked open, he pulled the right wing of the gate inward and motioned them wordlessly through the weeds and up the steps to the commissariat's front office.

From the dim of the unlit interior, Commander Voltaire rose smiling to greet them, offering his hand. Javier couldn't muster any real irritation over the disappearing act he'd pulled the last time they had had an appointment. He accepted the no-pressure Paradise handshake, and even held on to it a bit longer than he would have considered doing in the States. Straight men held hands in Paradise sometimes, Javier had observed, while they talked in low voices about matters of importance. It was less a display of affection than a way of raising the level of trust.

Voltaire's hand was slightly warm and perfectly dry. Javier had always respected the guy—a decent man who worked in near impossible conditions, doing the best that he or possibly anyone could do. Voltaire had a knack for diplomacy, and was a persuasive, sometimes poetic speaker of the liquid tongue of Paradise. Javier had seen him defuse a couple of situations that might otherwise have gone to a firefight.

Dayshon was giving them the hairy eyeball; Voltaire was the first to release his hand. He sat down in his desk chair and reached back to flip the light switch behind. Nothing happened. Voltaire glanced at the bare bulb hanging over head, but said nothing. Blackouts were the norm in Capetown, in any building where the state was responsible for furnishing electricity; all present knew that perfectly well.

Voltaire reached into a desk drawer and pulled out a fat bound document sandwiched in baby blue plastic covers. Javier had seen a lot of these things since Essential Solutions had been employed in Paradise: plans, programmes, agendae. They were produced by deep thinkers in frosty air-conditioned suites in the capital and handed to you by stunningly beautiful, sullenly severe women in heels and skirts so high and tight they could barely get across the room.

The relationship of such documents to reality on the steaming ground of Paradise was generally right around zero. Voltaire plopped his on the desk, riffled the creamy pages with a thumb, let it fall shut.

"*Ah bon, mezami,*" he said. "*La securité...*"

His Holiness was bound and determined to conduct ceremonies for the Paradise Bicentennial in Capetown in a few weeks' time—there would be foreign dignitaries and all that sort of thing, so security here was of paramount interest, yet dauntingly difficult to obtain. For example, the jail in back of Voltaire's office still had a gaping hole in its wall, since a disaffected Phantom (locked up on orders from His Holiness) had been broken out with the help of a tractor a couple of months before—along with forty-odd members of his gang and a similar number of operators from the death-squads directed by the military junta that had preceded his Holiness's populist regime.

The HNP's first response to the jailbreak had been to decamp from Capetown altogether—but since then they had cautiously crept back to occupy the commissariat and most of the old colonial part of the city. The popular neighborhoods and outlying area were divided, and often disputed, between Rosemond, leader of the Phantom contingent, and the leader of the old-guard death squads who called himself Jean Toro. These days, in the wee hours, there was activity even in areas ostensibly secured by the HNP. Small-arms fire had punctuated Javier's periods of sleep throughout the previous night, making a variation from the whine of mosquitoes and the noise Dayshon and the girls were making on the other side of the very unsoundproof wall.

With the electricity off at the commissariat, the computers didn't work, and the telephones were out as well. Chickens and little long-eared black shoats kept wandering in and out of the hole in the jail wall—there didn't seem to be much to forage inside. Commander Voltaire was an honest man, Javier had always felt; he was a realist too and when Javier pressed him about guaranteeing security for the upcoming State visit, Voltaire reminded him that the HNP was never intended to be a military force. He wondered if Chen Blan might help him obtain a generator for the commissariat, or a couple of operational vehicles, or some ammunition for their twelve-gauges and forty-four revolvers...

In the course of this conversation a *greffier* stamped in to the office from the back, saluted smartly and presented his arm—the Annie Oakley classic. There was something familiar about him. Javier stole a second glance and recognized the same starveling individual who had opened the gate for them an hour earlier. The cap and tunic and big jump boots and especially the shotgun seemed almost to have doubled his presence. And pride. Don't forget that, Javier told himself, as the *greffier*, following Voltaire's gesture, posted himself in the knee-high weeds out by the front gate, as sternly upright as if he were standing guard at Buckingham Palace.

Javier began to think seriously about finding some way to get Voltaire some better arms and equipment. The most obvious way would be to buy the stuff back from the Phantoms, who seemed to be getting plenty of munitions and transport somehow.

"It's fucked up," Dayshon said, as they walked out the commissariat gate.

"Tell me about it," Javier said.

"What could I tell you you don't already know?" Dayshon shrugged and climbed into the car. "What do you want to do now, anyway?"

Javier looked at the sky and then at his watch. "Let's go up to the Chateau," he said. "See if anything interesting happens on the way."

The Chateau had been erected on a mountaintop a few miles out of Capetown, by the first black ruler of a liberated Paradise, two hundred years ago. His Holiness would be obliged to perform commemorative ceremonies there, but the road to the mountain crossed territory now controlled by Rosemond or by Jean Toro. On the ride out Javier stopped often, to buy a coke or a beer and to stretch and let himself be seen and generally to let it be known that he was interested in talking to either or both of those leaders. The stops and the rough roads stretched an hour drive to something like three.

The Chateau sat atop its faraway peak like Noah's Ark on Ararat—it was fairly recognized as the eighth wonder of the world, but the perennial insecurity of Paradise had flushed out all the tourists long ago. The last mile of switchbacks to the fortress wasn't drivable. They left their driver to defend the car against the small army of hawkers who'd converged on the lone vehicle, and humped it up the hill on foot, followed by another contingent of the hopefully desperate who'd backed off to a respectful distance once made aware these visitors had guns.

Someone had run up ahead of them with a cooler of cold drinks. Javier accepted the beer Dayshon bought for him and pulled at it thirstily. From the battlements they could see the curve of the ocean and the outlying buildings of Capetown on the far side of the coastal plain—and to the east the forested mountains of the border between Paradise and the marginally more prosperous neighbor on the other side of the island. Javier felt elated, transformed—it was the way the vertigo struck him here. Since arriving in the north he'd switched his camo bandanna for a red one, to reinforce the Chen Blan legend. The locals claimed that the air in the gorges that dropped away from the Chateau was full of spirits. That if you weren't careful they would take you down.

"We're here, we're queer, we're Irish!" Javier said. Or whoever it was that was using his mouth. The Javier Connell who'd dropped out of Peabody and joined the military seemed aeons and aeons away from this place and the person who occupied it. "So far so good."

"We don't have His Holiness with us," Dayshon pointed out.

"True," Javier admitted. "What kind of fucked up?"

"Well," Dayshon picked up the hours-old thread with scarcely a wobble. "His Holiness has been raining guns down on the Phantoms for years now, just on the general theory that they're probably more or less on his side. Only sometimes like in the case of Rosemond for example, they really don't stay on his side..."

"Right," said Javier, "But what I'd like to know, who's arming Jean Toro and his crew?"

"Voltaire, for one."

Javier looked at him.

"What the hell do you expect?" Dayshon said. "The U.S. shut down aid since two thousand over some quirk in that fucking election and HNP hasn't been getting paid since then."

"So they're selling guns to the guys who're gonna shoot them with the guns they sold them..."

"That's it, brother," Dayshon said. "Like you heard today, HNP would love to get equipment and ammo and stuff, but they're spending whatever they can scrounge to buy crackers for their kids or whatever." He pointed eastward, toward the dark tree line of the border. "You know, since His Holiness abolished the Army, about half the ex-military has been sitting there in contra camps and *they're* getting armed by the far-right whackadoos in our own State Department, bro. They're sitting over there right now waiting for their day."

Javier felt the rush he'd been riding begin to fade. He turned in the opposite direction. "Beautiful sunset," he murmured.

"Oh yeah," Dayshon. "When it goes down, it's gonna be dark, and you notice we don't have an armored vehicle."

But nothing much happened during their return to Capetown. The next day they spent sitting around the hotel pool, scanning the harbor-front with their binoculars, and watching groups of scouts from either Rosemond or Jean Toro cruise through to case the joint. Otherwise the hotel seemed empty, but Myrième and her cousins and Dayshon's children made the most of the pool.

At twilight, Rosemond turned up himself. Warier, Jean Toro sent an emissary. Both wanted to offer Chen Blan honor and respect. Beyond that they made no assurances.

"Hmm," said Dayshon, once the girls and the kids had left the dinner table and Son-Son had served them a post-prandial rum. "I guess we could fly him up there on a helicopter."

"Like the dictators did in the bad old days," Javier said. "It makes the wrong impression."

"Then we need about twenty more guys, I think. You know, we can't like leave *nobody* in the capital."

"Yeah. I'll let Harold know when I go back. His Holiness will have to pony up for it of course."

"You know, if Rosemond could strike a deal with Toro they'd have this town sewed up," Dayshon said. "HNP will fold if you blow on them. And why do you think Rosemond wanted to know if we were representing the U.S. Government?"

"Because he knows damn well we're not," Javier said. "He's pulling our chain is all."

That night he slept even more poorly. The hotel's internet connection had failed and he couldn't send email or monitor his cameras. The sound of people having sex next door seemed to get to him more than it used to. Between his fitful doses of sleep it occurred to him that Rosemond and Jean Toro had somehow survived several months penned up in the same corral, and to wonder if either or both of them were in touch with the U.S. Government themselves. On the flight back to the capital he slept more soundly, snoring through the little plane's teeth-rattling jolts through air pockets.

From their post in the palace, Javier sent a message to Harold about Dayshon's request for reinforcements. The answer came quicker than he thought.

He found Dayshon waiting with Jared in his Holiness's anteroom—an airless cul de sac that got the noise of the window unit in the office beyond but none of its cool. When His Holiness, a reedy little man with bulbous glasses, came out to embrace Javier, a rivulet of cold air licked out behind him, then retracted when he went back to his meeting and closed the door.

"Speak of the Devil," Javier said. Over his shoulder he'd glimpsed the commander of HNP's so-called SWAT team seated at the conference table. He jerked his jaw at Dayshon, who used his hand-radio to call Fan-Fan to relieve him on guard, then followed Javier to one of the roof-top sniper posts.

"Harold got back to me double-quick," he said, having checked both ways down the long empty gallery.

"That's good."

"Yes and no. He doesn't want to send more guys over for Capetown. Says you should draw down on our local talent and liaise tighter with the Panthers."

"Sh..."

Dayshon shook his head. "We can't develop more locals in time. Not to where we could count on them. And the Panthers... well, Clement is in with His Holiness now."

"I saw him," Javier said. The SWAT team, which was more like a special forces group in thin disguise, was leaner and meaner and better-armed than the regular HNP. Both Harold and Javier had had a hand in training the group back in '96 and '97. Now they were quartered in the old Army barracks, the blue roof just outside the Palace compound—he could see it from where they stood on the gallery. Though a tougher unit than anything regular HNP could offer, Javier didn't think the SWAT team could compare to any Stateside elite corps. They wore black jumpsuits and black forage caps that, against their universally jet black skin, did make them look pretty scary. Calling them the Black Panthers might have been somebody's idea of a joke.

"Clement's all right," Dayshon said. "As far as he goes."

"Sure he is," Javier said. "But if His Holiness could really trust the Panthers, what would he need with us?"

"You know it," Dayshon said. "I know it—"

Together they gazed beyond the iron spears of the Palace fence across the Champ de Mars. The wide esplanade was quiet today—the demonstrations were on break, since on Sunday there was little for them to disrupt. A few washerwomen were busy hanging wet garments on the outstretched arms and brandished weapons of the numerous heroic statues.

"And Harold knows it," Javier said. "Something's not right."

Eleven

Back in Miami, Paradise and all its problems seemed as distant as the dark side of the moon. Javier went back to his regular schedule, flying his desk at the Essential Solutions office. Paradise wasn't the only client, after all.

Most evenings he came home and gave Eva a cooking lesson, by the way as he fixed supper for the three of them. When Kristina had been put to bed, Eva would often return quietly to the room where Javier was. She sat on the couch, a blank cushion between them, and watched TV, or if he was playing the piano she looked at her missal—he didn't think she actually read any of it, so seldom did she turn a page. There was always an M-16's worth of space between them.

After the first couple of nights, the sleeping arrangement didn't seem so strange. It was like having a cat in the bed with him, he thought... if you were allergic to cats and couldn't touch it. He was careful never to touch Eva, not so much as a fingertip.

Kristina had sometimes slept in the bed with him and Helena (Javier liked it; Hell didn't). When Hell was AWOL on a many-days tear Javier always shared his bed with Kristina, which was reassuring to them both, but once Helena was gone for good he thought he had better put a stop to that—the picture was already crooked enough if Child Protective Services was ever to take a close look at it.

He lay on his back, watching the vine shadows toss on the ceiling, wakeful but calm. Eva had turned toward the rifle, drawing up her knees; the fingers of one hand curled around the barrel. Javier was thinking how the smooth metal must be warmed by her touch when he realized her sleeping breath was crossing the barrier, raising the fine hairs on his fore-arm.

Don't stop, he thought, as his eyes drifted shut. A deep relaxation spread out from his spine. This tiny sensation was more delicious than anything their two bodies had ever transacted, before the M-16 was put in its place. How many times at morning or evening he had, in fact, felt something much like it. When turning through the shared space of kitchen or courtyard, they might have almost touched but didn't quite—those brushes raised a pleasant prickling on his skin, the same electricity he was feeling now.

Though Eva made no more sound than a ghost, Javier always knew, if he saw her or not, the moment she had entered a room. Some gyroscope in him had tuned itself to the grace of her movement, which replayed now in flashes on the backs of his eyelids, as her light breath across his arm continued to calm him. Eva dicing onion, as he'd showed her, on a wooden board. Lowering herself lightly over her heels to talk to Kristina, seriously, head to head. The way her whole body released from the balls of her feet when she raised her arms and stretched to set a stack of plates on a high shelf.

The turning movement Eva used to swing Kristina up from the floor to her hip, and then from hip to shoulder. Kristina was smiling at him across Eva's shoulder, and Eva was looking the other way, across the courtyard toward the sound of purling water. Her head was tilted slightly down on the long graceful neck, as if she was looking at something in the fishpond, but Javier had no idea at all what she saw...

There were times when he felt like they'd come through a strong passion to calm on the other side, like long-married people are supposed to do, like a pair of leaves blown down in a storm and drifting now on suddenly stilled water. But most the time he understood that couldn't be true at all.

Weekends Eva sometimes went somewhere on her own; as often she'd do whatever Javier and Kristina were doing. Two or three weeks had gone by in this way. One Saturday Eva was tagging along when Javier dropped Kristina off to a birthday party at an arcade in Ocean Ridge. Pick-up in two hours. Javier and Eva left the clatter of the games and walked across Old Ocean Boulevard and down onto the beach.

It was blazing hot, and the strand was dotted with coolers and beach umbrellas—not so much a family crowd here, Javier thought. They had walked a couple of hundred yards on the burning sand when Eva stopped and hauled her long cotton crew-neck dress off over her head. Underneath she wore a one-piece green suit that covered more than most other women on the beach could have claimed, and yet Javier noticed that she was attracting a lot more attention than most other women, as they wandered further south along the surf line.

They kept going until they were far enough away from the public access that crowds dwindled and then almost completely disappeared. Three guys with a case of beer and a jug of tequila made up the last outpost—Javier clocked them as they passed. The death metal they were playing on their big boom box depressed him, and he picked up his pace.

"Swim?" he said, once the music was out of earshot, stopping to peel off his own sweat-soaked shirt. Eva shook her head, the tight braids whipping. She was looking at the sand between her feet. It would be that simple, he thought, to take her hand and lead her out into the water with him. If not for the M-16.

"I don't know how to swim," she said.

"You can learn," he told her. He had taught Kristina.

Eva shook her head again, not looking at him.

"All right," he said. "I just want to cool off a bit."

He walked out through the weak low breakers till he was in waist deep, then dove and swam parallel to the beach in the blue water. Ten minutes later he stopped and rolled over and floated easily in the salt billow, the sun hot and red on his eyelids, imagining Eva floating beside him, supporting her with a palm beneath the small of her back.

There was a bit of a pull to the south, and he swam back toward the point where he had left her somewhat more slowly. Eva stood shin-deep in the surf, staring anxiously into the rollers beyond.

"What are you looking for," he asked as he came toward.

"Sharks," she said.

"What?" He wanted to tell her there weren't any sharks, but of course the ocean was full of them. He had practically never lied to Kristina, with exceptions only for the worst emergencies, and this would also be like lying to a child. That left him with nothing to say, and after a moment Eva turned from him and walked up on the shore. She scooped up her dress from sand and went in the direction they had come, the dress bunched in her left hand. He put his shirt back on—he burned easily—and followed a few paces behind her. The bathing suit was cut deep at the back and the puzzling edge of that tattoo, or whatever it was, kept peeping into the V at the base of her spine.

"Solange! Yo, Solange!"

It was the trio with the tequila and death-metal boom-box, cat-calling, and he looked up and down for whoever it was they might be talking to, but there was nobody on this stretch of beach but there was no one on this stretch of beach but him and Eva, and in fact two of the guys were coming out to intercept her, it appeared. Javier trotted to catch up.

"Solange!" It was the biggest guy, with the deep bronzed beer-belly and the 8-Ball Posse tattoo. "You not gone walk by like you don't know us."

"She doesn't know you," Javier said, glancing at Eva for just a second before he turned his attention back to the three men approaching. She was too dark-skinned to turn pale exactly but he could tell the blood had left her face.

"We know *her*." The second man, not so deeply tanned, was leaner and taller—his dirty blond hair was pulled back with a leather shoe string and there was small vertical scar through his left eyebrow. "*Oh yeah. Inside and out—know what I'm sayin?*"

"No fucking idea," Javier said. "She's with me."

"Don't worry about it!" 8-Ball said with a gold-toothed grin and a blast of tequila breath. He laid a beefy hand on Javier's shoulder. "She's been with a lotta guys."

Javier shifted his weight imperceptibly. "You know," he said. "If that hand is still touching me by the time I count three I'm going to take your whole arm off and beat you over the head with it."

Eva had barely had time to begin to think that she was going to have to give up and start fucking them all right away to keep Mister Connell from being hurt when there was a nasty crunching sound and the man with the 8-Ball tattoo whirled around Javier as if he had been whipped around a post by a high wind, and then plowed face-first into the sand. Javier and the second man were coming to meet each other like two magnets except the attraction turned into repulsion when Javier drew a little circle with the point of his elbow on the other man's chest and he too slammed into the sand as hard as if he had been dropped from a plane.

"Three," said Javier. He was shimmering all over and didn't seem to notice that his shirt had been torn half off of his left shoulder—there were some hairline scratches there where 8-Ball's nails had grazed him. "I count kind of fast when I'm upset," he said to the third man, who was backing rapidly away toward the umbrella and the cooler. "You might want to get your asshole friends to the hospital," he said. "Especially him." The second man had rolled to his side and was coughing blood into the palm of his hand. "I might have hit him a little hard."

Kristina was sitting by herself, wan and trembling, chewing a twisted rope-end of her hair, when they returned to the arcade. Javier ran to her, lifted her up.

"I don't know what's the matter?" Marlene, the

mother of the birthday girl, was saying. "I don't think anybody did anything to her?"

"It's all right." Javier held the girl against his warm bare skin—he'd stuffed the torn shirt into a trash barrel below the steps to the arcade. "It happens. Thanks for having her." Already he was carrying her toward the car. He caught a glimpse of Eva's face in the side mirror, focused on Kristina, who was looking back at her over his shoulder.

"What is it, kid?" he whispered to Kristina as he set her down to open the back door of the car. "Want to talk to me?"

"Mommy," she said, pulling herself back toward him. "I saw Mommy's ghost."

Javier crouched beside her. "It's all right. It's not gonna get you." Eva's face above them was unreadable to him. He hugged Kristina and patted her back. She wasn't crying. She was numbing out. She stiffened slightly when he lifted her but not so much he couldn't fit her in the car-seat. He fastened the belts and kissed her forehead.

"Some days just don't go right," he said to Eva as he straightened up. She only looked at him, or through him, with the same expression of mystical patience he had seen so many times before. He held the door for her to get into the back seat beside Kristina. His office gear was still occupying the shotgun seat. He caught Eva's eye in the rearview mirror as he backed out, calm, neutral—she was holding Kristina's limp hand.

By the time they parked in the garage under Javier's house, Kristina had passed into ordinary sleep. Eva managed to extract her from the car seat and transfer her, still sleeping, to her bed. When she woke forty minutes later she seemed to have forgotten her trouble and no one said anything more about it.

Javier sat at the piano bench, gliding idly through a Chopin Nocturne, Opus 48, Number 1, Lento, long limpid phrases full of darkness. Eva was sitting on the floor of Kristina's room, her back resting against the girl's mattress, listening to her breathing as she slept. She had a capacity for stillness which also seemed strangely familiar to him; again he wasn't sure why. But now she was rising, silent as a cat, and now she was moving toward the room where he was. She stopped in the door frame. He stopped playing and turned on the bench to face her.

"There's no such thing as Cognobits," she said.

"What?" Javier didn't at first remember that particular cover story; when he did he could only drop his eyes with a muted laugh. "No. Okay. As far as I know there's not."

Her eyes kept tracking him as she crossed the room to the couch and sat down lightly on the front edge of it.

"You called the office, didn't you?" he said.

Now it was her turn to mask a smile. Javier got up

and began to pace—to the dark glass door onto the courtyard, back to the piano again. He flipped down the wooden lid to cover the keyboard.

"I think I told you how many classical musicians there are in my family," he said to the wall. "It gets a little claustrophobic sometimes. Well, one day a recruiter came through. I did a training course for the Rangers and I did better than I thought I thought I would. By the time Somalia got finished, I'd been tapped for Delta. I went to Haiti after that. Then Afghanistan, after nine-eleven..."

Eva followed him into the kitchen, where he got down a bottle of rum from a cabinet above the refrigerator and poured himself two inches in a water glass. He showed the bottle to her and she shook her head.

"I had ten years in by that time." He took a drink and set the glass down. "I lost a couple of friends in Mogadishu. I don't know why that took so long to sink in." He shook his head. "A guy from my team had some start-up money for a private company so a couple of us went in with him on that."

"You're mercenaries."

"That's kind of an ugly word, don't you think?" He finished the rum and rinsed out the glass. As he paced back toward her she caught hold of his fingers and stood studying his palm as if she wanted to tell his fortune. A thrill trembled in him, like the point of the needle. I'm touching her, he thought. I'm holding her hand. Then she raised her eyes to his face.

"You didn't worry about your hands?" she asked him.

"What? My ivory-tickling fingers?" He wiggled them within her grasp. "No. Not really. I don't know why not." A warm breeze came in through the open glass doors and he turned his face in that direction. "I saw a guy pick up a grenade one time," he said. "Somebody had just lobbed it into our Humvee and he was planning to throw it back. One second he had a hand there and the next second it was just... this bloody mist." He shook his head. "That guy had been a soldier his whole life, practically. I doubt he ever even knew he had a hand before that."

"Did he die?"

"No, he lived and he went back to Iowa. He's driving a combine with a mechanical arm." Javier disengaged and went to slide the kitchen door shut. "That grenade would have done in half the people in that transport if he hadn't picked it up. You just don't know what's going to happen. No use thinking about it, in a way. If I hadn't got out when I did I'd be riding around Baghdad right now probably, with a bulls-eye this big on the back of my head."

He paced toward her. "You just want to be safe," he said. "To be safe, you have to put the enemy out of the way of harming you."

He had her complete attention, he saw. "Come on," he said. "I'll show you how it's done."

Kristina was sleeping soundly—he made sure of

that first. In the bedroom, the screensaver city built and dissolved in silence on the computer screen. He shut the bathroom door.

"I'm not going to hurt you," he said. He caught her wrist and her left elbow, T-stepped and threw her lightly onto the bed. She landed on her back, gasping and after a moment sat up with a smile.

"It's like flying," she said.

"Sure," Javier said. "If we're playing nice and you get a soft landing." He took her hand and pulled her back toward him. "You got joint locks, here on the wrist, here at the elbow, at the shoulder and all the way back to the shoulder. You want to play nasty, you twist the locks through when you make the throw and some of those joints are going to break."

But he sent her into the air as lightly as a feather, and she landed easily on the mattress. The same hot shimmer of action radiated from him, as it had on the beach that afternoon, and she felt warmed by it, though not frightened now. She lay on her back in the bed as if floating in a warm red sea. Javier was smiling at her, a little quizzically.

"Take that down, why don't you," he said, pointing at the veiled mirror. "We can see what we're doing that way."

Eva sat up and caught the corner of the sheet and pulled it down in a blue swirl atop the pillows. She stood up and moved toward him.

"It's a hip movement, mainly," he said, taking

her arm and nodding at their images in the mirror, poised like dancers waiting for the first notes to send them into motion. "You get your grip and do your T-step like so. That puts your body into kind of a coil, like a spring, and to complete the throw you just let it unwind."

He flipped her again, in slow motion this time, and kept hold of her hand, leaning into her as she unfurled on the bed. There was something in the flying sensation that eased her wonderfully, as if a knot drawn tight inside her was slowly coming loose.

"You fall well," Javier was saying. "If you tuck your chin a little that way on the landing—then you won't get your head slammed. Yeah. You got a feel for this." He was drawing her back up onto her feet. "Now you this time."

She took him by the wrist and elbow and T-stepped, watching the movement in the mirror, feeling the point of her hip bump the top of his thigh—"Don't stop," Javier was saying, and she unwound and he went sailing onto the bed, as lightly, easily as he had thrown her.

"Good one!" he said, bouncing back up. "Do it again—you got a good feel."

In fact he was throwing a lazy hand toward her face and her first impulse was to flinch, or then just to accept the blow, but then she felt how she could blend his movement into one of her own and send it through and away from her. She felt the same flying sensation all through her body, though his was the body flying this time. The knot in her entrails came completely undone, as easily as if someone had pulled the loose end of a shoelace bow.

"Oof," said Javier, rubbing his arm as he sat up. "Yeah, if you throw with *authority* like that, the guy probably won't get up very fast... but we're not playing for money, remember?" He got up and moved toward her. "Also, if a guy wants to grab you, you can use that same hip twist to break away."

By intuition she turned in his grasp, bending her knees and then popping them straight, but this time she didn't let go. She came with him, flipping over him as he landed and coming to rest on the other side of him on the mattress, which billowed up beneath her like a wave. A pleasant dizziness swam behind her eyes, and for a moment she imagined walking further into salt water, floating idly on her back as Javier had done that day—maybe there wouldn't be any sharks or the sharks that there were would not come near her. Both flushed with their movement, they lay lightly touching, shoulder to shoulder and hip to hip. She opened her eyes and saw the kaleidoscoping shards of the screensaver city beginning to reassemble. The hot smell of action still came off the man. She molded against him, turning up on her side, feeling that same diffuse glow of warmth she sometimes had felt cuddling with Alfie. She kissed Javier, pressing her cushiony lips against his thin ones. His eyes were startled. At first he didn't resist or respond.

She had comparatively little experience with kissing like this. She tried it again. The warm glad feeling didn't scatter, after all. It settled toward a point deeper in her body. *You just don't know what's going to happen.* His mouth yielded and opened to the tentative probing of her tongue. For so long she had known exactly what was going to happen but now she didn't and she didn't care. There wasn't any machine gun between them. Petals unfurled from around the warm red coal, opening one after the other like unfolding wings. *You just want to be safe*, he had said, but she had never felt safe before now. Now there was nothing between them at all, and they rocked together on a long slow tide, the warm glad feeling rising till it filled the world.

When she came a little to herself again they were both under the sheet that had covered the mirror and Javier was looking at her face, amazed—tears were standing in his eyes.

"My God," he said. "That was really you."

Twelve

Êve, O Êve O Êve… my girl's come home. To her most secret self. See how she flows back into her own body. The vessel broken so many times over by the hard use of others is made whole again. It is hers, in this moment, to own and enjoy.

For now it's safe for *Brise* to leave her. To sail up and away around the earth's receding curve, to the mountain and the cave where molten candle wax fills the three jars.

When Êve needs *Brise* again, she'll call. And *Brise* has many houses, not just Êve. Wherever there's an emptiness there am I.

But my girl is so full of her love and the man's that she doesn't remember the hollowness she knew. See how they stir again in the sheets, ready to bring their hearts together another time, moving in harmony, their bodies moving together like a song. My girl never knew it could be like that. Men taught her many things, but not that thing.

So far from the days not long ago when she whistled like the hungry wind in an empty bottle, yearning for the vessel that could carry her away from where she suffered, desperate as any other spirit wandering between the world and the other world *anba dlo*, she doesn't recall how furiously she was searching when she found Eva Aguilar, a skin so recently shed it was still warm when she writhed into it.

The dead ones are the best, her friend had taught her, and it's true. For him it's true, and for her it's true, but not for *Brise*.

Thirteen

The twelve-seater plane popped through an air pocket and for a spooky few seconds seemed to be in free fall. All the home-comers to Paradise aboard clutched the rickety seat-rests and turned gray with fear. Javier's gut rolled over too. Then the wings caught the air and the plane leveled off, banking over the coastline of the island. Javier peered through the scarred plastic porthole to his right. Through patches in the cloud below, the deforested hills of Paradise appeared, like the baggy, wrinkly hide of a rhino.

Beside him Rico sat silent and glum. And the other passengers seemed also to be lost in dark thoughts. Normally, this little flight to Capetown was a festive affair. Return to Paradise was a party. But anyone going back there today was doing it for lack of a less evil choice.

Though the plane had stabilized, Javier's stomach continued to turn. It was a bad time to be leaving his girls. He'd felt the same, he remembered, leaving

Helena and the baby behind on his last joyride to Afghanistan. But that was much different—a real war against a serious enemy, with no idea of when he'd be back and a reasonable chance he might never be. So it made no sense at all that this run should feel worse.

The plane banked and turned sharply inland, following the gravelly shoal of a half-dry river bed. Rico's heavy shoulder lurched into Javier as the plane pivoted on the tip of its right wing. The Fort Lauderdale flight took a left-handed approach to the Capetown airport, skirting the cliffs of the vast, boney mountain behind the town, zooming down into the green declivity of the plain. Through the porthole Javier saw another small aircraft approaching from the south, the general direction of the capital—a flyspeck at first but growing at an alarming rate. He nudged Rico and pointed, mentally calculating angles. Air traffic control in Capetown was a speculative affair and really for the most part hardly necessary.

He lost sight of the other plane as their own screeched down on the landing strip—it was directly behind them now, he thought, and that wasn't reassuring. He was on his feet almost as soon as the plane was on the ground, following Rico as he squeezed himself forward through the low narrow tube of the compartment. The copilot, a young Latin woman, waved them furiously back to their seats, but Rico ignored her, opening the hatch and flipping the steps out himself. A wave of heat sucked into the cabin, along with the snapping of small arms fire and the sound of tearing metal.

Javier straightened and caught at his head with one hand to secure his hat against the wind, which came even harder than usual across the landing strip. The other plane had heeled over not thirty feet from them, one wing crumpled on the burning concrete, a pool of fuel spreading from the broken tank. To his astonishment he made out the visage of Commander Voltaire through the windscreen, his hands releasing the yoke as he twisted out of the pilot's seat. A dozen-odd HNP officers tumbled out and made for the low clustered buildings of the airport—less eager for combat, Javier thought, than fearful that the plane behind them might explode. He wouldn't have been so keen either if he were them, since all they had were revolvers and the stupid Annie Oakley pump shotguns. The firing on the airport road was obviously full auto.

One of the HNP drew the same conclusion, apparently—he dropped his weapon and broke for the bush. Javier pounced on the abandoned gun, skidding to one knee. The wind ripped his hat off and took it for good. A figure bulked up by an armored vest paused in a gap between two of the low tin-roofed airport structures and let off a burst in their direction. Javier returned fire with the shotgun he'd recovered. Without a stock, the weapon recoiled so hard that the shot went high, and his wrist twisted painfully behind the pistol grip. "Fuck it!" he cried, racking the pump and holding the hot barrel down hard against the top of his raised knee—the second round went truer and Javier scored a knockdown. The shells must be loaded with heavy buckshot, he thought, and that, at least, was a good thing.

He got up, feeling in the air that the knee had torn out of his pants with his slide, and a fair amount of his skin along with it. The tails of the red rag he'd worn under the lost hat whipped from their knot along the tendons of his neck—*Chen Blan!* the cry went up from the fire zone. Fear and admiration swirled together—*Chen Blan!* Or it might have been an auditory hallucination.

"What did you do that for?" Rico said, turning from his explanation to the pilot, a big bluff flyboy whose muscle-bound body filled the whole hatch of the plane, that there would be an unexpected change in the flight schedule. "Not in the order of op, *compañero.*"

"To get their heads down for a minute, okay? Stop them—" Javier broke off and moved past Rico toward Voltaire, who was unloading an armload of assault rifles from the tail compartment of the plane he'd flown in.

"*M pa konnen w konn volé,*" Javier shouted at him. I didn't know you could fly. Voltaire grinned and shrugged as if to say necessity was the mother of many unexpected skill sets. Half a dozen HNP were lingering to receive these better weapons. Javier snagged an M-16 for himself and one for Rico, passing his shotgun to one of the police, and ran back toward the other plane.

"Come on," he said to Rico, handing him the second rifle.

"We can't do that," Rico said. "We don't stay with this plane it's not gonna be here when we come back."

"Get the key then," Javier said. He glanced into the cockpit where the copilot sat biting her lips in her seat, then turned and ran at a crouch toward the customs shed. Encouraged, the HNP formed up and followed him. Javier kicked in the door of the building and went in, covering the corners with the rifle's nose as he moved, but it was empty, except for a jumble of cartons. The front windows were glassless but barred against theft. He squatted below the sill of one and peered out. Fire came back at him from a battered Humvee clustered around with home-armored four by fours at the mouth of the airport road to his left. These men were uniformed and bulked up with body armor. A gang of marauders in civvies had run out ahead of them to begin torching the little buildings on the other side... tin roofed shacks that were restaurants or bars or offices for the several little one-horse airlines of the region.

"Would you look at this shit!" Rico hissed in his ear. "It's over. HNP is completely outgunned..."

"We got to get Dayshon, anyway." Javier squeezed

a burst at a man sighting on him from across the hood of the Humvee. The man jerked backward and dropped out of sight. *Chen-Blan!*

Rico seemed to have heard it too. He grimaced at Javier: "Don't get carried away."

Javier broke from the side door of the customs building and stopped, on his way to the embarkation shed, to look at the first man he had knocked down with the shotgun; one of the buckshot had snagged him in the throat, and he was bleeding out onto the packed dirt of the pass-way between the buildings.

"Would you look at this shit?" Rico asked again, kicking the M-16 away from the dead man's hand, then probing the armored vest with his toe. "This is U.S. Army Kevlar, yo. And we're out here with fucking T-shirts on."

Javier squeezed through a tear in the chain-link fence and ducked in the door of the embarkation shed, looking in all directions at once over the barrel of his rifle A couple of women and children crouched in grim silence in a corner of the cement block walls. Near the forward door a big black man in cornrows twisted up from a rank of plastic waiting room chairs, a six-shooter in either hand, like Buffalo Bill.

"Hold your fire, goddammit," Rico shouted. "It's us."

Dayshon lowered his pistols and grinned. "Oh man, I didn't think you were coming. I didn't think anybody was."

"Yeah, well we ain't staying," Rico said. "Come on.

We got a plane to catch."

"What about Voltaire and his crew?" Javier said.

"Do you see them anywhere?" Rico shouted, and Javier noticed that he didn't.

"They figured this thing out faster than we did," Rico said. "Than you did, I mean. We got to cut them loose."

"Right," Javier said. "I thought that's why I quit the military."

"Worry about that tomorrow if you're still alive. It ain't about that today, *compañero*. It's just you and me and Dayshon. We got him. Let's go."

But Dayshon was herding the women and kids out of their corner, toward the embarkation door. They moved in a tight trembling pack, but they didn't whimper or make any noise. People in Paradise didn't cry when they were hurt. They were used to being hurt and knew that crying didn't help. The women were young; Stateside they'd have been thought children themselves. Even in this moment of stress there was something in the way they moved... Dayshon put his hand in the small of one's back, and at that Javier recognized Myrième, Mimette, Manilise. The children were probably Dayshon's, or some of them were. But there were five of them altogether so they couldn't all be Dayshon's. Enough of them to fill most of the plane they'd arrived in.

There were no more shots coming across the landing strip, but they went crouching across the coverless space anyway, till they came up under the wing of the plane. Javier looked back. Smoke had begun to curl from the windows of both the embarkation and the customs shed. He saw Voltaire at the wheel of a flatbed truck, jumping a curb south of the embarkation waiting room to go cross-country, headed in the general direction of the camp Javier's A-team had occupied in ninety-five. A few men in the open back of the truck were still firing their weapons, though with no apparent target. The truck disappeared in dust among the scrubby bayahonde and cactus trees.

"Jesus, put out that cigarette," Javier snapped at Dayshon, who was sucking on a Comme Il Faut as the pool of gas from the plane Voltaire had wrecked crept toward his boots.

Rico was herding passengers out of the plane. "Ladies and Gentlemen, you have arrived at your destination of Capetown." He paused; there was no reaction. "Ah... arriving passengers need to get off so departing passengers can get on." He peered out the hatch. "Yo, Chen Blan—you want to translate?"

"What, we're just gonna ditch them here?" Javier said.

"Do you see another plane? We got to get Dayshon and his family out. That's what we're here for."

But now the passengers did begin to creep slowly down the stairs, squinting uneasily at the burning airport.

"It's not about you," Rico told them. It wasn't clear to Javier whether he meant that the fighting wasn't over them or that there was nothing personal in throwing them off the plane. A young man stopped to confer with Myrième, who pointed to the mouth of a trail on the far side of the landing strip from the burning buildings. The passengers began to file in that direction. The young wore hip-hop garb from Miami but the older ones dressed up for these flights: the men in neat business attire, the woman in stockings, elaborate hats, tottering on high heels. A man looked back at Javier.

"Chen Blan," he said, almost without expression, without fear and certainly with no admiration.

Bound for the capital, the little plane bounced through air pockets over the mountains, rising and falling in steep swoops and darts. Dayshon's women and children slept in their rickety seats. Javier stared through the yellow plastic of his porthole. He couldn't get that parting stare out of his field of mental vision. Since the mission in the nineties he'd been a true believer in Paradise. But now it was breaking very bad. He'd been so drunk with love the last few days he'd barely attended to the bad news smoking out of the island.

Then yesterday Rico had come out with the news that Harold was sending them both down. His Holiness was requesting reinforcements. Sixty-five more men.

"Have we even got that many on call?" Javier said. "I don't think we got half of that."

"It don't matter," Rico said. "We're not taking more guys down there. We're supposed to pull out the guys we got."

"What?" Javier said. "We have a contract with these people." But it was more than a contract. He knew Rico felt that too.

"I don't like it either," Rico said. "I don't think Harold likes it any better."

"So what the hell is he doing it for?"

Rico switched his long speckled braid. "The Feds were in to see Harold this morning," he said. "While you like *overslept?* Suits from State. The shit is coming straight out of the White House. Or else the Jesse Helms foreign policy division."

"No," Javier said. "We don't answer to those assholes."

"Right," Rico says. "That's what I thought too."

Willow covered Eva's hand with her own. They were facing each other across the spinning pottery wheel. Willow's touch was feather-light—not even guidance, but reassurance only. The orb of clay spun against Eva's fingers, as the jar swelled and asserted its shape, whole against the form of her hand. Willow's eyes made a firmer contact, limpid blue pouring freely into Eva's honey brown.

"There," she said finally, let go and sat back. Eva looked up and let the wheel coast to a stop.

"You did it," Willow said. "You're done."

The classroom was empty except for the two of them, and Kristina making clay animals at a table under the windows. The jar on the wheel made its last declining revolutions. It was simple, tapered to the bottom and top, almost like the shape of an egg, with just the suggestion of a lip at the opening, and big enough to carry water from a well.

"Let's put it in to fire with the others," Willow said. She carried the jar to a blind corner of the room and set in the top layer of the kiln, setting up little ceramic cones around it, arranging it symmetrically with the others. Eva watched. Then Willow stopped and put a finger tip to her lip.

"That kid can really concentrate," she said, looking at Kristina. "It's kind of eerie." But when she turned to Eva her smile was bright. "I think we can fit a couple of her beasties in before we close it."

Kristina glanced up for a second at Willow, then returned to pushing her clay animals about, murmuring to them as she did it.

"This can go," Willow said, picking up a fish with bulbous eyes and a long waving tail. "These two, no..."

"Why not," Kristina looking up, tossing her hair back.

"Air pockets," Willow said. "The way you put the legs on, they'll blow in the heat. You can take them home with you, though. They'll keep soft if you put them in a plastic bag. You can still play with them."

Kristina nodded, lowered her eyes.

"And this one," Willow said, lifting a blunt four legged object. "Is it a cow?"

"Buffalo," Kristina said.

"Of course a buffalo. We'll do the buffalo and the fish."

She arranged the animals in the kiln and shut the lid. "I'll fire these tomorrow," she said. "You can get them Thursday. If the storm doesn't hit."

Opening the throat of her coverall, she looked at Eva. "And you pass the course!" she said brightly. "Or you would've, if you'd ever signed up for it."

Eva looked away from the blue question in her eyes. Willow stepped out of her coverall, gave it a shake and began to fold it. She was dressed a bit more attentively than usual, in a silk blouse, and there were pearly snaps on her slim black jeans.

"Are you busy?" Willow said.

Eva looked like she didn't understand the question.

"I could take you to dinner," Willow said. "You and Kristina."

"We'll take you," Eva said. "I know a place."

Thirty minutes later, following Eva's directions, Willow parked in a set-back strip mall in downtown Miami. Most of the businesses were dark, but a rich smell poured from a grimy glass door with small letters stenciled on it. La Différence. Inside it was dark and the tables were empty. Some heavy women moved in the shadows behind a counter where a couple of cab drivers sat, scooping food from throw-away foam containers and murmuring something that sounded like French. Willow had had French in college but she couldn't pick a word out of this.

The vinyl table cloth was sticky. Willow wanted to ask Eva if she was sure of this place, but the girl was uncharacteristically confident and she didn't want to spoil it.

"*Gen lanbi?*" Eva called to the counter.

"*Wi genyen.*"

"*Bay nou twa lanbi tannpri.*"

"What are we getting?" Willow said.

"It's a kind of conch." Eva studied the red and black checks on the table. Willow leaned back and looked up at the dim ceiling, where old grimy Christmas tinsel bellied among curls of sticky paper well dotted with flies.

"I might just go for the chicken, you know? Any conch I ever tried was like—tire rubber."

"This is different," Eva said, with sudden animation. "Tender. They use papaya." She pointed to a basin of peels and pulp.

"Okay," Willow said. "I trust you."

Eva was looking at her carefully, as if she meant much more than she'd intended. But the food came very quickly. It must have been already prepared.

There were long slices of conch in a red sauce and rice with green cashews and a side plate of oval fried plantain.

"But this is good!" Willow said. "I never had any conch like this."

"It's *lanbi*." Eva said. "Same animal. Different food."

"So how did you know about this place?" Willow said. "You can't come here often. You'd weigh four hundred pounds."

She tried a couple of other conversational gambits, but this was not a place where people talked while they were eating. When the plates were mostly empty she asked Eva if she ate like this where they came from. Eva told her the same scraps of the story she'd heard before. The big Latin family in Brooklyn. She'd come south for school, to get out of the cold.

"What part of Brooklyn?" Willow said. "I lived in Williamsburg a couple of years. When I was in art school at the Pratt."

"The middle part," Eva said uneasily. A word from the license in her purse came to her mind. "Flatbush Avenue."

"That's a long street," Willow said. Then, as she felt Eva closing up, she dropped it.

"I can't believe I ate all that," she said. Eva was scooping the balance of Kristina's meal into a take-away box. Somehow she had paid the bill without Willow noticing.

"But I invited you," she said, as they moved toward

the door.

"It's okay," Eva said. "Mister Connell pays me. I don't spend much." She surprised Willow by taking her hand as they stepped outside. "You helped me too. You helped me extra."

"I wanted to help you," Willow said. She felt a tingle from Eva's hand, warm and light in hers, with no weight and no pressure, but she knew that little thrill was hers alone. "You needed to make that pot whole, I know. I couldn't tell you why but you did."

She waited, but Eva had dropped her eyes, though their hands were still pleasantly linked as they walked to the car, Kristina gamboling out ahead of them.

"Can you tell me why?"

Eva said nothing, but kept holding her hand, until they parted naturally to get into opposite sides of Willow's ancient blue Volvo. In the back, Kristina dozed, her bag of clay animals losing shape as she unconsciously pressed them into her leg. Willow played a flute CD, since nobody was saying anything much. Eva didn't seem ill at ease to her, but curiously blank. She gave brief directions, piloting them toward Morisco Bay along a bus route that she knew.

It seemed to Willow she ended up on a different street than the one where she'd dropped Eva off before. This time Eva led the yawning Kristina straight to a house door, instead of waiting on the curb for Willow to drive away. An imposing gate let into an archway, and she rolled down her window and waited while Eva punched a combination and fumbled with a key.

There was an unnerving whistle in the wind that drove in from the ocean a few blocks away. An ugly oversized red Hummer with tinted windows came nosing its way along the street from inland, pulsing a hip-hop beat from its mega-bass woofer. Something about it gave Willow the creeps.

As Eva locked the gate behind her, Willow leaned out her window and called. "Come get your things on Thursday, right?"

A hole of light opened into the courtyard beyond the arched gateway. In silhouette, Eva raised her hand. Then the door closed behind her and the gateway went dark. The thump of the Hummer's bass was over Willow's left shoulder now, as the gas-guzzler loitered its very slow way to the end of the block. She rolled up her window and pulled away, shaking her head as she switched from the breathy notes of the wooden flute to the weather news.

"The fuck they come up with these names from anyway?" Rico said, leaning in over Javier's laptop screen. On Google Earth, the dire pinwheel of tropical storm Ariadne moiled in the Caribbean, just southwest of Paradise's deep western bay.

"Greek mythology," Javier said. Rico snorted and turned away. After a moment Javier powered down his computer and walked up beside him to look out over the blacked-out capital. The night sky had lowered, heavy with cloud, and the wind off the bay had a knife edge to it. Behind him, the palace generators rumbled, and he could hear the voice of His Holiness shrilling from a TV set in one of the rooms of the balcony. Against all expectations, the palace's emergency systems were functioning smoothly. They had power, light, a sound internet connection via satellite. State TV broadcast an repeating loop of His Holiness, voice taut with repressed hysteria, exhorting his people to remain calm or, alternately, to rally round and defend democracy to the death.

But no one could be watching it. Hardly anyone. Twenty-four hours ago the rebels had destroyed the turbines at the dam that fed power to the city, and down toward the bay those few who owned generators had shut them off, since the noise and light would attract the most dangerous kind of attention now. Inland, a few points of light still glittered from fortified dwellings higher in the hills. Below the rooftop where they stood, torches moved across the park of the heroes. It was pretty, in a way. The red flares came singly from all directions or in small groups, then spiraled in to concentrate on a point where a hum of human voices rose, though they hadn't yet begun to chant their slogans.

"Shit on the boil," Rico muttered.

Someone let off a burst below, probably a Phantom

within the palace walls. Cries of rage and some more disorganized firing came from the cluster of torch-light in the park.

"*Not* a good idea," Rico grumbled. But there were no more shots from the palace and the commotion in the park died down.

What had happened was really quite bitterly simple. A week or so back, Rosemond had turned up dead on the docks of Capetown. Signs and portents strewn over his mangled body suggested that Phantoms had done the deed—which sent the blame to his Holiness, in theory. But maybe that theory was false. With Rosemond gone, most his crew had gone over to Jean Toro.

Then, at this most unpropitious moment, came the celebration of two hundred years of the independence of Paradise, and the grand ceremonies scheduled for the mountaintop Chateau. His Holiness had invited all manner of foreign dignitaries and they tried to go ahead with the scheme. Since the turn of events around Capetown had made the roads in the north unsafe, His Holiness and the other celebrants had to fly into the Chateau by helicopter. That was embarrassing enough all by itself. But next, in the midst of the exhortations, they were attacked in surprising force. Jean Toro had pooled his resources with all the ex-military men in the camps across the border. The Essentials team and HNP offered enough half-hearted resistance for His Holiness and his party to run back to their choppers and escape to the capital. Whereupon Toro and the old army men took over Capetown. His Holiness sent in his best shock brigade—the Black Panther special forces division which Javier and his A-team had helped to train a few years before. The Panthers were repulsed, with casualties.

That was when His Holiness hollered to Essential Solutions for reinforcements, and Javier came out of his love-struck daze to register what was really going on. After their short foray to the Capetown airport, the forces led by Jean Toro (or whoever in the old army network was really pulling Toro's strings) had begun to advance in reasonably good order into the south. There were only two roads from the capital to Capetown and both had quickly been cut off. The rebels were now at the capital's gate and there was really no obvious reason why they shouldn't go ahead and break in.

The capital's airport was still secure. When Javier's plane landed there from Capetown they found it freshly sandbagged and well patrolled by a contingent of sixty U.S. Marines who had flown in, "to secure the American Embassy." Otherwise the Marines were taking no action, and His Holiness's cries for more American aid got no answer, or the non-answer that the U.S. military was far too busy in Iraq to worry about Paradise now.

"Bullshit" Rico said now. "*Tu maldita madre!* Sixty

Marines could shut this thing down." He was saying what Javier already knew. They had been singing this song back and forth to each other since they arrived at the palace two days before. "That motherfucking *rebel army* is two hundred men max, armed and equipped. If sixty Marines can't handle that, why not send in sixty more? Hell, sixty of *us* could do it."

"Well," Javier said. "That's not what we got." In fact, following orders from Harold at the office, they had shipped out about half the Essential contingent before bad weather closed the airport. Then they'd drawn back whoever was left, with their arms and vehicles, into the palace compound. But like the Marines around the Embassy, they weren't supposed to do anything.

"Anyway," Javier brooded, "I think it's more like a thousand camped out there now. That tumbleweed picked up a lot of lint, rolling down from Capetown."

Rico hawked and spat over the rail. "You don't count those people. They just blow with the wind. Bust up the core and they'll all disappear."

"Right," said Javier. "You want to go do it?"

Rico looked at him. "I know *you* want to, *compañero*. But that's not what we been told."

Javier moved sideways and stood where he could stroke the barrel of the long sniper rifle. He could feel Fan-Fan watching him with interest from the shadows by the inner wall.

"You know what else," Rico said. "If your fucking

Greek hurricane decides to come ashore here, everybody's bet is gonna be off."

Eva opened the inner door and hurried Kristina into the courtyard. She stood for a moment looking back through the bars of the gate, deep in the shadow of the archway where she thought she could not be seen from the street. Willow's Volvo pulled away, the blue metal fenders dotted with salt-spots, old stickers for lost elections peeling from the bumpers. The blood-red Hummer still lingered on the block. The bass line from the big woofer pulsed, throbbing, thrusting itself toward her.

She went through the inner door and locked it behind her, reactivating the alarm. Kristina had gone into the kitchen; Eva could see her through the glass door, sitting on a high stool and unpacking her clay animals onto the table. She crossed the courtyard to the edge of the pool and stood watching the water flow in and out of the red clay jars, her hands lightly folded below her navel, just grazing her skin through the cloth of her cotton trousers. A red-gold koi nosed up between the broad flat lily pads, bending the surface of the water but not quite breaking through. It fell away, sinking into the frame of her own reflection. The gleam of golden scales disintegrating in the dim of the opaque water. But there was an uneasy edge in the wind that blew steady up from the southeast, and Eva could not sink entirely into the calm that usually absorbed her when she watched the fish.

In the kitchen she started a pot of rice and beans and put a couple of pork chops in to bake. She took off her sandals and carried them by their thongs into the bedroom. On the threshold she had that same feeling of being watched, but this time it didn't come from the dead cameras hidden in the corners of the room. The hard gaze probed toward her from the photo of Hell, face down on its oval frame. Eva put her sandals neatly away in the closet, then picked up the framed photo, keeping the image away from her and aimed at the carpeted floor, so that the hostile eyes could not rebound to strike at her from one of the mirrors. Since she and Javier had become lovers she had moved her clothes into the empty drawers of this bedroom but in the end she shoved the photo up under some shirts in one of the drawers he used. As she rested with the heel of her hand on the edge of the closed drawer it seemed that she heard the same bass line beating in her direction but when she tried to pick it out more clearly she could catch nothing but the keening of the wind outside the house.

Javier had left her a digital happy-snapper. She picked it up and walked quickly into the kitchen and took a couple of pictures of Kristina playing with the soft clay things she had made. Then she set down the camera and stooped to check the pork chops in the oven. The camera flashed and she turned her head and Kristina, giggling, caught her with her another shot as she was still stooped over.

"Hey you!" Eva straightened, snatched for the camera, but Kristina slipped down from the stool and eluded her.

"If you take one of me I can take one of you."

"Of my big behind you mean. Okay. All right. Don't drop it!" Eva stopped chasing her. "Here, let me have it. I'll take one of both of us." She set the timer and laid her cheek against Kristina's and the two of them beamed into the sudden brilliant light.

After supper Eva uploaded the snapshots to the computer and attached them to an email to Javier. Then she sat thinking for so long that the screensaver took over, building the fantasy city so that it could be shattered again. Behind her, the sound of bathwater rushed into the tub. She thumped the space bar and the screen emptied out.

We had a nice day today. Kristina and I went to pottery class. Kristina made a fish and a buffalo. They are going to be cooked in the clay oven by Thursday

She stopped typing. Kristina could have done better, she thought, as Kristina herself nudged up against her.

"Don't run around without any clothes on," Eva said. "You're supposed to go get in the tub."

"I wanna write Daddy." Kristina hooked one arm under Eva's elbow and began to peck out characters.

Lov u dad plese come hom son

"That's good, Kristina." Eva ruffled her curls. "Go jump in the tub before you catch cold."

Kristina ran toward the bathroom, heavy hair bouncing on her bare back. Eva sat for a moment with her hands curved over the keyboard, then typed quickly *Love you too* and pushed the button to send the message without a pause.

"Whatcha got on babycam, bro?" Rico leaned in, as if he meant to warm his face in the blue-green glow of Javier's laptop screen.

"Eva sent me these herself," Javier looked up. "I turned off that whole snoop system."

"Yeah?"

"You know," Javier said. "Sometimes you put your bet on trust."

"Right," said Rico, pulling his head out of the aura of the screen, then, "Hold on a minute. *That's* who you trust?"

"What?" Javier looked up. But he knew. His eyelids flashed the picture of the men he'd knocked down bleeding on the beach.

"Solange," Rico was saying. "I mean... okay, but with

your kid?"

Javier turned at the hip and stood up from his seat, and as if in an inverted tango step Rico moved out of his range, hands up, palms out, backing along the balcony as Javier advanced.

"I guess it's your business, eh?" Rico said. "You know how to pick them—that's all! That's all I'm saying."

"You don't think that might be saying too much?" Javier felt his whole brain turn pale. He was getting his best sense of the edge he must be on from Rico's placating tone and his wary grey regard. Rico looked like a man in a cage with a bear. Javier stopped and dropped his hands, giving Rico time to duck into the stairwell and disappear.

It was quiet tonight. The blackout continued. There were no torches on the esplanade before the palace. His Holiness wasn't broadcasting. He was hovering between the gilt-edged mirrors in the grandiose presidential suite downstairs, waiting for the thread to snap, the sword to drop. The "rebel army" was still poised on the edge of the capital, as if waiting for orders from somewhere else—somewhere in Washington, that was ninety-nine percent sure, at this point. The Marines, at the embassy, were sitting on their hands. Paradise was on its way back to hell and there was nothing he or Rico or Dayshon could do about it. They'd all have been back in Miami already, except flights were cancelled because of the weather.

Javier moved to the balcony rail, unconsciously stroking the cool barrel of the M-107 still cocked on its tripod there. Gusts tugged at the fronds of the tall palms in the garden below, bending the trunks toward the iron fence. When the wind dropped off he thought he could hear a sort of crowd turbulence, not very near but somewhere beyond the next fold of the mountain, where the highway from Capetown entered the capital from the north. Higher in the hills, a drum began a harsh dry rattle and then stopped.

Then the wind began again. Javier turned back and sat down in front of the laptop screen. Cute picture, a little silly: Eva bending over in front of the stove, looking back over her shoulder, surprised by the flash. A blunt edge of that near-invisible tattoo showed above the waistband of her pale linen pants.

Love you too

The computer pinged, and Javier shook his head when he saw it was Rico, just downstairs. He opened the email.

J. I know I'm out of line on this but

A hyperlink followed and that was all. With a stab of foreboding, Javier hit the link. He was soon wafted into a niche of "Spanish Eddie's Den of Delite." The place was not wholly unfamiliar, though he knew it mainly at second hand. Spanish Eddie ran a handful of bordellos in Miami and the Keys, and also stood by to send girls out on call. He would send girls to parties on occasion and he could furnish either coke or crank as a seasoning. None of it interested Javier much, but he and Rico both knew people who dipped into that stuff from time to time.

The name *Solange* flew in on a banner, just ahead of a sleek young black woman who certainly looked very much like his Eva. Kristina's Eva. Dropping her robe and raising her small high breasts to the camera—close on her face as her tongue thrust out, probing toward the lens. Eyes seductively lidded, dead under the lashes. He'd seen that before. Whenever anyone showed him a porn site he always sensed somebody with a cattle prod standing just out of the frame. Some hootchy-cootchy music started up and he hit the mute button.

To the rush of the wind through the palms behind him, Solange danced, writhing her torso, grinding her hips. She was wearing nothing but red high-heeled fuck-me shoes, with the straps winding up the curve of her calf—he remembered Eva was wearing them too, the first time. At the end of the short routine she spun around and deeply stopped, grasping her ankles, showing her teeth upside down through the V of her legs, parting her cheeks and lips for the camera, which now zoomed in on the tattoo, dark letters just barely distinguishable from the glossy black skin on which it was printed, but now so brightly lit it was legible.

**El
Culo
Mio**

It must be a sort of trademark, Javier realized; probably all Spanish Eddie's girls had it. As the image disintegrated, a crawl came across the bottom of the screen; directions as to how Solange's services might be procured. Or might have been. Because certainly this particular page was well out of date... if anything was certain.

He booted up his webcam system, pointlessly, since he had turned it all off at the base. The screen fed back only darkness, his own reflection dimly visible in the ambient glow that spread onto the balcony from the stadium lights that lit up the palace perimeter inside the high iron fence. He didn't actually think there was some porn movie going on at his house, where he couldn't see it—not without him being there to costar, anyway. No, she and Kristina would be eating pancakes and making clay animals and feeding the fish and taking their bath and going to bed. She curled up into him like a big limber cat, once he'd taken the M-16 out of the bed, and he could reach around and count the ebony knobs on her long back, until she complained that it tickled, snuggling into him to mute the complaint. The damn tattoo was slightly raised—he could feel the edges of it like the surface of a ribbon, and with a sinking feeling he realized now it was not so much a tattoo as a brand. And yet he had felt the same bruised tenderness for her that he'd felt with Hell at the beginning, maybe even part of the middle—Oh God, he thought, Rico's right, I do know how to pick them.

And he missed Eva. Whoever she was. He started a search engine and began to type.

Eva Aguilar New York.

Eva Aguilar Brooklyn New York.

Eva Aguilar Flatbush Avenue.

That simple—he could have done it months ago, if he had really wanted to. This Eva Aguilar looked nothing like his. Olive skin, wide mouth and a long hooked nose—no beauty certainly but she had nice eyes and you could have thought her pretty if you wanted her to be. It might have been a graduation picture or maybe a prom: a studio shot with drapes and flowerpots in the background, a halo of soft focus around the edge of image, and the light putting stars in the pleasant warm eyes as they looked toward a future she'd never see. Eva Aguilar was just

twenty years old when she had died two years before—killed in a car wreck over in Jersey.

He shut the computer and moved down the stair-
well, checking himself as he moved, cat-footed, tight-
ening the knot of his red bandanna around his head.
The door was open onto the corridor that led to the
Presidential suite, and Jared stood with a couple of
Phantoms outside the double doors to that sanctum.
They raised hands to Javier as he kept going down.

No sign of Rico, which suited him fine. Rico would
dig in and wait for things to cool out. Rico sometimes
went to a party—had he maybe fucked Solange? Not
worth thinking about, Javier decided, or tried to de-
cide. He jammed on the straw hat he'd bought to replace the one blown away on the Capetown airstrip,
and stalked through the blaze of security light toward the spear-pointed iron gates and the darkness
beyond them.

Paul Desrosiers was on the gate, talking to a couple of Phantoms who lingered outside the bars. The
three of them looked relaxed enough—the Phantoms
dangling nine millimeter pistols easily over the
iron crossbars. Paul had been one of Javier's train-
ees for the Panther team, and he was still wearing
their scary black jumpsuit and black forage cap. The
Phantoms stood back, slipping their weapons under
their shirt tails. Paul saluted smartly as Javier came
up and though his eyes looked a little uncertain, he
didn't hesitate to open the gate. A good thing too,

since Rico had spotted him from the Palace and was shouting from a second floor balcony—*Yo! Javier! You can't go out there!*

But Javier was already gone, sucked into the hot velvet envelope of darkness.

The real heavy weather was turning away from them. He could feel that. The wind was flagging. It blew hard for a minute or two, then dropped off, then puffed again and failed. Now and again a rain drop whipped against him, but he didn't think it would really rain. It was still overcast though, and he couldn't see shit. Halfway across the square of the heroes the lights of the Palace stopped penetrating and it was darker than the inside of a pig's gut.

South of the square the shops were all barred, iron shutters double-locked across the *vitrines*. Javier felt his way along the shutters, making his way forward one very cautious step at a time, for he remembered that somewhere on this block was a hole that could drop you twenty feet down into a sewer. No lights in the buildings, not so much as a candle, and there seemed to be no one out on the street. The past couple of nights had been loud with Phantoms driving around, shooting at stray dogs and shadows, but now even they seemed to have gone under cover. The "rebel army" might not be much, but the Phantoms wouldn't stand up to them long whenever the army did move on the town.

He was moving downhill, toward the salt smell of the bay, picking his way around the edge of a big heap of garbage. He could hear pigs foraging in the rot and then, surprisingly, he saw them too—their razor backs picked out in a sudden blaze of headlights. Shit. The pigs grunted, pricked up their long black ears and ran. Javier was pinned in a cone of light. He could feel the shape of the plastic Glock, tucked into his waistband at the small of his back, but if he reached for it he thought he'd get shot. It could be just that simple to die. All you had to do was be stupid and then run out of luck.

Kaché blan! the Phantoms were shouting, astonished to see a white person wandering these streets tonight. *Eh blan! sa w'ap fe?*

We're negotiating, Javier thought. If they just came in closer he'd have a few options. The front vehicle was backlit by a second, and he could see the knobs of heads in the bed of the first truck, a couple of gun barrels pointing to the sky.

Sé maché m'ap maché, he called. Just taking a walk. It wasn't a very good story, but he didn't have a better one. He smiled queasily, raised his open hands palm out, then took the risk of pulling off his hat.

Chen Blan! a voice hissed. *Gadé, sé Chen Blan li yé.*

A muted conversation followed. Javier couldn't quite make it out. But then both sets of lights went out.

Okeh, Chen Blan, the same voice said cautiously.

Ou met alé.

He was free to go. *Mesi mezami!* he said, settling the straw hat back over his red bandanna, sidling along the shuttered wall in the grateful darkness. Brake-lights on the second truck suffused them all in a red glow, and a couple of men sitting on the tailgate raised their palms to him solemnly as he went past.

Even now he didn't turn back. His eyes were adjusting just a bit: below him he could just make out the roofs of the Iron Market. His mind kept crawling like an ant hill. *Chen Blan. Chen Blan.* He couldn't make out if that was just an idea of him that other people had or if it was an avatar of his true self that he from time to time projected. Sometimes he felt he'd possessed *Chen Blan* more fully than he'd ever lived as Javier Connell. But now he was neither of them. He was nothing, an atom drifting in the dark.

How did you know who anyone was really? He'd certainly called it wrong with Hell. Maybe it made more sense to blame himself than her. She'd been a hard-partying girl when they met and for sure it was nothing she ever tried to hide. Of course he'd never have married her either if she hadn't been nine-and-a-half months pregnant when he first came back from a black-ops excursion to Yemen. No surprise really if she couldn't stick the wife-and-mother act for long, though no one would necessarily have expected she'd go back on the rock and take to beating up her own kid.

You're dead. Who had that been, the voice coming out of Javier's mouth? *You're dead and you just don't know it yet.* Whoever it was, Hell had believed it with all her shriveled heart and run away as fast as her shaky legs would carry her.

He was thinking about Hell because he didn't want to think about Eva, who wasn't Eva, who wasn't Solange either because obviously that was just some made-up whore-name, who was nothing and nobody, an atom drifting in the dark. A green luminescent speck appeared on what was probably the other side of the street from him, and Javier stopped moving, bent his knees slightly, rolled his weight to the balls of his feet. Despite the humidity the hair on his forearms was standing on end, and really, he wanted to laugh at himself, because he'd let two truckloads of Phantoms roll up on him without the least presentiment, and now he'd flipped into red alert over the glow of some other insane pedestrian's watch dial.

How fucked-up is that? The comment came from yet some other personality, a long way off, maybe somewhere near Rico back at the palace, and Rico was right—he had no business being out here. The other guy was just as frozen. If he kept straining his eyes Javier thought he could begin to make out the aura of a light-colored shirt.

It was going to go down soon, he realized. Something in the dead calm made him know it. The rebel army was going to be let off their leash and the

Phantoms would be scattered back to the wind and His Holiness would be killed or deported, and the whole fruit-basket would turn over. Now. When the sun came up there would be no rules. Once in a while there was a day with no rules in Paradise, and then a lot of old scores got settled, and of course Chen Blan was bound to appear on a couple of scorecards around the capital. He had to be back inside the palace compound before dawn. But he had reached the waterfront now, and he turned and walked west over the lumpy colonial cobblestone, tracking his way by a ribbon of steel he could probe out with the toes of his shoes, a vestige of an abandoned railway that once ran to the port.

It was still too dark to see a damn thing, but he heard the lap of waves on the breakwater, and somewhere out ahead of him was a speck of orangey light, from a candle or an oil lamp, and he was heading for it, though he didn't why. If that light was out on a boat he had a good chance to walk spang in the water. There was a little mag-light in his pants pocket, two double-A cells worth of illumination, but if he switched it on he'd be very conspicuous, and of course there were millions of eyes in the dark. Somebody was always watching you in Paradise. You were never, ever alone. He was thinking of that when a puff of sour breath struck his cheek and a human body hurtled into him, in utter silence and completely invisible, with momentum enough to rock him back on his heels. Reflexively his arms wrapped around the other, smaller man, who trembled in his embrace like a rabbit, then shook himself free and fled.

Javier was shaking too, fingertips jittering as he checked that his gun was still there, the knife still strapped to the inside of his left calf. The guy had been completely inside him. All the way. And no warning, he'd had no idea. He was out here rolling the dice with his life. But whose life was it? He remembered no matter what he was Kristina's dad, so he'd have no excuse if he got himself killed. He was still walking up toward the light.

Presently he found himself on a dirt path, ascending some sort of promontory that stretched past the breakwater into the bay—a feature he didn't remember being there. A dirt pile maybe, or a big garbage mound? A couple more pigs snorted and scooted away from him in the dark. There was a little ambient light reflected from the gasoline-smelling water, and he could just make out the cock-eyed pattern of a cluster of shanties slapped up out of scraps of cardboard and tin.

A waist-high picket gate secured the door of the hut where the candle burned, except it was open, as if somebody had just stepped out. Javier entered without grazing a picket, without touching any part of a wall or a door, though the rusty tin sign that served as a roof was so low he had to bow his head. A blue-skirted Madonna stood on the table, which was covered with a white cloth. Eva had one just like it in her room, he realized. Our Lady of Sorrows. There was water in a tin cup to the Madonna's right and at her left a gourd rattle, and the table was laid with the beads and bones and thunderstones one typically saw at these little shrines. A couple of Catholic devotional images were tacked to the wall behind the altar: the Black Madonna, and the guy on the horse.

Javier sat down cross-legged on the packed dirt floor. He was tired. His legs were tired and his arms were tired and his head was the most tired of all. He felt all his limbs going soft like ropes of licorice, and his sense that he must remain wary went floating away like a spark on the wind. The candle flame blurred as his eyes half closed and he felt his whole personality draining away down the back of his neck, swirling away into darkness, and really that was the deepest relief, because he had never wanted to be the fourth generation pianist at Juilliard or the swashbuckling Special Forces dude or the psycho vet who terrorized his wife or the guy who came home and fucked the *au pair.*

An eye that flew around like God on a pair of owl wings looked down on Javier Connell peeping into his laptop screen, peering out through the lenses all over his house like the ravenous ghost staring out of the mirrors, hungering for Eva's blood and heartbeat, her vitality, her life. There was no person there to be afraid anymore, just fear itself, black and rippling up and down his spine—with a start he opened his eyes and found he was looking past the blue Madonna to the black one. Her torn cheek and ferocious eyes and the way she held the child up toward him like a sword.

The fear stopped and his breath resumed. Whoever it was who called herself Eva had told him, when he showed her how to use the gun, *I will never let anything happen to her.* And that was true. It wasn't about him or even about Kristina really. Somehow it was true to whoever she was.

Pale tendrils of daylight crept into the shack, and Javier roused himself, stood up and stretched cautiously, careful not to dislodge the makeshift roof with his head. He felt peaceful, relaxed, though stiff from sitting in half-lotus position throughout the late watches of the night.

He dipped his fingers in the cup of water and tapped the cool damp to the back of his head, then shook a few drops onto the dirt floor. Stooping, he slipped out through the picket and straightened fully. At first light the calm was almost surreal, the bay as still as a sheet of glass. A couple of shirt-tail kids were staring at him from the doorways of other shanties. Javier yawned and looked down the trail. A young woman in a thin white shift was traversing the cobblestone street toward the port, balancing an enormous tin tray of fruit on her head, inevitably, never mind the risk, because no doubt she had family to feed and the men who'd be killed in the fighting today still wanted a plantain for breakfast first.

She moved with same languid grace they all had, swimming through the heavy air. Javier couldn't believe how long it had taken him to process it: Eva, whoever she was, was from here.

One of their rat patrol trucks came rattling over the remains of the railroad track, with Rico standing up in the truck bed, hands on the grips of the belt-fed machine gun. In a minute he was going to look over and spot Javier.

"Jesus Christ on the cross, where the hell have you been?" Rico said. "*Hijo de la puta*, am I glad to see you."

Fourteen

By Thursday morning the faint and far-away keening in the wind had turned into a constant whistling drone. Eva and Kristina walked on the beach at low tide. Kristina's idea: her daddy had taught her that rough weather could toss up more shells. There were not very many interesting shells, but the charged atmosphere electrified the two of them and they chased each other up and down the long strand, where the sand had gone pale under the purple sky. The wind came very hard from the southeast, blowing up bucket-size clots of foam and whipping them over their heads into the sea oats that speckled the dunes. No one else was on the beach.

In the afternoon they caught a bus to Lake Reed Community College. Traffic was unusually heavy, Eva noticed, but it was all going the other way. The parking lot, usually three-quarters' full at this hour, was almost entirely empty.

"Oh," Kristina said, her face falling. "They're closed."

"No, but she's here." Eva pointed to Willow's blue Volvo. Taking Kristina's hand, she led her down toward the entrance door. A plastic garbage can lid sailed over their heads in the wind like a giant Frisbee. The can itself followed, more slowly, rumbling on its side across the pebbled concrete.

The front door was locked. Eva rattled it while Kristina pouted, then pressed her face to the cloudy glass. The lights were out along the long corridor, but she could make out a pale flicker of movement back in the dim, like watching fish scales turn beneath the surface of the pool. The flicker resolved into Willow's slim figure, cradling a box in one hand and dragging a two-wheeled cart with the other.

"What are you doing here?" she said, parking the cart to open the door.

"We came for the fish," Kristina said brightly. "And the buffalo."

Willow's mouth stayed open. "Right," she said, after a moment. "And the vase, I guess. Haven't you heard about the storm?"

"A gale," Eva said, glancing over her shoulder.

"It's a Class Five hurricane, for Christ's sake," Willow said. "You didn't watch the news?"

"We watch cartoons," Kristina said. "The news is boring."

Willow released a thin smile. "Sometimes yeah, sweetie. But not today."

"You're here," Eva pointed out.

"I'm not staying! I wanted to get my equipment out before the building goes underwater." Willow looked into Eva's eyes, then shook her head. "All right, we'll get your stuff. Hurry."

In her classroom Willow moved with quick compressed care, lifting the fired clay from the kiln. She showed Eva a roll of bubble wrap she could use to pack her vase. She found a small box for Kristina's animals and a larger one for Eva. As they worked, the body of a gull thunked into the glass and fell away. It was unclear if the bird had flown into the window out of disorientation or if it had simply been hurled there by the wind.

"How did you get here anyway," Willow said as they hastened down the hall toward the exit.

"On the bus." Eva shrugged.

"The bus. The busses are running? Jesus." Willow looked back at her, thinking. "Look, you both better come with me."

Eva nodded. "If you can take us back to Morisco Bay."

Willow started to say something, didn't. The wind was blowing so hard against the door they had to try together to push it open. Kristina came out laughing with excitement, her thick curls swirling all around her head.

Willow turned on the radio when they got in the car. "Would you please listen to that?" she said. "I can't take you back to Morisco Bay. The whole area is being evacuated. It's not even legal for you to stay there."

"We have to wait for Daddy," Kristina said.

"Yes," Eva said, in as certain a tone. "We must wait. He will be coming back soon."

"How?" Willow's voice was reedy with frustration. She was straining both cars to hold the car on the road against the crosswinds. "He's not coming back on a plane. There's no flights."

"We have to stay in the house," Eva said. "It's the safest place."

"Listen to me. There's already looting in downtown Miami. Do you know what that means? It's coming this way."

Her eyes locked with Eva's. Blue to black. "The house is the safe place." Eva said, slower and with more assurance than before.

"All right," Willow said. "No, goddammit!—It's not all right. But I don't suppose I can force you to come." In fact she had already turned into their street. "Could we call the guy, does he have a cell phone? See if he really wants you to stick this out."

Eva dug in her purse, pulled out a scrap of paper and offered it.

"Okay," Willow reached to the dash for her phone. But Eva and Kristina were already getting out of the car. Willow dropped the phone and caught at Eva's sleeve. The slender arm slipped through her hand like a shadow.

"It's safe in the house," Eva said. "Don't worry."

Across the harbor it was dead calm. Gasoline slicks spiraled on the surface of the pale green water. Far out, the triangular sail of a *ti voilier* pricked the horizon. Fan-Fan sat behind the wheel of the jeep, discreetly watching Javier as he passed the cab to vault up into the bed beside Rico, then turned to mutter something to Paul Desrosiers, who sat in the passenger seat beside him. Uphill, in the direction of the Palace, the echoing thump of a twelve-gauge shotgun was answered by a full-auto crackle.

"What's the news?" Javier said.

Rico switched his long gray braid. "You tell me. You're the one out scouting all night."

Javier shrugged, looking over the roof of the cab to where he had been. The shanties, cobbled together from cardboard and tin, were propped together like a card castle on a heap of earth beyond the breakwater. An old man leaned on a stick by the picket gate to the *hounfor,* gazing back at the truck through rheumy eyes.

"How about your end?" Javier said.

"Well. The Phantoms are driving around shooting at anything that moves." Rico waved in the direction of another noisy gunfire exchange. "What else is new? His Holiness got a delegation from the embassy last night."

"Ours?" Javier said. "Well, that's sort of interesting."

"Right. They're offering him a ride out of the country."

"Really," said Javier. "What's he think of that?"

"He doesn't like it," Rico said. "But I think he'll probably take it. The barbarians are at the fucking gate, right. They'll fly him out if he's willing to go. If not they'll open the gate and feed him to the barbarians. There's guys out there been waiting to kill him for years."

"And the strings on them go back to DC in the end."

"You know it," Rico said. "It's over. All bets are off."

It was glassily still along the length of tattered pavement… Since that solitary market woman at the break of dawn, not a soul had passed. The shops were shuttered down to their sills. Even the old man had disappeared from view in the shantytown on the garbage island.

"Not a good time to be out on the street," Javier remarked.

"No," said Rico. "And another thing. You notice that hurricane's not here no more?"

Javier looked toward him.

"It turned around and went to Miami."

"Fuck!" Javier said. "I—"

"There's no flights," Rico reminded him. "The airport's locked down. And you couldn't fly in there now anyway."

"I can't just sit here." Javier stared at him.

"Not here, no. Not on the street." Rico rolled his

shoulders. "We can go hunker down at the Palace. Wait it out. There's sixty Marines already in there."

Javier shook his head. "We'll be stuck for a week."

"True," said Rico. "So I thought, we could maybe try to requisition a boat."

"You want to leave Dayshon?"

"Dayshon's already got his whole family with him. The Marines will secure the Palace—if His Holiness leaves."

"What if he doesn't?"

"He will," Rico said. "He may be crazy but he's not suicidal." He drummed his fingers on the roof of the cab. Fan-Fan peered out at him, then drew his head back in.

"Me, I got no reason to stick around," Rico said. "We'd live through it, but it's gonna be real depressing, I think." He kicked a duffel with his toe. "I threw your shit in a bag," he said. "Most of it, anyway. Who knows when you might want a toothbrush?"

Eva filled her vase with fresh water and carried across the courtyard to the maid's room. Wind lashed her braids around her face, but she walked slowly, solemnly, feeling the wholeness of the vessel thrum between her palms. The blue and white figure of Erzulie Freda still stood where she had placed it when she first came here, between the tightly folded red cloth and a new candle, sleek and fat in its glass jar.

She crouched and set the vase on the floor before

the altar, dipped her fingers in and shook a little water on the ground. *Se dlo m'ap jete pou sa nou pa we yo.* That was Man Brigitte's voice echoing in her head ; she had done so sometimes in the room they shared at the Duclos house, before. She stood, and lit the candle with a wooden match, and cupped her hands for a moment around the warmth of the flame. The shadow of Erzulie stretched long against the far wall. Eva stood back. *Tout bagay sou posisyon.* She left the room, closing the door quietly behind her, leaving the candle burning within the walls of the jar.

The rain swept almost horizontally across the courtyard. It stitched the surface of the fish pond, pocked into the skin of her face as she hurried toward the sliding glass door. Kristina laughed gaily as the wind rushed in with her, then, once Eva had dragged the door shut, returned to watching cartoons on cable. On the bottom of the screen a crawl reiterated the progress of the storm and the governor's order to evacuate Miami, Fort Lauderdale, Palm Beach...

Eva went to the kitchen and dried her face on a dish towel. She got out a package of chicken breasts from the refrigerator and sliced them on a slab of white plastic. According to what Javier had told her she sliced the mushrooms on a separate, wooden board. The knife was a good one, with a long, triangular blade, heavy and extremely sharp. She used the flat of it to crush a clove of garlic, diced it fine, wiped the blade and thrust the knife into a slot in the butcher block that held the others of the set.

Her cooking was more confident now. She made chicken and mushrooms with a lot of butter for Kristina's taste, brown rice with carrots, frozen spinach with a dash of lemon and soy. It seemed a special night because of the storm, so they ate in front of the TV, watching a tape of an old movie, *All Dogs Go to Heaven*. Eva recognized a couple of scenes and realized she must have seen it before, in one of her other lives—there'd been a fund of children's videos in the basement where she'd stayed with Nadya. They'd helped her to learn English, but...

She pushed the memory from her, got up to do the dishes. When the movie was done she gave Kristina her bath, then set about brushing and combing the mass of strawberry hair... She'd done the same for Marie Angelique Duclos, in another life, less lovingly and under more duress—then another unwanted image jabbed her: blood on the white stone stairs. It was unusual for such memories to leak from the sealed compartments where they were storied—maybe something to do with the storm. She closed her eyes a moment, picturing the altar across the courtyard: water clear and still inside the vase, the calm and soulful face of the blue-robed figure in the candlelight, the shadow stretching long on the rear wall.

"What is it, Eva?" Kristina, restless before, had stilled in her hands. She was peculiarly alert to any adult's change of mood. Something she'd learned from her experience. This time Eva blocked the image, the idea, before it reached her. It was the storm, swirling all her lives together—she felt that certainly. She opened her eyes.

"It's all right," she said. "*Está bien.*" Leaning a little forward she laid her cheek against Kristina's, meeting the girl's watchful eyes in the mirror.

"*Te amo,*" she said.

"I love you too," said Kristina. "And Daddy."

Later Kristina was restless again, agitated by the weather. She couldn't settle herself to sleep, and finally Eva got in bed beside her, held her till her breathing slowed. She slept herself an hour or so, while the wind slashed and roared outside. Then something woke her and she untangled herself from the sleeping child and crept into the front room to turn on the television: weather channel on mute. The whirling blade of Hurricane Ariadne sliced into the tip of South Florida like a paring knife cutting into a thumb. Reporters stood under lights in the wind, gesticulating, mouthing in silence.

Eva had drawn the heavy drapes across the doors and all the windows, in case maybe glass would break, but the hacienda style of the house helped armor it against the wind. The house was the safest place. Javier had told her that, and disclosed to her a couple of safety features which before she had only dimly suspected. She drew back a curtain and looked across the way. A crack of light framed the door to the maid's room; inside, the candle still burned. The fish pool was overflowing a little and wide puddles stood on the tile of the courtyard. But the sills letting into the house were high.

She went down into the basement: it was still dry. In a closet beside the firing range was the emergency power: a bank of car batteries and, as a second line of backup, a small gas generator. When she came out of the closet, the range target startled her: life-sized image of a thug hulking off the rear wall. As if it were a real intruder. Shreds of paper hung from bullet-holes that perforated the ugly drawing. She laughed at herself and went back upstairs.

She woke next time to the clunk of power going out, sudden cut in the hum of the refrigerator and the hiss of the central air. The wind's shriek, though, seemed a bit further off. No reason to rise. She held Kristina's warmth to her. To her own surprise she slept again.

The morning was peculiarly calm, and the house, without air-conditioning, was hot and clammy at the same time. Eva pulled back the blinds from the kitchen doors, opened the sliding glass panel. The sun reflected from a sheet of water that had risen nearly flush with the sill, and she laughed aloud when she saw one of the koi from the pool swim by, a quarter-inch below her toes.

Was the water rising still? She went down to the basement. Indeed there was an inch or so of water on the floor. She bit her lower lip, wondering if she should spend emergency power on the pump. Yes, she must, because if the water kept rising in the basement it would eventually drown the batteries.

The sump pump came on as soon as she threw the emergency power switch. She gassed the generator, pulled the cord a time or two till it turned over. The generator was set up to keep the batteries charged. When she stepped back it seemed to her the water was receding.

On her way back up the steps she heard the doorbell buzzing. Strange. It hardly ever happened, except for some private courier service, needing a signature for a package. But that would hardly be true today. Rescuers, maybe, she thought as she waded ankle deep across the flooded courtyard. There had been pictures of rescue on the TV when she first woke the night before, paramedics plying the streets of downtown Miami in small motorboats or sometimes canoes, people reaching up to lowering helicopters from the roof-tops of their drowning houses. She opened the door without thinking

"*Mi corazon!*" Eduardo spread his arms wide for her. "Is a small world, no? A very small world."

The truck bed had been armored in an ad hoc manner, with four extra doors butt-welded to provide side walls. The back was open, except for the tailgate. While Rico manned the belt machine gun, Javier settled facing the rear, resting the barrel of the M-107 sniper rifle, which Rico had thoughtfully brought along, in a dent on the top edge of the tailgate.

They drove north along the Grand Rue, with the harbor spooling away to the left. Presently their view of the water was blocked by the walls around the commercial port. Some men were using sledgehammers to break jagged holes through the masonry while others walked in and out of the passages thus opened, carrying off whatever they could from the depots inside—foodstuffs for the most part, vast bags of rice or crates of canned goods. Some of the looters stopped what they were doing to stare uneasily at the armed truck as it rattled by. Most ignored it altogether. Apart from the smoldering roofs of the depots it might almost have been a normal work day.

"They always put too much sand in the blocks," Rico said. "One good tap and the wall comes down."

"Doesn't look too promising from the transportation point of view," Javier muttered.

"Not here, no," Rico said. "There's another place better."

A big green SUV with smoked windows skidded into the next intersection and opened fire on them. With a nasty metal-scraping sound, something like a big horsefly blew across the back of Javier's neck. He whipped his head around, found himself looking into the street through a bullet hole in a butt-welded door. Desrosiers lazily draped an Uzi out the passenger side window, and, shooting one-handed (as Javier had many times admonished him not to do), caved in the windshield of the attacking vehicle.

The tail-gate pinged and Javier turned toward it. A couple of guys with their heads wrapped in t-shirts were busting on them with handguns from the partial cover of the doorways behind. Their marksmanship was not very good, however, and with his eye in the scope it was easy enough for Javier to take them out. As he capped the second one, Rico wrenched the M-50 around on its mount and drenched the SUV in heavy fire till it began to sink into the potholed street on its punctured tires. Javier twisted back and snatched at his pant leg.

"It's dead already!" he said. "Save some ammo."

Rico stopped firing. Fan-Fan already had them through the intersection, comfortably out of the intended kill zone.

"That went well," Rico said.

Javier ran his finger around the inside of the bullet hole through the jerry-rigged door. "Armor could be a little stouter," he mentioned.

Rico shrugged, then rapped on the cab roof. "Left here!" he shouted.

"*Á gauche*," Javier seconded. Fan-Fan made the turn with a screech. Just beyond the walled area of the port a chewed spit of land had been built high with shanties. Here the roadway was no more than a trail. Several dreadlocked youths popped up from either side of it, brandishing assault rifles. But they lowered them quickly when Rico spun the 50-caliber machine gun around.

"It's Phantom Central down here," Javier said.

"Sure it is," said Rico. "With luck we won't stay long."

The promontory's edge was lined with rotting pilings where several wooden fishing boats were moored—and two black cigarette boats, one already standing off, its powerful motor throbbing. The other appeared to be unmanned, but since the cockpit was covered with a fiberglass cap it was hard to be exactly certain.

"There's your vessel," Rico said. "Oh shit!"

A muscle-bound man in a mesh t-shirt and a Chicago Bulls baseball hat popped out of one of the shanties and made for the tethered boat, scurrying up and down over a garbage heap with the ruthless agility of a crab. In response the boat motors thrummed to life. Javier jumped out of the cab, raising his right hand in peaceable greeting, checking the Glock in the back of his waistband with his left.

"Koute, monche!" he called *"Nou bezwen—"*

Chicago Bulls pivoted and caught his balance on a piling, bringing something up and around from a sling under his arm. Then he flipped over backwards into the suddenly bloody water as the M-50 machine gun roared. A Latin-looking man with a mustache and a loose khaki bush shirt popped out of the cockpit with something else in his hands. Another M-50 burst knocked him over the stern.

It was quiet then. Javier looked back at Rico.

"What," Rico said. "Diplomacy has failed."

"It has now," Javier said.

Rico lit a cigarette and jumped down from the truck bed, the M-50 and its tripod gathered under one arm.

"They'd of killed us both if we gave them the chance, *compañero*. You think they're gonna give up their good just because you want to go to Miami? And once they start running with the Colombians... It's all over."

Javier shrugged, then moved cautiously up toward the boat, the grip of the Glock now warm in his palm. The sleek hull bumped against the piling, engines rumbling, churning white froth. The body of the Colombian in the khaki shirt rocked face-down in the narrow wake, blood from his torso spreading through the dirty water. There was no one else aboard the boat. Rico vaulted over the gunwale and moved to the controls.

"Cast off, will you," he said to Javier. "No real reason to wait around here."

Javier tucked the Glock in the front of his pants and went to unfasten the bowline. He clambered up on the swelling fiberglass hull, stowed the rope and raised a hand to Fan-Fan and Desrosiers.

"*Kenbe fem, mezami!*"

Desrosiers, who'd climbed in the back to man the big machine gun, tossed him a languid wave. Fan-Fan was busy backing the truck away from the waterside.

Javier slid backwards down the curve of the bow and dropped into the cockpit. "You sure you know how to run this thing?" he asked Rico.

"What does it look like?" Rico snorted. He'd already turned the go-fast around; the bow thrust high above the water as he opened the throttled and steered toward the horizon line beyond the bay. "I was a Seal before Delta. Of course I can run this boat."

"Excellent," said Javier. "Then I guess you also know how long it's gonna take us to get to Miami."

"Maybe eight hours if everything's perfect," Rico said. "But you know, the odds against that are real high."

They ran for two hours, north by northeast, keeping the shore of Paradise just in sight on the horizon. A couple of small planes stitched the skyline, buzzing like mosquitoes. From the larger towns of the coast, plumes of black smoke rose.

"Payback time," Rico mused, glancing up from the navigation screen.

Javier didn't answer. He rooted in the duffel to see what Rico had managed to grab. His laptop was there, and most of his clothes, a kit bag with toothpaste and razor. He flipped open his cell phone. A missed call message chirped. When he punched for the message he heard a strange woman's voice, obscured by static.

"⊠⊠⊠don't know ⊠⊠but—⊠⊠⊠your, ⊠⊠⊠Eva's pottery ⊠⊠⊠⊠⊠⊠⊠⊠ at Lake Reed—So ⊠⊠⊠⊠⊠ dropped her and ⊠⊠⊠⊠⊠⊠⊠ house in Morisco ⊠⊠⊠⊠⊠⊠⊠ evacuating because of the ⊠⊠⊠⊠⊠⊠⊠bring them with me but they wouldn't ⊠⊠⊠⊠⊠⊠⊠⊠⊠."

"Dammit!" Javier tried calling back—then tried the house. No go either way.

Rico was looking at him. "You must have a four-band phone there, sport."

"For what it's worth," Javier dropped the phone back in the duffel. "I don't know. I couldn't make out most of the message but it seems like they're still at the house and they probably shouldn't be."

"The direct hit was south of there, last thing I saw. I'll get you there as fast as I can." Rico faced the windscreen, pulled back on the stick. The bow of the go-fast lifted, and the tip of the northwestern peninsula fell away behind them.

"*Hasta la vista Paradiso*," Rico said. "Hello Atlantic Ocean."

There weren't storm seas, but the swells on the open ocean were larger. The go-fast raced across them with a regular thumping rhythm.

By mid-afternoon they were cruising through the shallow water south of the Bahamas. The sun had disappeared into a powdery haze, and to the west the horizon line was black.

"I don't think we ought to run right into that." Rico said, and throttled down. "Let's lay up in the lee of one of these sand bars and see if it doesn't start to clear."

The motor burbled slowly and the boat rocked more queasily in the swells. Javier scouted through the lockers, found some crackers and a pop top can of Spam.

"That's it?" Rico said, accepting a smeared cracker with a grimace. "We must have hit them before they were done loading. Which reminds me— You ought to find the coke and get rid of it. We don't want to get snarled up in a rare case of drug interdiction actually functioning."

"Me?" said Javier

"You," said Rico. "I got to keep the bow of this thing up the wind or it'll flip over while we're not paying attention."

After an hour of probing at the bulkheads with a two foot long screwdriver Javier had come up with two ten-gallon cans of extra fuel and, wedged into fishing rod cases, several long objects wrapped in black plastic, about the size of extra-long baguettes. Rico nicked the end of one with a combat knife and shook some white crystalline powder into his palm.

"Oh yeah," he said. "Hold this a second." He passed Javier the yoke and dug in his duffel, coming up with a small plastic pouch which he filled with a generous ounce of the coke.

"Ah... what're you doing?" Javier said.

"Girls like it." Rico slipped the bag in his shirt pocket.

"What girls?"

"Some girls," said Rico, buttoning the flap. "Don't worry. I'll ditch it if anything happens. If there's any law enforcement happening in Miami, which I doubt."

Javier slit the black bundles one by one and poured the cocaine over the stern. To their north, a couple of high-rise hotels thrust up from a sand-strip so low they couldn't actually see it over the waves on which they rocked. It was almost ominously still.

"You know, if we'd run in a little closer we might have actually sold some of this shit," Rico said.

"Not our mission," said Javier.

"I don't think there's anybody out on the beach either." Rico squinted at the hotels' dark windows. "Bad weather."

"We miss you," Eduardo said. "Oh.." he placed his meaty hands over the jangle of gold trinkets that lay in the deep V of his half-unbuttoned Hawaiian shirt, as if he meant to open his very heart to her. "Everbody miss Solange so *much*. So why she have to go and leave us lonely?"

Behind him a red Hummer purred on the curb, up to the hubcaps in flood water. The windows were tinted so she couldn't see who else might be inside.

The sealed vehicle emitted a subwoofer bass note so low it was less a sound than a muffled blow to her vitals. *Doom. Doom.*

"*Venga, querida,*" Eduardo crooned. "*Venga aqui.*" He had thrust his forearm through the bars of the gate and was beckoning her with his curling fingers. Sick fascination benighted her like a numbing drug. For so long she had been trained to obey.

"*Venga al Papi.*" Eduardo hummed. His odor of lubricant and cologne was familiar. It was Hell who had given her up, she knew. It was true what he said, the world was too small. She watched his fingers, furling and unfurling in the dim light of the archway like seaweed underwater. Everything he was saying must be inevitable. She remembered that Hell's key hadn't worked when she came. Eduardo would not have a working key either. If he did have one, he'd already be in. She jerked back and slammed the door behind her and leaned her back against it, breathing. It was crushingly hot and still, the sun lost in a bright haze above. Her legs were rubber. When she collected herself enough to open the hatch in the door and look out, Eduardo was no longer in view.

She splashed across the courtyard and went back in the house. Kristina still slept. The phones were dead. Thanks to the emergency power, the computer was on. No internet, but the local network was working. She summoned the mind of Trix and powered up Javier's web cameras. One gave an exterior view of the front.

On the screen, the red Hummer made a U turn, throwing up a silent curve of bright water. It popped one wheel over the curb and slowly snuggled itself against the stucco wall of the house. The door sprang open and Red Mickey got out. Eduardo boosted him to the roof of the SUV.

Eva leapt away from the computer and with stiff fingers spun the combination dials of the drawer beneath the bed. She sat on the bed with the M-16 across her knees, her mind for the moment completely blank, shaking so hard the gun barrel jittered. On the computer screen she saw Red Mickey's feet and ankles on the roof of the Hummer and then they disappeared from the top of the frame and Eduardo stepped back and craned his head upward.

Breathe, relax, squeeze. That was what Javier had said, but it didn't do anything for her now. Javier was far away. Red Mickey would be on the roof of the maid's room, where the candle still burned in the jar and water stood still in the vase she had made. That stillness seemed to calm her a little and she moved her mind toward it, remembering Willow's guiding hands over hers, shaping the soft clay as the wheel spun round. Steady now, she got up, raising the rifle as she stepped into the doorframe.

Red Mickey crouched on the roofline, one hand spread on the red tiles, then cautiously raised himself erect and peered down toward her. The polish of the gunstock smooth against her cheek. *Breathe, relax, squeeze.* She remembered not to spend the whole clip. A shower of red tile chips sprayed up from the roof to the right of Red Mickey's slightly bowed legs.

"Fuckin' shit!" Red Mickey exclaimed.

Eva raised the gun barrel a degree and rotated her whole torso to the left as she pressed the trigger again. Red Mickey did a back-flip and vanished, leaving an empty patch of sky behind him.

She heard a small choked sound behind her, and when she turned the gun turned with her. Kristina stood barefoot in her nightshirt, both hands folded across her mouth. *BonDye.* Eva propped the gun inside the door frame and ran to pick her up.

"It's all right," she said, feeling the child still stiff in her arms, holding her body tightly away. "It's safe in the house." She stroked Kristina's back, reached under the mane of hair to the taut tendons of her neck. "I'll keep you safe. I will never let anything happen to you." As the child relaxed slightly into her chest, she felt her own determination harden.

Javier came awake with a start, shocked at himself that he'd slept at all, straining his eyes into sudden darkness. He couldn't remember what he had dreamed. The pitch of the boat's motor had changed. Rico stood behind the controls, his face weirdly lit by the glow of the GPS screen.

"Back with us, are you?" Rico said.

Javier pulled himself upright and arched his back. Constellations streamed over the night sky.

"Clear skies and plain sailing." Rico said. "We're going to Florida, *amigos.*"

"You get anything on the radio?" Javier said. They'd spent the earlier part of the evening still drifting west of the Bahamas, spinning the dial for the news of the storm.

"Miami's a federal disaster area," Rico said. "For all the good that does anybody. President Punk is sending a battalion of DC street-sweepers or something like that. Whatever he's got available, *entiende?*"

"Situation normal," Javier said.

"Don't you know it," Rico said. "Nobody's doing anything that works."

At four a.m. a lumpy dark line began to coalesce on the western horizon. Off the boat's stern, the sky was lightening just a little. Javier thought he heard morning cries of a few shore birds.

"If that's Miami," Rico said, "the power's seriously out."

"What's the GPS say it is?"

"Boca," said Rico, glancing down at the screen. "You know, I think we're just gonna have to run in there. I dumped those gas cans in the tank while you were sleeping. And this thing doesn't come with a paddle."

The sun came slicing through the horizon as Rico idled the boat into the channel; both men squinted in the sudden brilliance. The big trapezoidal marina was strewn with the wreckage of capsized sailboats, some still lashed to floating docks that had ripped loose from their moorings. For a couple of minutes neither of them spoke. To their port side a cormorant broke the oily surface and shook droplets from its scrawny head.

"Where's all the people?" Rico said finally.

"Evacuated," Javier said, full of foreboding. He scrambled up on the go-fast's high bow and caught hold of a line "Come on and let's get docked already. I want to get up to the house."

Rico had thoughtfully tossed a couple of MP5 submachine guns into one of their bags. Javier carried his by the pistol grip in his right hand, his duffle bag riding high on his left shoulder. The houses near the marina looked as if they had been flooded, but the water had gone down.

"Well," said Rico. "I don't think the busses are running today."

Javier frowned and picked up his pace. There seemed to be no vehicles around at all except for an old station-wagon up on blocks. Somebody had driven them all away.

"Hold up." Rico caught up with him and stopped him with a hand on his shoulder. Javier looked up. In the middle of the next block a posse of dreadlocked black men were handing boxed televisions through the broken display window of a store and stacking them onto a wooden pallet. One of them turned and flourished a nine-millimeter pistol, waving them off.

Rico brought his MP5 to his shoulder and popped off a round. The dreadlocked youths scattered, hitting the deck. The one with the pistol rolled inside the broken window without returning fire.

"Come on!" Javier said, pushing down Rico's gun barrel. "You can't just shoot people. This is the United States."

"I seriously think the United States is taking the day off," Rico said. "If not the whole week. And that was a warning shot, you know. If I'd wanted to shoot him I'd have shot his ass—"

"Let's just walk the other way," Javier said. "They don't have anything we can use. We seriously need to score some transportation here."

When they turned the next corner, they came nose to nose with a Nissan Pathfinder, idling quietly by the curb. Rico hissed and spun into a doorway. Javier broke the other way, raising his weapon before he'd even identified the threat. Half a dozen men in flak jackets and fatigue caps were working their way down the block, all of them raising their assault rifles to attack. Javier, crouching behind an overturned newspaper box that gave him fairly inadequate cover, sighted on a bear-paw logo on the cap of the man nearest him, who seemed to have drawn a bead on Rico.

"Hold your fire!" Rico called. "You're dealing with the pros here, fellas."

From inside the Pathfinder a bullhorn squawked. "I'm getting out of the car, you hear me? No worries. Just stepping out of the car."

Javier squeezed down a little tighter. He could feel sweat drizzling down his spine. The passenger door of the Pathfinder creaked open and a seven-foot tall black man with wraparound sunglasses and a gleaming shaved head stood up in the middle of the street.

"Enrique?" he said, shading his eyes with one shovel-sized hand.

"Karl?" Rico lowered his weapon a notch. "What the hell are you doing here?"

"Assisting local law enforcement."

"My hairy ass!" Rico said. "The local law enforcement has beat feet to the nearest landlocked state."

Javier decided to risk getting up. The man whose head he'd been about to blow off looked at him through a pair of aviator sunglasses. In large chunky capitals, the word BLACKWATER was stenciled from his shoulder seam to his cuff.

The black man shrugged. "So we're filling a need," he said. "We're subcontracting for FEMA, if you gotta know."

"Really," Rico said. He hitched up the MP5. "You know, Karl, I don't want to be crude about this but we kinda sorta need to requisition your vehicle."

"What?"

Rico jerked his jaw at Javier. "My man here has got to check on his family."

All eyes and several gun barrels turned Javier's way.

"Um," Karl said. "I don't want to disrespect your problem. But a whole lot of people seem to be in that situation today."

Javier's finger twitched in the trigger guard. Don't move, he told himself. Don't look funny.

"You know what, though," Karl said. "There's a Nissan dealership two blocks back of us and three to the left. Still a couple of trucks left on the lot. Or there were."

"Terrific," said Rico. "Keys in them?"

"You said you were pros," Karl reminded him. "Work it out for yourself."

The eye of the hurricane passed on, but the eye of *Brise* stayed here. All through the night I held my girl up, while she worked to comfort the child. Eve, O Eve, she lit her candle and poured water for Erzulie Freda, but in the back of her mind, at the top of her spine, she knew that *Brise* was near.

Brise watched her on the path of her becoming, all the way to here from there, where the woman balanced her heavy belly up the mountain, stepped carefully over the trilling spring, crossed the waxy shoots of aloe, and delivered her charge inside my cave. In airless dark inside that orb my girl turned weightlessly, until the curtains of the door drew back and she looked out and saw my candles, and breathed and cried for the first time, felt the first pang of her fight to live for both herself and for me.

Now *Brise* belongs to her, more than she to *Brise*. But if I free her from her service, I am still here to serve her, at her need.

When the storm had passed she was still troubled in her spirit. She fretted over what would happen next, because she knew that something would. But everything has already happened, though the world keeps turning on itself, and fails to find an ending.

Kristina had gone deadly quiet since Eva shot Red Mickey off the rooftop. A well-protected child may scream or weep in the face of danger. The unprotected child chooses silence. So Eva understood Kristina's quiet, and yet it chilled her. For much of the day, the girl was impossible to distract. The koi still swam in the flooded courtyard but Kristina would not pay attention to them. She sat with her nose an inch from the TV, watching a Disney clip over and over, "Pink Elephants on Parade." Eva found the psychedelic pachyderms rather frightening, and she thought that maybe Kristina did too.

The phones were still dead, and the cable was out, and the internet was down. She found a little headphone radio that Javier sometimes wore on a run. The reception was iffy but she was able to pick up a couple of reports of general mayhem all over the Miami area in the wake of the storm. It had been the same when she was small, at the house in Bel

Air—whenever there was a change of government, they locked the gate and barred the doors and lay quiet until things returned to normal. But Eva never thought of those days and it unnerved her to be thinking of them now.

With Kristina occupied by the television, she cleaned the rifle and put in a fresh clip. The basement pump seemed to be getting ahead of the water down there, and by late afternoon the water had mostly drained from the courtyard. She chivvied the koi back into their pool and did her best to mop the mucky tiles.

There was plenty of food for her to make supper, and by suppertime Kristina had calmed down considerably. She was still quiet but no longer rigid with fear. Eva let her get by with a sponge bath, since the hot water supply was short. She sat by her bedside stroking Kristina's back with her fingertips until the girl slept.

She had turned off the AC to save power, so it was uncomfortably hot and clammy, but normally that wouldn't have kept her awake. She didn't know she had slept at all until some subtle noise woke her—the thump of the refrigerator going dead again, or the pump in the basement choking itself silent. She sat up, knowing the power was finished, both the generator and batteries sucked dry. If Javier didn't return today they would be down to a couple of flashlights and the last car battery that powered the emergency gates.

Morning light poured in through the bedroom windows. After all, she had slept later than she thought. There was a slight mildew smell, from flooding in the basement probably. She pulled on drawstring pants and a T-shirt and went out into the courtyard for a breath of fresh air.

The tiles were still tacky under her bare feet. She didn't quite know what to do to get them properly clean. The sound of a car gliding down the street outside distracted her from that concern. She heard the engine slow, then rev up to a desperate pitch. The red Hummer exploded through the wall to the left of the entryway, in a cloud of plaster dust, splinters and chips of red tile.

She froze for a very long, dangerous moment before she turned and ran for the M-16. Her first burst went wild and then the rifle jammed. Two men got out that she didn't recognize, dangling blunt little firearms in their hands. Then Eduardo was walking toward her, wary at first, beginning to smile as he saw she was helpless. Her finger jerked uselessly against the dead trigger. He was almost on the threshold when she remembered to pull the lever that sent the emergency gates slamming shut.

A mesh of high-grade steel now divided her from them. Through it, Eduardo's face was blurry, as if underwater. To trigger either gate was to trigger them both. Kristina's bedroom was also sealed off, or should be if the thing worked properly. There had been interior barriers in the Bel Air house too, similar in principle, if lower-tech. She remembered now that they hadn't helped much.

The mesh was just too fine for Eduardo's fingertips to go through. Experimentally he probed the surface. "You keel Miko," he said softly. "My frien' won't eat or fuck or fight no more. Never no more, because of you."

"*Se pa zanmi w, se esklav w li te ye,*" she told him. He wasn't your friend, he was your slave. Eduardo pressed his chubby cheek against the mesh. "*El culo mio,*" he said murmured. "We'll be together very soon."

Without knowing she would do it she drew the rifle over her head and hammered the stock at him through the mesh. Eduardo sprang back with a shout, raising one hand to his face. One of the men with him fired at the wall, and a round came through, whining like a wasp within the sheltered space.

Eva gasped and ran to Kristina's room. The girl had huddled in the corner of her bed, her body rigid when she touched it. She thought for a moment, then snatched off the covers and used them to make a pad in the bottom of the bathtub. When she returned, Eduardo was peering in through the mesh of the second gate.

"Is a little beauty!" he said in his syrupy voice. "But you never told Eduardo, that you have this for me."

Hastily she picked up Kristina, tucking her head

to her shoulder so she wouldn't have to see him. "*Ou pa janm touche'l*" she hissed. You'll never touch her. She rushed Kristina into the bathroom and laid her down on the folded blanket and coverlet in the tub. She dragged the mattress of the child's bed and positioned it over the tub rim so it came up to Kristina's chin.

"Cozy!" she said.

Kristina returned her a thousand-yard stare. Eva ran back into her room and grabbed the rug with the cat's head up from the floor.

"Here's kitty to stay with you," she said. "Just be still and you'll be fine." But of course she didn't need to tell Kristina to be still.

They were trying to break down the bedroom wall with a tire tool and a jack from the Hummer. The plaster crumbled easily enough, but Javier had thought to reinforce it with steel bars inside and these they could not break down. Eva clawed at the M-16, but Javier had not told her what to do if it jammed. She couldn't even get the clip loose. Her next best hope for a weapon would be in the kitchen—outside the gates.

"Fuck it," said Eduardo. "It's taking too long."

She heard the Hummer's engine rumble back to life, then rev. Its front end slapped into the sliding doors, shattering the glass and tearing the metal as it thrust halfway across the passage to the emergency gate.

"No, no." Eduardo's voice. "Don't hit it so fast. We don't want to hurt her, see? I mean we want to hurt her slowly."

Obediently the Hummer crept forward till its bumper pressed into the gate. Eduardo's voice, "Okay now, a little more gas."

Eva ran into the bathroom and locked the door on the far side. Kristina's long stare dug into her back. She couldn't bear to look at her. The motor chugged and grumbled louder and she could hear the sound of metal tearing. She pushed the button to lock the second bathroom door and went back into the bedroom, pulling it shut behind her.

The Hummer was backing away from the torn gate. Carefully Eduardo peeled back the mesh. "You don't need those guns," he said to the men behind him. "She is only a little *puta*. Use your *chimbos* to teach her who she is."

She clawed at the face of one and kicked up sharply at the other but one of the men caught her wrists together in one huge hand and the other yanked her head back by the braids. Eduardo came toward her, touching the bruise on his cheek with a fingertip before he reached for her face. She couldn't stop herself from flinching, but he only caressed her cheek with his palm.

"Doan worry," he said. "I'm not going to hit you. We only will fuck you until you are dead."

He turned from her then, and tried the bathroom

door, frowning when it refused to turn. He set his shoulder against the door as if he would break it but then relaxed.

"We doan need to frighten this little girl," he said. "No." He strolled to the computer and picked up a paper clip from the desk beside. With the straightened tip he fished in the hole in the center of the door knob until there was a little click and the knob turned.

Eduardo held up the paperclip, then tossed it to the carpet. "So easy," he said, looking back at her. "No reason to fight it." Then to the men. "Doan bother me now. I need some time to be with my girl."

Very softly he opened the door, stepped through and pushed it too behind him. The man who'd been holding Eva's braids let go and stepped back to unbuckle his belt. She leaned into the man who was holding her wrists, relaxing her body, pouring her mind empty. A high wind rushed into the cave on the mountain, flattening the flames of the candles in the three-chambered jar. Then the flames leapt straight and higher than before.

Se Bris mwen rele! Vini mwon Brise!

The whirlwind spiraled in the tight space of the bedroom and with the strength of *Brise* in her bone marrow she twisted and flung the man away from her so hard that he shattered the big mirror above the headboard and slumped down stunned onto the bed. She snatched up an icicle shard of the mirror and turned to the other, who tripped on his dropped trousers as he lunged at her and fell with his whole weight on the point of the mirrored glass as she jerked it up into him, supporting her right hand with her left and feeling the edge of the glass slice into her palm as the point snapped off deep inside him and he collapsed past her, face down on the floor.

The other was pushing himself up from the bed and she flung the broken glass in his face as he straightened groggily. Then she ran for the kitchen, not looking back, only feeling he was gaining on her as his head cleared and his focus sharpened, her whole intention bent on the butcher block on the kitchen, the clutch of black handles curling from the slots. She had just time to draw a knife and turn as he rushed on her. The handle bruised her sternum when the point caught on something and then pierced it. She turned out from under his weight and let him fall, leaving the knife inside his body, reaching back over him in almost the same motion to pull another knife from the block.

Light and rapid as a cat, she ran back through the bedroom, laying her bare feet down gently the carpet, to make no sound. The bathroom door had drifted open, and she could see the back of Eduardo's head— he was still standing, rapt, above the bathtub, so hypnotized by his own obsession he noticed nothing else.

The molasses stream of his crooning voice curled around the door frame—all the same words he'd used on her before. Catching his hair short at the scalp, she jerked his head up and saw his eyes flash white in the mirror as the triangular blade went gliding across his throat.

To Kristina she said, "Don't look."

It was scarcely ten miles from Boca Raton to Morisco Bay but they kept having to double back where flooding had made the roads too deep to risk. Rico had had to hotwire the Pathfinder, and as he pointed out it would be time-consuming to do it all over if they drowned the motor. They made a tortuous way north, in a sort of Greek key pattern sketched by circumstance.

"I can't figure out what's harder to process," Rico said. "That Karl went with fucking Blackwater or that Blackwater's contracted with fucking FEMA."

"I can't help you that one," Javier said. "I don't really have that much invested either way."

"You think Harold ought to get us cool logos and shit?" Rico turned to him.

"Not really," Javier said. "That bear paw makes a terrific target."

"A contract with FEMA though, that could be good," Rico turned his eyes back on the road. "That is the *taxpayer's dollar,* yo."

Javier didn't answer. He watched the roadside. In

the parking lot of a strip mall, egrets fished in knee-deep water. Between two low buildings he saw a man gliding by on a surfboard, sitting up cross-legged and using a broken board as a paddle.

"Check it out," Rico said, and tapped him on the shoulder.

Looking down in the other direction from the raised road-bed, Javier saw a wraith-like flame burning underwater. "Weird, he said. "What do think it is?"

"I don't know." Rico shook his head. "A gas main, maybe." He kept staring. Not far from the sunken flame a long oblong object floated. With a ripple in the water it spread its dead arms like seaweed.

"Come on, let's go."

Rico pressed the accelerator and the Pathfinder rolled forward, tires slipping a little in the wet. He turned his head toward Javier.

"Was that Solange who called your phone?"

"Some friend of hers," Javier said. "Don't call her that." He realized he couldn't call her Eva either any more. "She's come a long way to be where she is."

Rico looked at him curiously. "Where's that?"

"With me," Javier said.

"Oh, man..." Rico said, and Javier tensed, but Rico was looking at something else—a bus that had dropped from an interstate overpass, caught in a crosswind probably, and lay crushed on its side, surrounded by a scatter of white baseballs that had rolled to a stop all around it. A half-dozen teenagers in numbered jerseys lay where they had been thrown from the vehicle.

"*Dios mio,*" Rico muttered as they passed. A breeze came up, catching the mesh of a blond boy's sleeve; it looked as if the corpse were waving. Rico tapped the brake.

"It's the wind," Javier said. "We can't help them. And anyway Blackwater's got the contract."

Rico didn't laugh, but he kept going. Silence, except for damp air rushing through the half-open windows. They'd turned the corner of the playground now and were only a couple of blocks from the house. Javier's fingers danced on his knees.

"Uh-oh," Rico said, and hit the brake a little too hard, so that the car stalled. But they had already reached the target. Rico was looking at the jagged tear in the courtyard wall beside the entryway, a halo edged with ripped wire mesh and broken stucco. "Something's not good here."

Javier's heart pulsed up his gullet. But he was already pulling out his key ring and pushing it at Rico. "Go in through the basement," he said. "God knows what's going on in there. If it's still happening we'll take them two ways."

"Check," Rico said. He opened the car door quietly and sidled around the corner of the house.

Javier stepped out, boots squelching in the flooded street. MP5 at the ready, he crept toward the hole in the wall. At the edge of it he stopped to listen, flexing his knees. There was nothing to hear but the sound of water running somewhere. He whipped in, crouching, pivoting to cover every corner of the courtyard with his eyes and the machine gun's snout. But there was no movement anywhere. A red Hummer, its body dented and scraped from end to end, was heeled down on a flat tire, a few yards back from the ripped emergency gate to the bedroom.

The doors of the house gaped at him like black holes into nothingness. He scooted up to the Hummer's rear bumper and peered into the house from cover of the car.

Eva, whoever she was, came out through the broken gate to the bedroom. Kristina was riding on her left hip, one arm around her neck, the other reaching toward Javier. He looked past them, eyes darting around them to probe at whatever might still be in the house behind them.

Rico appeared in the kitchen doorframe. "Holy Mary, Mother of God," he said, scratching his head just above the root of his braid. "Tell Harold he needs to sign this babe up."

"We're secure?" Javier called to him.

"*Oh* yeah," Rico said. "It's... dead quiet in here." He shook his head and withdrew from the doorway.

Javier laid his weapon down behind the Hummer and stepped out into the open. He could see that Kristina was all right because he knew what she looked like when she wasn't. Kristina still held out her hand to him but she didn't seem to want to get down. And Eva, Eva didn't look much hurt. She had cut her palm and her t-shirt was torn and there were two vertical brownish streaks of something on her left cheek. What was he going to say to her?

I just want to know who are, he thought. I just want to know who you really are. She seemed to still be moving toward him, or maybe he was moving toward her. Medusa locks snaked around her head. Her eyes a little startled, but warm.

"Eve," he said. "Oh Eve." The way that name would be pronounced in Paradise.

Be yourself, he wanted to tell her. But he saw that she already was.

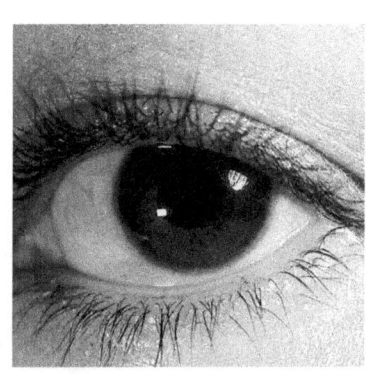

About Gabrielle Chavela

According to the Haitian Constitution of 1987,
"The cult of personality is categorically forbidden."
Gabrielle Chavela respects this law.